NO FEAR SHAKESPEARE

KING LEAR

D0009856

SPARK
NOTES

SPARKNOTES is a registered trademark of SparkNotes LLC.

Spark Publishing
A Division of Barnes & Noble
120 Fifth Avenue
New York, NY 10011
www.sparknotes.com

Please submit all comments and questions or report errors to www.sparknotes.com/errors

ISBN-13: 978-1-5866-3853-5
ISBN-10: 1-5866-3853-X

Library of Congress Cataloging-in-Publication Data

Shakespeare, William, 1564–1616.
    King Lear / edited by John Crowther.
        p. cm.—(No fear Shakespeare)
    Summary: Presents the original text of Shakespeare's play side by side with a modern version, with marginal notes and explanations and full descriptions of each character.
    ISBN 1-58663-853-X (pbk.) ISBN 1-41140-047-X (hc.)
    1. Lear, King (Legendary character)—Drama. 2. Inheritance and succession—Drama. 3. Fathers and daughters—Drama. 4. Young adult drama, English. 5. Kings and rulers—Drama. 6. Aging parents—Drama. 7. Britons—Drama. [1. Shakespeare, William, 1564–1616. King Lear. 2. Plays. 3. English literature—History and criticism.] I. Crowther, John (John C.) II. Title.
    PR2819 .A25C76 2003
    822.3'3—dc21
                        2003004312

Printed and bound in the United States

12 13 14 15 SN 30 29 28 27

There's matter in these sighs, these profound heaves.
You must translate: 'tis fit we understand them.

(Hamlet, 4.1.1–2)

FEAR NOT.

Have you ever found yourself looking at a Shakespeare play, then down at the footnotes, then back at the play, and still not understanding? You know what the individual words mean, but they don't add up. SparkNotes' *No Fear Shakespeare* will help you break through all that. Put the pieces together with our easy-to-read translations. Soon you'll be reading Shakespeare's own words fearlessly—and actually enjoying it.

No Fear Shakespeare puts Shakespeare's language side-by-side with a facing-page translation into modern English—the kind of English people actually speak today. When Shakespeare's words make your head spin, our translation will help you sort out what's happening, who's saying what, and why.

NO FEAR SHAKESPEARE

As You Like It

The Comedy of Errors

Hamlet

Henry IV, Parts One and Two

Henry V

Julius Caesar

King Lear

Macbeth

The Merchant of Venice

A Midsummer Night's Dream

Much Ado About Nothing

Othello

Richard III

Romeo and Juliet

Sonnets

The Taming of the Shrew

The Tempest

Twelfth Night

KING LEAR

Characters ix

CHARACTERS

King Lear—The aging king of Britain and the protagonist of the play. Lear is used to enjoying absolute power and to being flattered, and he does not respond well to being contradicted or challenged. At the beginning of the play, his values are notably hollow—he prefers his two older daughters' obvious flattery over the actual devotion of Cordelia, and he wishes to maintain the power of a king while unburdening himself of the responsibility. Nevertheless, Lear inspires loyalty in subjects such as Gloucester, Kent, Cordelia, and Edgar, all of whom risk their lives for him.

Cordelia—Lear's youngest daughter, disowned by her father for refusing to flatter him. Cordelia is held in extremely high regard by all of the good characters in the play—the king of France marries her for her virtue alone, overlooking her lack of dowry. Cordelia remains loyal to Lear despite his cruelty toward her, forgives him, and displays a mild and forbearing temperament even toward her evil sisters, Goneril and Regan. Despite her obvious virtues, Cordelia's reticence makes her motivations difficult to read, as in her refusal to declare her love for her father at the beginning of the play.

Goneril—Lear's ruthless oldest daughter and the wife of the duke of Albany. Goneril is jealous, treacherous, and amoral. Shakespeare's audience would have been particularly shocked at Goneril's aggressiveness, a quality that it would not have expected in a female character. Goneril challenges Lear's authority, boldly initiates an affair with Edmund, and wrests military power away from her husband.

Regan—Lear's middle daughter and the wife of the duke of Cornwall. Regan is as ruthless as Goneril and as aggressive in all the same ways. In fact, it is difficult to think of any quality that distinguishes her from her sister. When they are not egging each other on to further acts of cruelty, they jealously compete for the same man, Edmund.

Gloucester—A nobleman loyal to King Lear whose rank, earl, is below that of duke. The first thing we learn about Gloucester is that he is an adulterer, having fathered a bastard son, Edmund. Gloucester's fate is in many ways parallel to that of Lear: he misjudges which of his children to trust. Also like Lear, Gloucester suffers tremendously for his mistakes.

Edgar—Gloucester's older, legitimate son. Edgar plays many different roles, starting out as a gullible fool easily tricked by his brother, then assuming a disguise as a mad beggar to evade his father's men, then carrying his impersonation further to aid Lear and Gloucester, and finally appearing as an armored champion to avenge his brother's treason. Edgar's propensity for disguises and impersonations makes him a complex and at times puzzling character.

Edmund—Gloucester's younger, illegitimate son. Edmund resents his status as a bastard and schemes to usurp Gloucester's title and possessions from Edgar. He is a formidable character, succeeding in almost all of his schemes and wreaking destruction upon virtually all of the other characters.

Kent—A nobleman of the same rank as Gloucester who is loyal to King Lear. Kent spends most of the play disguised as a peasant, calling himself "Caius," so that he can continue to serve Lear even after Lear banishes him. Kent is extremely loyal but gets himself into trouble throughout the play by being exceptionally blunt and outspoken.

Albany—The husband of Lear's daughter Goneril. Although Albany allows Goneril, Regan, and Cornwall to abuse their power, Albany himself is good at heart, eventually denouncing and opposing their cruelty and treachery. Yet Albany is indecisive and lacks foresight, not realizing the evil of his allies until quite late in the play.

Cornwall—The husband of Lear's daughter Regan. Unlike Albany, Cornwall is domineering, cruel, and violent, and he works with his wife and sister-in-law Goneril to persecute Lear and Gloucester.

Fool—Lear's jester. The Fool uses double-talk and seemingly frivolous songs to criticize Lear for the latter's foolish mistakes.

Oswald—The steward, or chief servant, in Goneril's house. Oswald obeys his mistress's commands and helps her in her conspiracies.

KING LEAR

ACT ONE
SCENE 1

Enter KENT, GLOUCESTER, *and* EDMUND

KENT

I thought the king had more affected the Duke of Albany
than Cornwall.

GLOUCESTER

It did always seem so to us. But now in the division of the
kingdom, it appears not which of the dukes he values most,
for equalities are so weighed that curiosity in neither can
make choice of either's moiety.

KENT

(indicating EDMUND*)* Is not this your son, my lord?

GLOUCESTER

His breeding, sir, hath been at my charge. I have so
often blushed to acknowledge him that now I am brazed
to it.

KENT

I cannot conceive you.

GLOUCESTER

Sir, this young fellow's mother could, whereupon she
grew round-wombed, and had indeed, sir, a son for her
cradle ere she had a husband for her bed. Do you smell
a fault?

KENT

I cannot wish the fault undone, the issue of it being so
proper.

GLOUCESTER

But I have, sir, a son by order of law, some year older than
this, who yet is no dearer in my account. Though this knave
came something saucily to the world before he was sent for,
yet was his mother fair, there was good sport at his making,
and the whoreson must be acknowledged.—Do you know
this noble gentleman, Edmund?

ACT ONE
SCENE 1

KENT, GLOUCESTER, *and* EDMUND *enter.*

KENT

> I thought the king preferred the Duke of Albany to the Duke of Cornwall.

GLOUCESTER

> We used to think so too. But the way he's divided the kingdom recently, nobody can tell which of the dukes he favors more. He's split the kingdom so evenly that it's impossible to see any indication of favoritism.

KENT

> *(pointing to* EDMUND*)* Isn't this your son, my lord?

GLOUCESTER

> Yes, I've been responsible for his upbringing. I've had to acknowledge that he's my son so many times that now I can do it without embarrassment.

KENT

> I can't conceive of what you mean.

GLOUCESTER

> You can't conceive? Well, this guy's mother could conceive him all to well. She grew a big belly and had a baby for her crib before she had a husband for her bed. Do you smell something naughty?

KENT

> Well, I wouldn't want to undo the naughtiness, since the boy turned out so well.

GLOUCESTER

> But I have a legitimate son a few years older than this one, and I don't love him any more than I love my bastard. Edmund may have snuck into the world a little before his time, but his mother was pretty, we had a fun time making him, and now I have to acknowledge the guy as my son.—Do you know this gentleman, Edmund?

EDMUND
No, my lord.

GLOUCESTER
25 *(to* EDMUND*)* My lord of Kent. Remember him hereafter as
my honorable friend.

EDMUND
My services to your lordship.

KENT
I must love you and sue to know you better.

EDMUND
Sir, I shall study deserving.

GLOUCESTER
30 He hath been out nine years, and away he shall again.

Sennet.

The king is coming.

Enter one bearing a coronet, then King LEAR*, then the Dukes
of* CORNWALL *and* ALBANY*, next* GONERIL*,* REGAN*,*
CORDELIA*, and attendants*

LEAR
Attend the lords of France and Burgundy, Gloucester.

GLOUCESTER
I shall, my lord.

Exit GLOUCESTER

LEAR
Meantime we shall express our darker purpose.—
35 Give me the map there.—Know that we have divided
In three our kingdom, and 'tis our fast intent
To shake all cares and business from our age,
Conferring them on younger strengths while we
Unburdened crawl toward death.—Our son of Cornwall,
40 And you, our no less loving son of Albany,
We have this hour a constant will to publish

EDMUND

No, I don't, my lord.

GLOUCESTER

(to EDMUND*)* This is Lord Kent. Remember him as my friend and an honorable man.

EDMUND

Very pleased to meet you, my lord.

KENT

I look forward to getting to know you better.

EDMUND

I'll try to make myself worth your knowledge.

GLOUCESTER

He's been gone for nine years and he's leaving again soon.

Trumpets announce the arrival of King LEAR.

The king is coming.

A man bearing a crown enters, followed by King LEAR, *the Dukes of* CORNWALL *and* ALBANY, *then* GONERIL, REGAN, CORDELIA, *and attendants.*

LEAR

Go escort the lords of France and Burgundy, Gloucester.

GLOUCESTER

Yes, my lord.

GLOUCESTER *exits.*

LEAR

In the meantime I'll get down to my real business.— Hand me that map over there.—I hereby announce that I've divided my kingdom into three parts, which I'm handing over to the younger generation so I can enjoy a little rest and peace of mind in my old age.— Cornwall and Albany, my loving sons-in-law, I now want to announce publicly what each of my daughters will inherit, to avoid hostilities after I die. The

Our daughters' several dowers, that future strife
May be prevented now.
The two great princes, France and Burgundy,
45 Great rivals in our youngest daughter's love,
Long in our court have made their amorous sojourn,
And here are to be answered.—Tell me, my daughters,
(Since now we will divest us both of rule,
Interest of territory, cares of state)
50 Which of you shall we say doth love us most
That we our largest bounty may extend
Where nature doth with merit challenge?—Goneril,
Our eldest born, speak first.

GONERIL
Sir, I do love you more than words can wield the matter,
55 Dearer than eyesight, space, and liberty,
Beyond what can be valued, rich or rare,
No less than life, with grace, health, beauty, honor,
As much as child e'er loved or father found—
A love that makes breath poor and speech unable.
60 Beyond all manner of so much I love you.

CORDELIA
(aside) What shall Cordelia speak? Love, and be silent.

LEAR
Of all these bounds, even from this line to this,
With shadowy forests and with champains riched,
With plenteous rivers and wide-skirted meads,
65 We make thee lady. To thine and Albany's issue
Be this perpetual.—What says our second daughter,
Our dearest Regan, wife of Cornwall? Speak.

REGAN
Sir, I am made of that self mettle as my sister,
And prize me at her worth. In my true heart,
70 I find she names my very deed of love—
Only she comes too short, that I profess

two great princes of France and Burgundy, vying for the hand of my youngest Cordelia, have been at my court a long time and will soon have their answers.— My daughters, since I'm about to give up my throne and the worries that go along with it, tell me which one of you loves me most, so that I can give my largest gift to the one who deserves it most.—Goneril, my oldest daughter, you speak first.

GONERIL

Sir, I love you more than words can say. I love you more than eyesight, space, and freedom, beyond wealth or anything of value. I love you as much as life itself, and as much as status, health, beauty, or honor. I love you as much as any child has ever loved her father, with a love too deep to be spoken of. I love you more than any answer to the question "How much?"

CORDELIA

(to herself) What will I say? I can only love and be silent.

LEAR

I give you all this land, from this line to that one— dense forests, fertile fields, rivers rich with fish, wide meadows. This land will belong to your and Albany's children forever.—And now what does my second daughter Regan, the wife of Cornwall, have to say? Tell me.

REGAN

Sir, I'm made of the same stuff as my sister and consider myself just as good as she is. She's described my feelings of love for you precisely, but her description falls a little short of the truth. I reject completely any

Myself an enemy to all other joys,
Which the most precious square of sense possesses.
And find I am alone felicitate
75 In your dear highness' love.

CORDELIA
    (aside)   Then poor Cordelia!
And yet not so, since I am sure my love's
More ponderous than my tongue.

LEAR
To thee and thine hereditary ever
Remain this ample third of our fair kingdom,
80 No less in space, validity, and pleasure
Than that conferred on Goneril.—But now, our joy,
Although our last and least, to whose young love
The vines of France and milk of Burgundy
Strive to be interessed. What can you say to draw
85 A third more opulent than your sisters? Speak.

CORDELIA
Nothing, my lord.

LEAR
Nothing?

CORDELIA
Nothing.

LEAR
How? Nothing will come of nothing. Speak again.

CORDELIA
90 Unhappy that I am, I cannot heave
My heart into my mouth. I love your majesty
According to my bond, no more nor less.

LEAR
How, how, Cordelia? Mend your speech a little,
Lest you may mar your fortunes.

CORDELIA
                                  Good my lord,
95 You have begot me, bred me, loved me. I
Return those duties back as are right fit—

joy except my love for you, and I find that only your majesty's love makes me happy.

CORDELIA

(to herself) Poor me, what am I going to say now? But I'm not poor in love—my love is bigger than my words are.

LEAR

You and your heirs hereby receive this large third of our lovely kingdom, no smaller in area or value than what I gave Goneril.—Now, you, my youngest daughter, my joy, courted by the rich rulers of France and Burgundy, what can you tell me that will make me give you a bigger part of my kingdom than I gave your sisters? Speak.

CORDELIA

Nothing, my lord.

LEAR

Nothing?

CORDELIA

Nothing.

LEAR

Come on, "nothing" will get you nothing. Try again.

CORDELIA

I'm unlucky. I don't have a talent for putting my heart's feelings into words. I love you as a child should love her father, neither more nor less.

LEAR

What are you saying, Cordelia? Revise your statement, or you may damage your inheritance.

CORDELIA

My lord, you brought me up and loved me, and I'm giving back just as I should: I obey you, love you, and honor you. How can my sisters speak the truth when

Obey you, love you, and most honor you.
Why have my sisters husbands if they say
They love you all? Haply when I shall wed
100   That lord whose hand must take my plight shall carry
Half my love with him, half my care and duty.
Sure, I shall never marry like my sisters,
To love my father all.

LEAR

But goes thy heart with this?

CORDELIA

105   Ay, good my lord.

LEAR

So young and so untender?

CORDELIA

So young, my lord, and true.

LEAR

Let it be so. Thy truth then be thy dower.
For by the sacred radiance of the sun,
110   The mysteries of Hecate and the night,
By all the operation of the orbs
From whom we do exist and cease to be—
Here I disclaim all my paternal care,
Propinquity, and property of blood,
115   And as a stranger to my heart and me
Hold thee from this for ever. The barbarous Scythian,
Or he that makes his generation messes
To gorge his appetite, shall to my bosom
Be as well neighbored, pitied, and relieved
120   As thou my sometime daughter.

KENT

                                        Good my liege—

LEAR

Peace, Kent.
Come not between the dragon and his wrath.
I loved her most and thought to set my rest
On her kind nursery.—

they say they love only you? Don't they love their husbands too? Hopefully when I get married, I'll give my husband half my love and half my sense of duty. I'm sure I'll never get married in the way my sisters say they're married, loving their father only.

LEAR

But do you mean what you're saying?

CORDELIA

Yes, my lord.

LEAR

So young and so cruel?

CORDELIA

So young, my lord, and honest.

LEAR

Then that's the way it'll be. The truth will be all the inheritance you get. I swear by the sacred sun, by the mysterious moon, and by all the planets that rule our lives, that I disown you now as my daughter. As of now, there are no family ties between us, and I consider you a stranger to me. Foreign savages who eat their own children for dinner will be as close to my heart as you, ex-daughter of mine.

KENT

But sir—

LEAR

Be quiet, Kent. Don't get in my way when I'm angry. I loved Cordelia most of all and planned to spend my old age with her taking care of me. *(to* CORDELIA*)* Go

(to CORDELIA*)*

                            Hence, and avoid my sight!—

125   So be my grave my peace as here I give
Her father's heart from her.—Call France. Who stirs?
Call Burgundy.—

                              Exeunt several attendants

                   Cornwall and Albany,
With my two daughters' dowers digest this third.
Let pride, which she calls plainness, marry her.
130   I do invest you jointly with my power,
Preeminence, and all the large effects
That troop with majesty. Ourself, by monthly course,
With reservation of an hundred knights
By you to be sustained, shall our abode
135   Make with you by due turns. Only shall we retain
The name, and all th' additions to a king.
The sway, revenue, execution of the rest,
Belovèd sons, be yours; which to confirm,
This coronet part between you.
(gives CORNWALL *and* ALBANY *the coronet)*

KENT

                         Royal Lear,
140   Whom I have ever honored as my king,
Loved as my father, as my master followed,
As my great patron thought on in my prayers—

LEAR

The bow is bent and drawn. Make from the shaft.

KENT

Let it fall rather, though the fork invade
145   The region of my heart. Be Kent unmannerly
When Lear is mad. What wouldst thou do, old man?
Think'st thou that duty shall have dread to speak
When power to flattery bows? To plainness honor's bound
When majesty falls to folly. Reserve thy state,

away! Get out of my sight!—I guess if she doesn't love her father, then I'll only have peace when I'm dead.— Call the King of France. Why is nobody doing anything? Call the Duke of Burgundy.

Several attendants exit.

Cornwall and Albany, you and your wives can divide this last third of my kingdom between you. If she wants to be proud, or "honest," as she calls it, she can just marry her own pride. I hereby grant to you two my crown and all the privileges that kingship brings. I'll live one month with one of you, the next month with the other one. All I ask is that you provide me with a hundred knights for my own entourage. I'll keep only the title of king, but you'll have everything else: all the authority and income that come with kingship. To confirm all this, take this crown to share between yourselves. *(he gives* CORNWALL *and* ALBANY *the crown)*

KENT

King Lear, I've always honored you as king, loved you as my father, obeyed you as my master, and thanked you in my prayers—

LEAR

I'm furious and ready to snap. Stay away or else I'll take my anger out on you.

KENT

Let your anger fall on me then, even if its sharpness pierces my heart. Kent can speak rudely when Lear goes mad. What are you doing, old man? When powerful kings cave in to flatterers, do you think loyal men will be afraid to speak out against it? When a majestic king starts acting silly, then it's my duty to be blunt.

150 And in thy best consideration check
This hideous rashness. Answer my life my judgment,
Thy youngest daughter does not love thee least,
Nor are those empty-hearted whose low sound
Reverbs no hollowness.

LEAR
                                        Kent, on thy life, no more.

KENT
155 My life I never held but as a pawn
To wage against thy enemies, nor fear to lose it,
Thy safety being motive.

LEAR
                                        Out of my sight!

KENT
See better, Lear, and let me still remain
The true blank of thine eye.

LEAR
                                        Now, by Apollo—

KENT
160 Now, by Apollo, King,
Thou swear'st thy gods in vain.

LEAR
O vassal! Miscreant!

ALBANY, CORNWALL
                        Dear sir, forbear!

KENT
Do, kill thy physician, and the fee bestow
Upon thy foul disease. Revoke thy gift,
165 Or whilst I can vent clamor from my throat,
I'll tell thee thou dost evil.

LEAR
Hear me, recreant! On thine allegiance hear me.
That thou hast sought to make us break our vows,
Which we durst never yet, and with strained pride
170 To come betwixt our sentence and our power,
Which nor our nature nor our place can bear,

Hold on to your crown and use your better judgment to rethink this rash decision. On my life I swear to you that your youngest daughter doesn't love you least. A loud mouth often points to an empty heart, and just because she's quiet doesn't mean she's unloving.

LEAR

Kent, if you want to stay alive, stop talking.

KENT

I never considered my life as anything more than a chess pawn for you to play off against your enemies. I'm not afraid to lose it if it helps protect you.

LEAR

Get out of my sight!

KENT

Learn to see better, Lear, and let me stay here where you can look to me for good advice.

LEAR

Now, I swear by Apollo . . .

KENT

By Apollo, King, you're taking the names of the gods in vain.

LEAR

Oh, you lowlife! Scum!

ALBANY, CORNWALL

Please stop, sir.

KENT

Sure, kill the doctor who's trying to cure you and pay your disease. Take back your gift to Albany and Cornwall. If you don't, then as long as I'm able to speak I'll keep telling you you've done a bad, bad thing.

LEAR

Listen to me, you traitor. You'll pay the price for trying to make me go back on the vow I made when I bequeathed my kingdom to them. I've never broken a vow yet. You tried to make me revise my judgment on my youngest daughter, disrespecting my power as

Our potency made good, take thy reward:
Five days we do allot thee for provision
To shield thee from diseases of the world.
175   And on the sixth to turn thy hated back
Upon our kingdom. If on the next day following
Thy banished trunk be found in our dominions,
The moment is thy death. Away! By Jupiter,
This shall not be revoked.

KENT
180   Why, fare thee well, King. Sith thus thou wilt appear,
Freedom lives hence, and banishment is here.
(to CORDELIA*)*
The gods to their dear shelter take thee, maid,
That justly think'st and hast most rightly said!
(to REGAN *and* GONERIL*)*
And your large speeches may your deeds approve,
185   That good effects may spring from words of love.—
Thus Kent, O princes, bids you all adieu.
He'll shape his old course in a country new.

Exit KENT

Flourish. Enter GLOUCESTER *with the King of* FRANCE, *the Duke of* BURGUNDY, *and attendants*

GLOUCESTER
Here's France and Burgundy, my noble lord.

LEAR
My lord of Burgundy.
190   We first address towards you, who with this king
Hath rivaled for our daughter. What in the least
Will you require in present dower with her
Or cease your quest of love?

king—which I can't put up with either as a ruler or as a person. This is your punishment: I'll give you five days to gather together what you need to survive, then on the sixth day you'll leave this kingdom that hates you. If the day after that you're found in my kingdom, you die. Now get out of here! I swear by Jupiter I'll never revoke this punishment.

KENT

Farewell, King. If this is how you act, it's clear that freedom has been banished from this kingdom. *(to* CORDELIA*)* I hope the gods will protect you, my dear girl, for thinking fairly and speaking correctly. *(to* REGAN *and* GONERIL*)* And you two, I hope your actions carry out your grand promises of love, so that big words can bring big results. Farewell to all of you. I'll carry on my old life in a new land.

KENT *exits.*

Trumpets play. GLOUCESTER *enters with the King of* FRANCE, *the Duke of* BURGUNDY, *and attendants.*

GLOUCESTER
Here are the rulers of France and Burgundy, my lord.

LEAR
My lord the ruler of Burgundy, I'll speak to you first. You've been competing with this king for my daughter. What's the least that you will settle for as a dowry?

A dowry is a payment traditionally made to a husband by his father-in-law at the time of marriage.

BURGUNDY
Most royal majesty,
I crave no more than hath your highness offered.
195 Nor will you tender less.

LEAR
Right noble Burgundy,
When she was dear to us we did hold her so,
But now her price is fallen. Sir, there she stands.
If aught within that little seeming substance,
Or all of it, with our displeasure pieced
200 And nothing more, may fitly like your grace,
She's there, and she is yours.

BURGUNDY
I know no answer.

LEAR
Sir, will you, with those infirmities she owes—
Unfriended, new adopted to our hate,
Dowered with our curse and strangered with our oath—
205 Take her or leave her?

BURGUNDY
Pardon me, royal sir.
Election makes not up in such conditions.

LEAR
Then leave her, sir, for by the power that made me,
I tell you all her wealth.
(to **FRANCE***)* For you, great King,
I would not from your love make such a stray
210 To match you where I hate. Therefore beseech you
T' avert your liking a more worthier way
Than on a wretch whom Nature is ashamed
Almost t' acknowledge hers.

FRANCE
This is most strange,
That she that even but now was your best object—
215 The argument of your praise, balm of your age,
Most best, most dearest—should in this trice of time

BURGUNDY

Your highness, I want nothing more than what you've already offered. I know you'll offer nothing less than that.

LEAR

Burgundy, I valued her highly when I cared about her. But now her price has fallen. There she is, over there. If there's anything you like about that worthless little thing, then go for it. She's all yours. But what you see is what you get—her only dowry is my disapproval. There she is.

BURGUNDY

I don't know what to say.

LEAR

She's got big flaws. She has no friends or protectors. I no longer love her. Her only dowry is my curse and banishment. So do you take her or leave her?

BURGUNDY

I'm sorry, sir, but nobody can make a choice like this in such circumstances.

LEAR

Then leave her, sir. I swear to God she's not worth anything more than what I told you. *(to* FRANCE*)* And as for you, great King of France, I'd never insult our friendship by encouraging you to marry a girl I hate. So I beg you to look around for a better match than this wretched creature that you can barely call human.

FRANCE

This is very odd. Until very recently she was your favorite, the object of all your praise and the delight of your old age. It's strange that someone so dear to you could do anything so horrible as to warrant this sud-

Commit a thing so monstrous to dismantle
So many folds of favor. Sure, her offense
Must be of such unnatural degree
220   That monsters it (or your fore-vouched affection
Fall into taint), which to believe of her
Must be a faith that reason without miracle
Could never plant in me.

CORDELIA
(to LEAR) I yet beseech your majesty,
225   If for I want that glib and oily art
To speak and purpose not—since what I well intend,
I'll do 't before I speak—that you make known
It is no vicious blot, murder, or foulness,
No unchaste action or dishonored step
230   That hath deprived me of your grace and favor,
But even for want of that for which I am richer:
A still-soliciting eye and such a tongue
As I am glad I have not, though not to have it
Hath lost me in your liking.

LEAR
Go to, go to. Better thou
235   Hadst not been born than not t' have pleased me better.

FRANCE
Is it no more but this—a tardiness in nature
Which often leaves the history unspoke
That it intends to do?—My lord of Burgundy,
What say you to the lady? Love's not love
240   When it is mingled with regards that stands
Aloof from th' entire point. Will you have her?
She is herself a dowry.

BURGUNDY
(to LEAR)   Royal King,
Give but that portion which yourself proposed,
And here I take Cordelia by the hand,
245   Duchess of Burgundy.

den hatred. Her crime must be extreme and monstrous, or else your earlier love for her wasn't as true as it seemed. But it'd take a miracle to make me believe she could do anything that horrible.

CORDELIA

(to LEAR*)* Please, your majesty, I don't have a glib way with words and I only say what I mean. If I decide to do something, then I do it instead of talking about it. So I beg your majesty to let people know that it wasn't because I did something atrocious
that I fell from your favor. I didn't murder or commit any immoral or lustful act. I'm out of favor simply because I'm not a fortune-hunter and I don't have a smooth way with words—and I'm a better person because of it, even though it has cost me your love.

LEAR

Enough. It would've been better for you not to have been born at all than to displease me as you did.

FRANCE

You mean this is the whole problem, that she is shy and hasn't said everything she means to say and do?— My lord of Burgundy, what do you have to say to this lady? Love's not love when it gets mixed up with irrelevant outside matters. Will you marry her? She herself is as valuable as any dowry could ever be.

BURGUNDY

(to LEAR*)* King, just give me the dowry you promised me, and I'll make Cordelia the Duchess of Burgundy right away.

LEAR
Nothing. I have sworn. I am firm.

BURGUNDY
(to CORDELIA*)* I am sorry then. You have so lost a father
That you must lose a husband.

CORDELIA
Peace be with Burgundy.
250 Since that respects and fortunes are his love,
I shall not be his wife.

FRANCE
Fairest Cordelia, that art most rich being poor,
Most choice forsaken, and most loved despised!
Thee and thy virtues here I seize upon,
255 Be it lawful I take up what's cast away.
Gods, gods! 'Tis strange that from their cold'st neglect
My love should kindle to inflamed respect.—
Thy dowerless daughter, King, thrown to my chance,
Is queen of us, of ours, and our fair France.
260 Not all the dukes of waterish Burgundy
Can buy this unprized precious maid of me.—
Bid them farewell, Cordelia, though unkind.
Thou losest here, a better where to find.

LEAR
Thou hast her, France. Let her be thine, for we
265 Have no such daughter, nor shall ever see
That face of hers again. *(to* CORDELIA*)* Therefore be gone
Without our grace, our love, our benison.—
Come, noble Burgundy.

Flourish

Exeunt all but FRANCE,
GONERIL, REGAN, *and* CORDELIA

FRANCE
Bid farewell to your sisters.

LEAR

No, I'll give nothing. I won't budge on that.

BURGUNDY

(to CORDELIA*)* In that case, I'm sorry you have to lose me as a husband because you lost the king as a father.

CORDELIA

Peace to you, my lord of Burgundy. Since you love money and power so much, I won't be your wife.

FRANCE

Beautiful Cordelia, you're all the richer now that you're poor. You're more valuable now that you're rejected and more loved now that you're hated.
I'll take you and your wonderful virtues here and now, if it's okay that I'm picking up what others have thrown away. It's so strange that in neglecting you so cruelly, the gods have made me love you so dearly.— King, the daughter you've rejected is now mine, as Queen of France. No Duke of spineless Burgundy can take this treasure of a girl from me now.—Say goodbye to them, Cordelia, even though they've been unkind to you. You'll find a much better place in France than what you're giving up here.

LEAR

She's yours, King of France. Take her. She's no longer my daughter, and I'll never see her face again. *(to* CORDELIA*)* So get out of here. Leave without any blessing or love from me.—Come with me, Burgundy.

Trumpets play.

Everyone exits except FRANCE, GONERIL, REGAN, *and* CORDELIA.

FRANCE

Say goodbye to your sisters.

CORDELIA

270   The jewels of our father, with washed eyes
       Cordelia leaves you. I know you what you are,
       And like a sister am most loath to call
       Your faults as they are named. Love well our father.
       To your professèd bosoms I commit him.
275   But yet, alas, stood I within his grace,
       I would prefer him to a better place.
       So farewell to you both.

REGAN

       Prescribe not us our duty.

GONERIL

                                        Let your study
       Be to content your lord, who hath received you
280   At fortune's alms. You have obedience scanted,
       And well are worth the want that you have wanted.

CORDELIA

       Time shall unfold what plighted cunning hides,
       Who covers faults at last with shame derides.
       Well may you prosper.

FRANCE

285   Come, my fair Cordelia.

                                Exeunt FRANCE *and* CORDELIA

GONERIL

       Sister, it is not a little I have to say of what most nearly
       appertains to us both. I think our father will hence tonight.

REGAN

       That's most certain, and with you. Next month with us.

GONERIL

       You see how full of changes his age is. The observation we
290   have made of it hath not been little. He always loved our
       sister most, and with what poor judgment he hath now cast
       her off appears too grossly.

CORDELIA

Sisters, you whom our father loves so dearly, I leave you now with tears in my eyes. I know you for what you really are, but as your sister I'm reluctant to criticize you. Take good care of our father and show him the love that you have professed. I leave him in your care—but oh, if only I were still in his favor I could arrange for better care for him. Goodbye to you both.

REGAN

Don't tell us what our duty is.

GONERIL

You should focus instead on pleasing your husband, who's taken you in as an act of charity. You've failed to obey your father and you deserve to be deprived of everything that's been taken away from you.

CORDELIA

Time will tell what you've got up your sleeve. You can be deceitful in the short term, but eventually truth will come out. Have a good life.

FRANCE

Come with me, my dear Cordelia.

FRANCE and CORDELIA exit.

GONERIL

Sister, I have a lot to say about things that concern us both. I think that our father will leave here tonight.

REGAN

Yes, I'm sure he will—to stay with you. Next month he'll stay with us.

GONERIL

He's so flighty in his old age, as we keep noticing. He has always loved Cordelia best, and his bad judgment in disowning her now is obvious.

REGAN
'Tis the infirmity of his age. Yet he hath ever but slenderly known himself.

GONERIL
295 The best and soundest of his time hath been but rash. Then must we look from his age to receive not alone the imperfections of long-engrafted condition, but therewithal the unruly waywardness that infirm and choleric years bring with them.

REGAN
300 Such unconstant starts are we like to have from him as this of Kent's banishment.

GONERIL
There is further compliment of leave-taking between France and him. Pray you, let's sit together. If our father carry authority with such dispositions as he bears, this last
305 surrender of his will but offend us.

REGAN
We shall further think on 't.

GONERIL
We must do something, and i' th' heat.

Exeunt

REGAN

He's going senile. But then again he's never really understood his own feelings very well.

GONERIL

Yes, he was hotheaded even in the prime of his life. Now that he's old, we can expect to have to deal not only with his old character flaws, which have turned into deep-rooted habits, but also with the uncontrollable crabbiness that comes with old age.

REGAN

We'll probably witness many more outbursts from him, like banishing Kent.

GONERIL

There's still the King of France's farewell ceremony. Let's put our heads together. If our father continues to use his authority as usual, then his recent abdication of the kingdom will just hurt us.

REGAN

We'll have to think about it carefully.

GONERIL

We have to strike while the iron's hot.

They exit.

ACT 1, SCENE 2

Enter EDMUND *the bastard, with a letter*

EDMUND
Thou, nature, art my goddess. To thy law
My services are bound. Wherefore should I
Stand in the plague of custom and permit
The curiosity of nations to deprive me
5   For that I am some twelve or fourteen moonshines
Lag of a brother? Why "bastard"? Wherefore "base"?
When my dimensions are as well compact,
My mind as generous, and my shape as true
As honest madam's issue? Why brand they us
10   With "base," with "baseness," "bastardy," "base," "base"—
Who in the lusty stealth of nature take
More composition and fierce quality
Than doth within a dull, stale, tirèd bed
Go to th' creating a whole tribe of fops
15   Got 'tween a sleep and wake? Well then,
Legitimate Edgar, I must have your land.
Our father's love is to the bastard Edmund
As to the legitimate.—Fine word, "legitimate"!—
Well, my legitimate, if this letter speed
20   And my invention thrive, Edmund the base
Shall top th' legitimate. I grow, I prosper.
Now, gods, stand up for bastards!

Enter GLOUCESTER
EDMUND *looks over his letter*

GLOUCESTER
Kent banished thus? And France in choler parted?
And the king gone tonight, prescribed his power
25   Confined to exhibition? All this done
Upon the gad?—Edmund, how now? What news?

ACT 1, SCENE 2

EDMUND *enters with a letter.*

EDMUND

I only worship what's natural, not what's manmade. Why should I let myself be tortured by manmade social customs that deprive me of my rights simply because I was born twelve or fourteen months later than my older brother? Why do they call me "bastard" and "lowlife" when I'm just as gifted in mind and body as legitimate children? Why do they call us bastards "lowlifes"? Always "lowlife," "bastard," "lowlife," "lowlife." At least we bastards were conceived in a moment of passionate lust rather than in a dull, tired marriage bed, where half-sleeping parents monotonously churn out a bunch of sissy kids. All right then, legitimate brother Edgar, I have to have your lands. Our father loves me just as much as the legitimate Edgar. What a nice word that is, "legitimate"! Well, my legitimate Edgar, if this letter works and my plan succeeds, Edmund the lowlife will beat the legitimate. Look out, I'm on my way up. Three cheers for bastards!

GLOUCESTER *enters.* EDMUND *looks over his letter.*

GLOUCESTER

Kent's been banished just like that? And the King of France gone in a huff? And King Lear's abdicated his authority, making his kingship a ceremonial title only? All this so suddenly?—Edmund, what's going on? What's the news?

EDMUND
(*pocketing the letter*) So please your lordship, none.

GLOUCESTER
Why so earnestly seek you to put up that letter?

EDMUND
I know no news, my lord.

GLOUCESTER
30   What paper were you reading?

EDMUND
Nothing, my lord.

GLOUCESTER
No? What needed, then, that terrible dispatch of it into
your pocket? The quality of nothing hath not such need to
hide itself. Let's see.—Come, if it be nothing, I shall not
35   need spectacles.

EDMUND
I beseech you, sir, pardon me. It is a letter from my brother
that I have not all o'er-read. And for so much as I have
perused, I find it not fit for your o'erlooking.

GLOUCESTER
Give me the letter, sir.

EDMUND
40   I shall offend, either to detain or give it. The contents, as in
part I understand them, are to blame.

GLOUCESTER
(*taking the letter*) Let's see, let's see.

EDMUND
I hope, for my brother's justification, he wrote this but as an
essay or taste of my virtue.

GLOUCESTER
(*reads*)
45   "This policy and reverence of age makes the world
bitter to the best of our times, keeps our fortunes from
us till our oldness cannot relish them. I begin to find
an idle and fond bondage in the oppression of aged
tyranny, who sways not as it hath power but as it is

EDMUND

(pocketing the letter) No news, my lord.

GLOUCESTER

Why are you hiding that letter?

EDMUND

I don't have any news to report, my lord.

GLOUCESTER

What's that paper you were reading?

EDMUND

It's nothing, my lord.

GLOUCESTER

No? Then why did you have to stick it in your pocket in such a hurry? If it were nothing, you wouldn't need to hide it. Let's see it. Come on, if it's nothing, I won't need glasses to read it.

EDMUND

Please, sir, I beg you. It's a letter from my brother that I haven't finished reading yet. But judging from the bit I have read, it's not fit for you to see.

GLOUCESTER

Give me that letter, sir.

EDMUND

Now I'll offend you whether I give it to you or not. The problem is in what the letter says, as far as I can tell.

GLOUCESTER

(taking the letter) Let's see, let's see.

EDMUND

I hope for my brother's sake that he just wrote it to test my honor.

GLOUCESTER

(reads)

"The custom of respecting the elderly makes it hard for the young and healthy to live well, and keeps us without our inheritance until we are so old we can't enjoy our happiness anyway. The

50 suffered. Come to me, that of this I may speak more.
If our father would sleep till I waked him, you should
enjoy half his revenue forever, and live the beloved of
your brother,
                                    Edgar."
55 Hum, conspiracy? "'Sleep till I wake him, you should enjoy
half his revenue"—my son Edgar? Had he a hand to write
this, a heart and brain to breed it in? When came this to
you? Who brought it?

EDMUND
It was not brought me, my lord. There's the cunning of it.
60 I found it thrown in at the casement of my closet.

GLOUCESTER
You know the character to be your brother's?

EDMUND
If the matter were good, my lord, I durst swear it were his.
But in respect of that, I would fain think it were not.

GLOUCESTER
It is his.

EDMUND
65 It is his hand, my lord, but I hope his heart is not in the
contents.

GLOUCESTER
Has he never before sounded you in this business?

EDMUND
Never, my lord. But I have heard him oft maintain it to be
fit that, sons at perfect age and fathers declined, the father
70 should be as ward to the son, and the son manage his
revenue.

GLOUCESTER
O villain, villain! His very opinion in the letter! Abhorred
villain! Unnatural, detested, brutish villain—worse than

power of the elderly is starting to feel like a silly and foolish slavery to me, and they only enjoy that power because we let them have it. Come talk to me about this. If our father were dead you'd receive half of his revenue forever, and you'd have my undying love,

Edgar."

Hmm, what's this, a conspiracy? "If our father were dead, you'd receive half of his revenue forever"—my son Edgar? How did he bring himself to write such a thing? How could he have even entertained these thoughts in his heart? How did you get this letter? Who delivered it?

EDMUND

Nobody delivered it, my lord. That's what's clever about it. It was tossed into the window of my room.

GLOUCESTER

You're sure the handwriting is your brother's?

EDMUND

If he'd written nice things, I'd swear yes right away. But as it stands, I wish I could believe it wasn't.

GLOUCESTER

But it is his handwriting?

EDMUND

It's his handwriting, my lord, but I hope he didn't mean what he wrote.

GLOUCESTER

Has he ever tested out these ideas on you before?

EDMUND

Never, my lord. But I've often heard him argue that when sons are at their prime and their fathers are declining, the sons should be their fathers' guardians and manage their fathers' money.

GLOUCESTER

Oh, what a villain! That's just what he said in the letter. Evil villain! Monstrous, hateful, bestial villain!

brutish! Go, sirrah, seek him. I'll apprehend him.
75 Abominable villain! Where is he?

EDMUND
I do not well know, my lord. If it shall please you to
suspend your indignation against my brother till you can
derive from him better testimony of his intent, you shall
run a certain course—where if you violently proceed
80 against him, mistaking his purpose, it would make a great
gap in your own honor and shake in pieces the heart of his
obedience. I dare pawn down my life for him that he hath
wrote this to feel my affection to your honor and to no other
pretense of danger.

GLOUCESTER
85 Think you so?

EDMUND
If your honor judge it meet, I will place you where you shall
hear us confer of this and by an auricular assurance have
your satisfaction—and that without any further delay than
this very evening.

GLOUCESTER
90 He cannot be such a monster—

EDMUND
Nor is not, sure.

GLOUCESTER
To his father, that so tenderly and entirely loves him.
Heaven and earth! Edmund, seek him out, wind me into
him, I pray you. Frame the business after your own
95 wisdom. I would unstate myself to be in a due resolution.

EDMUND
I will seek him, sir, presently, convey the business as I shall
find means, and acquaint you withal.

GLOUCESTER
These late eclipses in the sun and moon portend no good to
us. Though the wisdom of nature can reason it thus and
100 thus, yet nature finds itself scourged by the sequent effects.
Love cools, friendship falls off, brothers divide, in cities

Worse than a beast! Go look for him. I'll arrest him. Horrid villain! Where is he?

EDMUND

I'm not sure, my lord. But it may be a good idea to restrain your rage until you find out exactly what he meant. If you go after him and then find out that you made a mistake, it would damage your reputation and greatly undermine his loyalty to you. I'll bet my life that he only wrote this letter to gauge my love for you, and for no other reason.

GLOUCESTER

Do you think so?

EDMUND

If you agree, I'll hide you somewhere where you can eavesdrop on us talking about it, and hear how he feels with your own ears. You won't have to wait longer than until tonight.

GLOUCESTER

He can't possibly be such a monster—

EDMUND

And I'm sure he isn't.

GLOUCESTER

—toward his own father who loves him so completely. Oh, God! Edmund, go find him. Gain his confidence for me, please. Manage him however you think best. I'd give up my rank and fortune to be free from my doubts.

EDMUND

I'll find him right away, sir, and carry out the business as well as I can. Then I'll let you know what's happening.

GLOUCESTER

These recent eclipses of the sun and moon don't bode well for us. Though science can explain them away, disasters still come after eclipses. Love cools off, friendships break up, and brothers become enemies. Riots

mutinies, in countries discord, in palaces treason, and the
bond cracked 'twixt son and father. This villain of mine
comes under the prediction—there's son against father.
105   The king falls from bias of nature—there's father against
child. We have seen the best of our time. Machinations,
hollowness, treachery, and all ruinous disorders follow us
disquietly to our graves. Find out this villain, Edmund. It
shall lose thee nothing. Do it carefully.—And the noble and
110   true-hearted Kent banished, his offense honesty! 'Tis
strange, strange.

Exit GLOUCESTER

EDMUND
This is the excellent foppery of the world that when we are
sick in fortune—often the surfeit of our own behavior—we
make guilty of our disasters the sun, the moon, and the
115   stars, as if we were villains by necessity, fools by heavenly
compulsion, knaves, thieves, and treachers by spherical
predominance, drunkards, liars, and adulterers by an
enforced obedience of planetary influence, and all that we
are evil in by a divine thrusting-on. An admirable evasion
120   of whoremaster man, to lay his goatish disposition to the
charge of a star! My father compounded with my mother
under the dragon's tail and my nativity was under Ursa
Major, so that it follows I am rough and lecherous. Fut, I
should have been that I am, had the maidenliest star in the
125   firmament twinkled on my bastardizing. Edgar—

Enter EDGAR

and pat on 's cue he comes like the catastrophe of the old
comedy. My cue is villainous melancholy, with a sigh like
Tom o' Bedlam. Oh, these eclipses do portend these
divisions! Fa, sol, la, mi.

break out, civil war erupts, kings are betrayed, and the bond between father and son snaps. This wicked son of mine confirms the prediction —son against father. The king acts unnaturally—father against child. We've seen the best our age has to offer. Conspiracies, fakery, betrayal, and disorder are all that's left until we die. Find out what this villainous Edgar is thinking, Edmund. You won't lose any respect. Just do it carefully.—And to think that the noble and loyal Kent has been banished, for the crime of telling the truth! It's strange, strange.

GLOUCESTER *exits.*

EDMUND

This is a classic example of the idiocy of the world: when we're down and out—often because of our own excesses —we put all the blame on the sun, the moon, and the stars, as if they forced us to be bad, or the heavens compelled us to be villainous or stupid. As if we become thieves and traitors according to astrological signs or obey planetary influences to become drunks, liars, and adulterers! As if some universal power pushed us into evil deeds! What a sneaky trick it is for lustful mankind to blame our horniness on some star! My father and mother coupled when the demonic moon was descending, and I was born under the Big Dipper, so it's inevitable that I'm rude and oversexed. Christ! I would have been what I am even if the most virginal star in the heavens had twinkled at my conception. Edgar—

EDGAR *enters.*

and, speak of the devil, here he comes, right on cue. I've got to play the role and sigh like a poor beggar.— Oh, these eclipses predict such disorder. Fa, sol, la, mi.

EDGAR

130   How now, brother Edmund? What serious contemplation
    are you in?

EDMUND

    I am thinking, brother, of a prediction I read this other day,
    what should follow these eclipses.

EDGAR

    Do you busy yourself about that?

EDMUND

135   I promise you, the effects he writes of succeed unhappily —
    as of unnaturalness between the child and the parent,
    death, dearth, dissolutions of ancient amities, divisions in
    state, menaces and maledictions against king and nobles,
    needless diffidences, banishment of friends, dissipation of
140   cohorts, nuptial breaches, and I know not what.

EDGAR

    How long have you been a sectary astronomical?

EDMUND

    Come, come. When saw you my father last?

EDGAR

    Why, the night gone by.

EDMUND

    Spake you with him?

EDGAR

145   Ay, two hours together.

EDMUND

    Parted you in good terms? Found you no displeasure in him
    by word or countenance?

EDGAR

    None at all.

EDMUND

    Bethink yourself wherein you may have offended him. And
150   at my entreaty forbear his presence till some little time hath
    qualified the heat of his displeasure, which at this instant so
    rageth in him that with the mischief of your person it would
    scarcely allay.

EDGAR

Hello, brother Edmund. What are you thinking about so seriously?

EDMUND

I was thinking about what an astrologer predicted the other day. He wrote about what these eclipses mean.

EDGAR

Are you spending your valuable time on that?

EDMUND

Oh, I assure you the things he writes about are wretched —things like divisions between parents and children, death, famine, broken friendships, political rebellion, treason against the king and noblemen, exiled friends, dissolved armies, adultery, and I don't know what else.

EDGAR

How long have you believed in astrology?

EDMUND

Come on. When was the last time you saw my father?

EDGAR

Why, last night.

EDMUND

Did you speak to him?

EDGAR

Yes, we talked for a couple of hours.

EDMUND

Did you leave on good terms? Did he express any dissatisfaction with you, either in his words or his face?

EDGAR

No, none at all.

EDMUND

Try to remember how you might have offended him, and try to avoid spending time with him until his anger has cooled a little. Right now he's so angry that even if he harmed you physically, he'd still be raging.

EDGAR
Some villain hath done me wrong.

EDMUND
155 That's my fear. I pray you, have a continent forbearance till the speed of his rage goes slower. And as I say, retire with me to my lodging, from whence I will fitly bring you to hear my lord speak. Pray ye, go. There's my key. If you do stir abroad, go armed.

EDGAR
160 Armed, brother?

EDMUND
Brother, I advise you to the best. Go armed. I am no honest man if there be any good meaning towards you. I have told you what I have seen and heard—but faintly, nothing like the image and horror of it. Pray you, away.

EDGAR
165 Shall I hear from you anon?

EDMUND
I do serve you in this business.

Exit EDGAR

A credulous father, and a brother noble—
Whose nature is so far from doing harms
That he suspects none, on whose foolish honesty
170 My practices ride easy. I see the business.
Let me, if not by birth, have lands by wit.
All with me's meet that I can fashion fit.

Exit

EDGAR

Some villain has told lies about me.

EDMUND

That's what I'm afraid of. I suggest you lay low until his rage cools a little. In the meantime, come home with me, and when the time is right I'll take you to talk to him. Please go. Here's my key. If you go outside, arm yourself.

EDGAR

Arm myself?

EDMUND

Brother, I'm giving you good advice. Arm yourself. I'd be a liar if I told you nobody wanted to hurt you. I've told you what I've seen and heard, but I've toned it down a lot. I've spared you you the full extent of the horror that threatens you. Now please go.

EDGAR

Will I hear from you soon?

EDMUND

I'll help you through this business.

EDGAR *exits.*

A gullible father and a brother who's so innocent that he can't suspect anyone else of wanting to hurt him— these are the two fools I need for my plan to work. I know exactly how to proceed. If I can't have an estate by birthright, then I'll get it by being clever. Any trick that works is good for me.

He exits.

ACT 1, SCENE 3

Enter GONERIL *and her steward* OSWALD

GONERIL
>Did my father strike my gentleman
>For chiding of his fool?

OSWALD
>   Ay, madam.

GONERIL
>By day and night he wrongs me. Every hour
>He flashes into one gross crime or other
5   That sets us all at odds. I'll not endure it.
>His knights grow riotous, and himself upbraids us
>On every trifle. When he returns from hunting,
>I will not speak with him. Say I am sick.
>If you come slack of former services,
10   You shall do well. The fault of it I'll answer.

OSWALD
>He's coming, madam. I hear him.

Hunting horns within

GONERIL
>Put on what weary negligence you please,
>You and your fellow servants. I'll have it come to question.
>If he distaste it, let him to our sister,
15   Whose mind and mine I know in that are one,
>Not to be overruled. Idle old man
>That still would manage those authorities
>That he hath given away! Now by my life,
>Old fools are babes again and must be used
20   With checks as flatteries, when they are seen abused.
>Remember what I have said.

OSWALD
>   Very well, madam.

ACT 1, SCENE 3

steward = person responsible for running the household

GONERIL *enters with her steward,* OSWALD.

GONERIL

Did my father hit one of my attendants for scolding his fool?

OSWALD

Yes, ma'am.

GONERIL

He constantly offends me. Every hour he comes out with some horrible new offense that puts us all on edge. I won't stand for it. His knights are getting out of control, and he himself reprimands us about every little detail. When he comes back from hunting, I'm not going to speak to him. Tell him I'm sick. And if you're not as attentive in serving him as you used to be, that'll be good. I'll take responsibility for it.

OSWALD

He's coming, ma'am. I hear him.

Hunting horns play offstage.

GONERIL

Be as lazy and neglectful as you like around him—you and the other servants. I want it to become an issue. If he doesn't like it, he can go live with my sister. I know she feels the same way about him that I do, and she'll stand her ground. That useless old man still thinks he can wield all the powers he's given away. I swear, old fools become like babies again. You can't just flatter them; you also have to discipline them when you see that they're misguided. Remember what I've told you.

OSWALD

Very well, ma'am.

GONERIL
And let his knights have colder looks among you.
What grows of it, no matter. Advise your fellows so.
I would breed from hence occasions, and I shall,
25 That I may speak. I'll write straight to my sister
To hold my very course. Go, prepare for dinner.

Exeunt severally

GONERIL

And make sure the servants are less friendly to his knights. Don't worry about the consequences. Tell your men as much. I want this to provoke confrontations, so I can give him a piece of my mind. I'll write to my sister and tell her my plans. Now go, set up for dinner.

They exit in opposite directions.

ACT 1, SCENE 4

Enter KENT *disguised*

KENT

If but as well I other accents borrow,
That can my speech diffuse, my good intent
May carry through itself to that full issue
For which I razed my likeness. Now, banished Kent,

5   If thou canst serve where thou dost stand condemned,
So may it come thy master, whom thou lovest,
Shall find thee full of labors.

Horns within
Enter LEAR *with attendant knights*

LEAR

Let me not stay a jot for dinner. Go get it ready.

Exit attendant

(to KENT*)* How now, what art thou?

KENT

10   A man, sir.

LEAR

What dost thou profess? What wouldst thou with us?

KENT

I do profess to be no less than I seem—to serve him truly
that will put me in trust, to love him that is honest, to
converse with him that is wise and says little, to fear

15   judgment, to fight when I cannot choose, and to eat no fish.

LEAR

What art thou?

KENT

A very honest-hearted fellow, and as poor as the king.

LEAR

If thou beest as poor for a subject as he's for a king, thou'rt
poor enough. What wouldst thou?

ACT 1, SCENE 4

KENT *enters in disguise.*

KENT

If I can disguise my voice as well as my appearance, then I'll be able to carry out my plan perfectly. I was banished, but hopefully I can serve the very king who condemned me. I love my master, and he'll find me very hard-working.

Trumpets play offstage. LEAR *enters with his attendant knights.*

LEAR

Don't make me wait for dinner even a moment. Get it ready immediately.

An attendant exits.

(to KENT*)* Well now, who are you?

KENT

A man, sir.

LEAR

What's your profession? What do you want from me?

KENT

Kent interprets "your profession" as "your declaration" rather than "your job."

I profess that I'm as good as I seem—I'll faithfully serve a master who trusts me, love those who are honest, talk with those who are wise and don't talk too much. I'm God-fearing, I fight if I must, and I don't eat fish.

LEAR

But who are you?

KENT

An honest guy who's as poor as the king.

LEAR

If you're as poor a subject as he is a king, you definitely are poor. What do you want?

KENT

20   Service.

LEAR

Who wouldst thou serve?

KENT

You.

LEAR

Dost thou know me, fellow?

KENT

No, sir. But you have that in your countenance which I
25   would fain call master.

LEAR

What's that?

KENT

Authority.

LEAR

What services canst thou do?

KENT

I can keep honest counsel, ride, run, mar a curious tale in
30   telling it, and deliver a plain message bluntly. That which
ordinary men are fit for, I am qualified in. And the best of
me is diligence.

LEAR

How old art thou?

KENT

Not so young, sir, to love a woman for singing, nor so old to
35   dote on her for anything. I have years on my back forty-
eight.

LEAR

Follow me. Thou shalt serve me. If I like thee no worse after
dinner, I will not part from thee yet.—Dinner, ho, dinner!
Where's my knave, my fool?—Go you, and call my fool
40   hither.

Exit attendant

Enter OSWALD *the steward*

KENT

To work as a servant.

LEAR

Who do you want to work for?

KENT

You.

LEAR

Do you know me?

KENT

No, sir, but there's something about your face that makes me want to serve you.

LEAR

What do you see in my face?

KENT

Authority.

LEAR

What work can you do?

KENT

I can be discreet in honorable matters, ride a horse, run, tell a good story badly, and deliver a plain message bluntly. I'm good at everything that ordinary men can do. The best thing about me is that I'm hardworking.

LEAR

How old are you?

KENT

Not young enough to fall in love with a woman because she sings well, but not old enough to dote on a woman for any reason. I'm forty-eight.

LEAR

Follow me. You'll work for me. If I still like you after dinner, I won't send you away yet.—Hey, dinnertime! Dinner! Where's my fool?—Go call my fool and have him come here.

An attendant exits.

OSWALD *enters.*

You, you, sirrah, where's my daughter?

OSWALD
So please you—

Exit OSWALD

LEAR
What says the fellow there? Call the clotpoll back.

Exit FIRST KNIGHT

Where's my fool, ho? I think the world's asleep.

Enter FIRST KNIGHT

45   How now? Where's that mongrel?

FIRST KNIGHT
He says, my lord, your daughter is not well.

LEAR
Why came not the slave back to me when I called him.

FIRST KNIGHT
Sir, he answered me in the roundest manner he would not.

LEAR
He would not?

FIRST KNIGHT
50   My lord, I know not what the matter is, but to my judgment
your highness is not entertained with that ceremonious
affection as you were wont. There's a great abatement of
kindness appears as well in the general dependants as in the
duke himself also, and your daughter.

LEAR
55   Ha! Sayest thou so?

FIRST KNIGHT
I beseech you pardon me, my lord, if I be mistaken—for my
duty cannot be silent when I think your highness wronged.

You, sir, where's my daughter?

OSWALD

I beg your pardon, sir—

OSWALD *exits.*

LEAR

What did that guy say? Call the numbskull back in here.

The FIRST KNIGHT *exits*

Where's my fool? You'd think everyone was asleep.

The FIRST KNIGHT *enters again.*

So what's going on? Where's that dog?

FIRST KNIGHT

He says your daughter's not feeling well, my lord.

LEAR

Why didn't the jerk come back to me when I called him?

FIRST KNIGHT

Sir, he told me quite bluntly that he didn't feel like it.

LEAR

Didn't feel like it?

FIRST KNIGHT

My lord, I don't know what's going on, but it seems to me that your highness isn't being treated as politely as before. The servants, the duke, and your daughter all seem to be treating you less kindly.

LEAR

Huh! Do you really mean that?

FIRST KNIGHT

Please forgive me if I'm mistaken, my lord—but I can't keep quiet when I think you're being insulted.

LEAR

Thou but rememberest me of mine own conception. I have
perceived a most faint neglect of late, which I have rather
60   blamed as mine own jealous curiosity than as a very
pretense and purpose of unkindness. I will look further
into 't. But where's my fool? I have not seen him this two days.

FIRST KNIGHT

Since my young lady's going into France, sir, the fool hath
much pined away.

LEAR

65   No more of that. I have noted it well. Go you and tell my
daughter I would speak with her.

Exit an attendant

Go you, call hither my fool.

Exit another attendant

Enter OSWALD

O you sir, you, come you hither, sir. Who am I, sir?

OSWALD

My lady's father.

LEAR

70   "My lady's father"? My lord's knave, your whoreson dog!
You slave, you cur!

OSWALD

I am none of these, my lord. I beseech your pardon.

LEAR

Do you bandy looks with me, you rascal?
(he strikes OSWALD*)*

OSWALD

I'll not be strucken, my lord.

KENT

(tripping OSWALD*)*
75   Nor tripped neither, you base football player.

LEAR

No, you're just reminding me of something I've also noticed. I've felt neglected recently, but I decided that it was more likely that I was being hypersensitive than that they were intentionally unkind. I'll look into it further. But where's my fool? I haven't seen him for two days.

FIRST KNIGHT

Ever since Cordelia left for France, sir, the fool has been depressed.

LEAR

Let's not talk about it. I've noticed it myself. Go and tell my daughter I want to speak with her.

An attendant exits.

And you, go call my fool.

Another attendant exits.

OSWALD *enters.*

You there, sir, come here please. Who am I, sir?

OSWALD

The father of the lady of the house, sir.

LEAR

"The father of the lady of the house"? You scoundrel! You lowlife son-of-a-bitch! You dog, you peasant!

OSWALD

I'm sorry, sir, but I'm not any of those things.

LEAR

Are you making faces at me, you scoundrel? *(he hits* OSWALD*)*

OSWALD

I won't be hit, my lord.

KENT

Football (soccer) was considered a lower-class game.

(tripping OSWALD*)* Or tripped, you lowlife football player?

LEAR

(to KENT*)* I thank thee, fellow. Thou servest me, and I'll love
thee.

KENT

(to OSWALD*)* Come, sir, arise, away! I'll teach you
differences. Away, away. If you will measure your lubber's
80   length again, tarry. But away, go to. Have you wisdom? So.

Exit OSWALD

LEAR

Now, my friendly knave, I thank thee.

Enter FOOL

(gives KENT *money)* There's earnest of thy service.

FOOL

Let me hire him too.—Here's my coxcomb.
(offers KENT *his cap)*

LEAR

How now, my pretty knave? How dost thou?

FOOL

85   *(to* KENT*)* Sirrah, you were best take my coxcomb.

LEAR

Why, Fool?

FOOL

Why? For taking one's part that's out of favor. Nay, an thou
canst not smile as the wind sits, thou'lt catch cold shortly.
There, take my coxcomb. Why, this fellow has banished
90   two on 's daughters, and did the third a blessing against his
will. If thou follow him, thou must needs wear my
coxcomb.—How now, nuncle? Would I had two coxcombs
and two daughters.

LEAR

(to KENT*)* Thank you, sir. You serve me well, and I'll love you for it.

KENT

(to OSWALD*)* Come on, sir, get up and get out of here! I'll teach you to respect your betters. If you want me to trip you again, then stick around. If not, get going. Go on. Do you know what's good for you? There you go.

OSWALD *exits.*

LEAR

Now, my friendly servant, thank you.

The FOOL *enters.*

(giving KENT *money)* Here's a token of my gratitude.

The fool is a professional court jester. Unlike other people, he doesn't have to be polite and may say whatever he wants, as long as he's funny.

FOOL

Wait, let me hire him too.—Here's my fool's cap, a token of my gratitude. *(he offers* KENT *his cap)*

LEAR

Well hello, my good boy. How are you doing?

FOOL

(to KENT*)* Guy, you'd better take my cap.

LEAR

Why, Fool?

FOOL

Why? For standing up for this unpopular king. No, if you can't adjust to political changes, you'll suffer for it. There, take my fool's cap. This guy here has banished two of his daughters and blessed the third one without intending to. If you work for him, you're a fool and should wear a fool's cap.—So how's it going, uncle? I wish I had two fool's caps and two daughters.

LEAR
Why, my boy?

FOOL
95   If I gave them all my living, I'd keep my coxcombs myself.
       There's mine. Beg another of thy daughters.

LEAR
Take heed, sirrah—the whip.

FOOL
Truth's a dog that must to kennel. He must be whipped out,
when Lady Brach may stand by th' fire and stink.

LEAR
100   A pestilent gall to me!

FOOL
Sirrah, I'll teach thee a speech.

LEAR
Do.

FOOL
Mark it, nuncle.
Have more than thou showest,
105   Speak less than thou knowest,
Lend less than thou owest,
Ride more than thou goest,
Learn more than thou trowest,
Set less than thou throwest,
110   Leave thy drink and thy whore
And keep in-a-door,
And thou shalt have more
Than two tens to a score.

KENT
This is nothing, Fool.

FOOL
115   Then 'tis like the breath of an unfee'd lawyer. You gave me
nothing for 't.—Can you make no use of nothing, nuncle?

LEAR

Why, my boy?

FOOL

If I gave them all I own, I'd have two fool's caps for myself. Here's mine. Ask your daughters for another one.

LEAR

Watch out, boy—remember I can whip you.

FOOL

I get whipped like a dog for telling the truth, while Lady Bitch gets to stand around the fire and stink the place up with her false words.

LEAR

A constant pain to me!

FOOL

I'll recite something for you, guy.

LEAR

Yes, do that.

FOOL

Listen up, uncle.
Have more than you show,
Speak less than you know,
Lend less than you owe.
Ride more than you walk,
Don't believe everything you hear,
Don't bet everything on one throw of the dice,
Leave behind your booze and your whore,
And stay indoors,
And you'll end up with more
Than two tens to a twenty.

KENT

That makes no sense, Fool. It's nothing.

FOOL

In that case it's like the words of an unpaid lawyer. You paid me nothing for it. Can't you make any use of nothing, uncle?

LEAR
Why no, boy. Nothing can be made out of nothing.

FOOL
(to KENT) Prithee, tell him so much the rent of his land comes to. He will not believe a fool.

LEAR
120 A bitter fool.

FOOL
Dost thou know the difference, my boy, between a bitter fool and a sweet fool?

LEAR
No, lad. Teach me.

FOOL
That lord that counseled thee
125 To give away thy land,
Come place him here by me.
Do thou for him stand.
The sweet and bitter fool
Will presently appear—
130 The one in motley here,
The other found out there.

LEAR
Dost thou call me fool, boy?

FOOL
All thy other titles thou hast given away that thou wast born with.

KENT
135 This is not altogether fool, my lord.

FOOL
No, faith, lords and great men will not let me. If I had a monopoly out, they would have part on 't. And ladies too—they will not let me have all fool to myself; they'll be snatching. Give me an egg, nuncle, and I'll give thee two
140 crowns.

LEAR

Why, no, boy. Nothing can be made out of nothing.

FOOL

(to **KENT**) Please tell him that his income is nothing, now that he's given his lands away. He won't believe a fool.

LEAR

You're a bitter fool.

FOOL

Do you know the difference, my boy, between a bitter fool and a sweet one?

LEAR

No, son. Tell me.

FOOL

Bring here
The gentleman who advised you
To give away your land.
You can stand in his place.
The sweet and bitter fool
Will appear right away.
The sweet fool in a fool's costume—that's me.
The bitter one is the other one—that's you.

LEAR

Are you calling me a fool, boy?

FOOL

Well, you've given away all your other rightful titles. The title of "fool" is the only one left.

KENT

This isn't entirely a joke, your highness.

FOOL

No. I wish I could be a complete joker—but so many lords and important men are also playing fools that I can't have a monopoly on it. Ladies too—they're always snatching away my role as the biggest fool.— Uncle, give me an egg, and I'll give you two crowns.

LEAR

What two crowns shall they be?

FOOL

Why—after I have cut the egg i' th' middle and eat up the
meat—the two crowns of the egg. When thou clovest thy
crown i' th' middle, and gavest away both parts, thou borest
145   thy ass o' th' back o'er the dirt. Thou hadst little wit in thy
bald crown when thou gavest thy golden one away. If I
speak like myself in this, let him be whipped that first finds
it so.

(sings)
>   *Fools had ne'er less wit in a year,*
150   >   *For wise men are grown foppish.*
>   *They know not how their wits to wear,*
>   *Their manners are so apish.*

LEAR

When were you wont to be so full of songs, sirrah?

FOOL

I have used it, nuncle, ever since thou madest thy daughters
155   thy mothers. For when thou gavest them the rod, and put'st
down thine own breeches,

(sings)
>   *Then they for sudden joy did weep*
>   *And I for sorrow sung,*
>   *That such a king should play bo-peep*
160   >   *And go the fools among.*
>   *Prithee, nuncle, keep a schoolmaster that can teach thy*
>   *fool to lie. I would fain learn to lie.*

LEAR

An you lie, sirrah, we'll have you whipped.

LEAR

Which two crowns would those be?

FOOL

Well, when I cut the egg in half and eat the whites, the yolk will be in two parts like two golden crowns. When you cut your own crown and kingdom in half and gave away both parts, you were as foolish as the old man in the old story who carries his donkey on his back instead of letting the donkey carry him. You didn't have much brains inside the bald crown of your head when you gave away the gold crown of your kingdom. If I'm telling the truth like a fool in saying all this, whip the first person who thinks I sound foolish.
(he sings)

> *Fools have had a hard time this year.*
> *They've been displaced by wise men who've grown foolish.*
> *These men no longer know how to use their brains,*
> *And they don't know how to behave except by foolishly imitating others.*

LEAR

When did you become so fond of singing, boy?

FOOL

I've been singing ever since you made your daughters into your mothers by giving them all your power. That's when you gave them the spanking paddle and pulled your pants down,
(he sings)

> *Then your daughters wept for joy,*
> *And I sang in sadness,*
> *Seeing such a king become*
> *A child and a fool.*
> *Please, uncle, hire a teacher who can teach your fool to lie. I want to learn how to lie.*

LEAR

If you lie, boy, we'll have you whipped.

FOOL

       I marvel what kin thou and thy daughters are. They'll have
165   me whipped for speaking true, thou'lt have me whipped for
       lying, and sometimes I am whipped for holding my peace.
       I had rather be any kind o' thing than a fool. And yet I
       would not be thee, nuncle. Thou hast pared thy wit o' both
       sides and left nothing i' th' middle. Here comes one o' the
170   parings.

       Enter GONERIL

LEAR

       How now, daughter? What makes that frontlet on?
       Methinks you are too much of late i' th' frown.

FOOL

       (to LEAR*)* Thou wast a pretty fellow when thou hadst no
       need to care for her frowning. Now thou art an O without
175   a figure. I am better than thou art now. I am a fool. Thou art
       nothing. *(to* GONERIL*)* Yes, forsooth, I will hold my tongue.
       So your face bids me, though you say nothing.
       Mum, mum,
       He that keeps nor crust nor crumb,
180   Weary of all, shall want some.
       (indicates LEAR*)* That's a shelled peascod.

GONERIL

       (to LEAR*)* Not only, sir, this your all-licensed fool,
       But other of your insolent retinue
       Do hourly carp and quarrel, breaking forth
185   In rank and not-to-be-endurèd riots. Sir,
       I had thought by making this well known unto you
       To have found a safe redress, but now grow fearful
       By what yourself too late have spoke and done
       That you protect this course and put it on
190   By your allowance—which if you should, the fault
       Would not 'scape censure, nor the redresses sleep
       Which in the tender of a wholesome weal
       Might in their working do you that offense,

FOOL

I'm amazed how similar you and your daughters are. They want to whip me for telling the truth, you want to whip me for lying, and sometimes I'm even whipped for keeping quiet. I'd rather be anything besides a fool. And yet I wouldn't want to be you, uncle. When you gave away pieces of your kingdom, it's as if you cut off pieces on both sides of your brain and left nothing in the middle. Here comes the owner of one piece.

GONERIL *enters.*

LEAR

What's going on, daughter? Why are you frowning like that? I think you've been frowning too much recently.

FOOL

(to LEAR*)* You were better off when you didn't have to care whether she frowned or not. Now you're a big zero, with no digit in front of it to give it value. I'm better than you are—I'm a fool and you're nothing. *(to* GONERIL*)* Yes, I promise I'll shut up. That's what you're telling me with that expression on your face, even though you don't say anything. Mum, mum, The man who gives away his crust and his crumbs Will discover that he needs some crumbs back. *(pointing at* LEAR*)* That guy is an empty pea pod.

GONERIL

(to LEAR*)* It's not just your fool here who can say whatever he wants, but your whole obnoxious entourage keeps whining and arguing, bursting out in intolerably vicious riots. Sir, I thought you could put an end to all this if I told you about it. But judging by what you've said and done recently, I'm worried that you don't mind this chaos, and even approve of it. If that's true, it's shameful. I realize that restraining your knights will damage your reputation with them—and under ordinary circumstances it would be unfortu-

Which else were shame, that then necessity
195   Will call discreet proceeding.

FOOL
For you know, nuncle,
The hedge-sparrow fed the cuckoo so long,
That it's had it head bit off by it young.
So out went the candle and we were left darkling.

LEAR
200   Are you our daughter?

GONERIL
Come, sir,
I would you would make use of that good wisdom
Whereof I know you are fraught, and put away
These dispositions that of late transform you
205   From what you rightly are.

FOOL
May not an ass know when the cart draws the horse?
Whoop, Jug! I love thee.

LEAR
Does any here know me? Why, this is not Lear.
Doth Lear walk thus? Speak thus? Where are his eyes?
210   Either his notion weakens, or his discernings
Are lethargied. Ha, sleeping or waking?
Sure, 'tis not so.
Who is it that can tell me who I am?

FOOL
Lear's shadow.

LEAR
215   I would learn that. For by the marks
Of sovereignty, knowledge, and reason,
I should be false persuaded I had daughters.

FOOL
Which they will make an obedient father.

LEAR
(to GONERIL*)* Your name, fair gentlewoman?

nate to have them see you as an ogre. However, this is an extreme situation, and it's more important to control it than to worry about how you'll look.

FOOL

You know, uncle,
A sparrow once raised a cuckoo in its nest
Until the cuckoo grew up and bit the sparrow's head off.
So the candle went out and now we're all in the dark.

LEAR

Are you my daughter?

GONERIL

Come on, sir. I know you're very wise, and I wish you would use some of that wisdom to snap out of this mood you've been in lately and be your true self again.

FOOL

Even an idiot knows when the normal order has been inverted and the cart is pulling the horse. Whoo-hoo, honey, I love you!

LEAR

Does anyone here know who I am? I'm not Lear. Does Lear walk and talk like this? Where are his eyes? Either his mind is losing its grip or his judgment is screwy.—Hey, am I awake? I don't think so. Who can tell me who I am?

FOOL

You're Lear's shadow.

LEAR

I'd like to find out who I am, since the obvious signs around me wrongly indicate that I've got daughters.

FOOL

Daughters who can make you obey them.

LEAR

(to GONERIL) What's your name, my dear lady?

GONERIL

220   This admiration, sir, is much o' th' savor
     Of other your new pranks. I do beseech you
     To understand my purposes aright.
     As you are old and reverend, should be wise.
     Here do you keep a hundred knights and squires,
225   Men so disordered, so debauched and bold
     That this our court, infected with their manners,
     Shows like a riotous inn. Epicurism and lust
     Make it more like a tavern or a brothel
     Than a graced palace. The shame itself doth speak
230   For instant remedy. Be then desired
     By her that else will take the thing she begs,
     A little to disquantity your train,
     And the remainder that shall still depend
     To be such men as may besort your age,
235   Which know themselves and you.

LEAR

     Darkness and devils!
     Saddle my horses. Call my train together.—
     Degenerate bastard, I'll not trouble thee.
     Yet have I left a daughter.

GONERIL

240   You strike my people, and your disordered rabble
     Make servants of their betters.

Enter ALBANY

LEAR

     Woe that too late repents!—
     (to ALBANY*)*   O sir, are you come?
     Is it your will? Speak, sir.—Prepare my horses.

Exit attendant

GONERIL

> This fake astonishment of yours is just like your other pranks. I'm asking you to understand my point of view. Since you're old and respected, you should be wise. But you're keeping a hundred knights here who are so disorderly, vulgar, and obnoxious that our noble court is starting to look like a noisy cheap hotel. They're such oversexed gluttons that I feel like we're living in a pub or a whorehouse rather than a respectable palace. It's shameful, and we have to make some changes right away. Please, as a favor to me—and if you don't do it for me, I'll do it myself—reduce the number of your knights a little. Keep the ones who are older, like you, and who act their age.

LEAR

> Hell and damnation! Saddle up my horses. Call my knights together. I won't bother you any more, you monstrous bastard. You're not really my daughter, but I still have one daughter left.

GONERIL

> You hit my servants, and your disorderly mob of knights treat their superiors like servants.

ALBANY enters.

LEAR

> You'll be sorry later, but it'll be too late. *(to ALBANY)* Oh, sir, are you here now? You decided to come? Answer me, sir. *(to attendants)* Get my horses ready.

An attendant exits.

Ingratitude, thou marble-hearted fiend,
245 More hideous when thou show'st thee in a child
Than the sea monster.

ALBANY
Pray, sir, be patient.

LEAR
(to GONERIL*)*   Detested kite, thou liest!
My train are men of choice and rarest parts
That all particulars of duty know
250 And in the most exact regard support
The worships of their name. O most small fault,
How ugly didst thou in Cordelia show,
Which like an engine wrenched my frame of nature
From the fixed place, drew from heart all love,
255 And added to the gall! O Lear, Lear, Lear!
(strikes his head)
Beat at this gate that let thy folly in
And thy dear judgment out!—Go, go, my people.

ALBANY
My lord, I am guiltless, as I am ignorant,
Of what hath moved you.

LEAR
260 It may be so, my lord.
Hear, Nature, hear, dear goddess, hear!
Suspend thy purpose if thou didst intend
To make this creature fruitful.
Into her womb convey sterility.
265 Dry up in her the organs of increase,
And from her derogate body never spring
A babe to honor her. If she must teem,
Create her child of spleen, that it may live
And be a thwart disnatured torment to her.
270 Let it stamp wrinkles in her brow of youth,
With cadent tears fret channels in her cheeks,

Ingratitude is always hideous, but an ungrateful child is uglier than a sea monster!

ALBANY

Please, sir, be patient.

LEAR

(*to* GONERIL) You disgusting vulture, you're a liar! My knights are the finest men who can attend a king, and they meticulously uphold their reputation. Oh, how ugly did Cordelia's small flaw appear! And now Cordelia's small flaw has bent me completely out of shape and sucked all the love out of my heart. Oh, Lear, Lear, Lear! (*he hits himself on the head*) Let me beat this portal that let my good sense out and my foolishness in!—Go, go, people.

ALBANY

My lord, I have no idea what's upset you, but whatever it is, I had nothing to do with it.

LEAR

That may be true, my lord. Ah, dear Nature, my goddess, listen to me! Change your plans if you ever intended for this woman to have children. Make her sterile and dry up her womb so that no baby will ever come out of her body and honor her. If she must give birth, make her child a bad seed who will torment her, give her a forehead wrinkled with worry, make her cry until her cheeks are sunken.

Turn all her mother's pains and benefits
To laughter and contempt, that she may feel—
That she may feel
275   How sharper than a serpent's tooth it is
To have a thankless child.—Away, away!

Exeunt LEAR, FOOL, KENT, FIRST KNIGHT,
and the other attendants

ALBANY
Now gods that we adore, whereof comes this?

GONERIL
Never afflict yourself to know more of it,
But let his disposition have that scope
280   That dotage gives it.

Enter LEAR *and* FOOL

LEAR
What, fifty of my followers at a clap?
Within a fortnight?

ALBANY
What's the matter, sir?

LEAR
I'll tell thee.
285   *(to* GONERIL*)* Life and death! I am ashamed
That thou hast power to shake my manhood thus,
That these hot tears which break from me perforce
Should make thee worth them. Blasts and fogs upon thee!
Th' untented woundings of a father's curse
290   Pierce every sense about thee! Old fond eyes,
Beweep this cause again, I'll pluck ye out

Let it be a wicked child who mocks the mother who cares for it. Make my daughter feel—make her feel how an ungrateful child hurts worse than a snake-bite.—Now let's leave. Go!

> LEAR, *the* FOOL, KENT, FIRST KNIGHT, *and attendant knights exit.*

ALBANY

Dear gods in heaven, what's the reason for this?

GONERIL

Don't even bother to ask the reasons. Just let him rant and rave. He's senile.

> LEAR *enters with the* FOOL.

LEAR

What, fifty of my knights dismissed all at once? In only two weeks?

ALBANY

What are you talking about, sir?

LEAR

I'll tell you. *(to* GONERIL*)* I'm ashamed that you have the power to upset me like this, as though you're worth the tears you're making me shed. Damn you! May you feel every pain a father's curse can bring! If I cry again because of you, I'll rip my eyes out of their sockets and throw them and their wet tears down to moisten the earth. Has it come to this? Then so be it. I have one more daughter who I'm sure is kind. When

And cast you, with the waters that you loose,
To temper clay. Yea, is 't come to this?
Ha? Let it be so. I have another daughter,
295   Who I am sure is kind and comfortable.
When she shall hear this of thee, with her nails
She'll flay thy wolvish visage. Thou shalt find
That I'll resume the shape which thou dost think
I have cast off for ever. Thou shalt, I warrant thee.

Exit LEAR

GONERIL
300   Do you mark that, my lord?

ALBANY
I cannot be so partial, Goneril,
To the great love I bear you—

GONERIL
                                    Pray you, content.
Come, sire, no more.—What, Oswald, ho!
(to FOOL*)* You, sir, more knave than fool, after your master.

FOOL
305   Nuncle Lear, nuncle Lear, tarry and take the fool with thee.
A fox when one has caught her
And such a daughter
Should sure to the slaughter,
If my cap would buy a halter.
310   So the fool follows after.

Exit FOOL

GONERIL
This man hath had good counsel—a hundred knights!
'Tis politic and safe to let him keep
At point a hundred knights, yes, that on every dream,
Each buzz, each fancy, each complaint, dislike,
315   He may enguard his dotage with their powers
And hold our lives in mercy?—Oswald, I say!

she hears what you've done to me, she'll tear up your wolflike face with her fingernails. And then you'll see that despite what you thought, I'll be as powerful as I was before. You'll see, I promise you.

LEAR *exits.*

GONERIL

Did you hear that?

ALBANY

Goneril, you know how much I love you, but still I have to say—

GONERIL

Shush, please. Come, sir, no more.—Oswald, come here! *(to FOOL)* And you, sir, you're more of a rascal than a fool. Go follow your master.

FOOL

Uncle Lear, uncle Lear, wait. Take your fool with you.
A fox you've trapped
And such a daughter
Should both be slaughtered,
If my fool's cap is worth a rope to bind them.
So the fool follows you.

The FOOL exits.

GONERIL

My father can't think straight—a hundred knights! Just imagine the risk we run in letting him keep a hundred knights around! He could use them to strong-arm us into bowing to every little whim of his, and keep us at his mercy.—Oswald, where are you?

ALBANY
    Well, you may fear too far.

GONERIL
    Safer than trust too far.
    Let me still take away the harms I fear,
320   Not fear still to be taken. I know his heart.
    What he hath uttered I have writ my sister.
    If she sustain him and his hundred knights
    When I have showed th' unfitness—

    Enter OSWALD *the steward*

OSWALD
    Here, madam.

GONERIL
325   How now, Oswald?
    What, have you writ that letter to my sister?

OSWALD
    Ay, madam.

GONERIL
    Take you some company, and away to horse.
    Inform her full of my particular fear,
330   And thereto add such reasons of your own
    As may compact it more. Get you gone
    And hasten your return.

    Exit OSWALD

             No, no, my lord,
    Though I condemn not, yet under pardon
    You are much more attasked for want of wisdom
335   Than praised for harmful mildness.

ALBANY
    How far your eyes may pierce I cannot tell.
    Striving to better, oft we mar what's well.

ALBANY

You may be exaggerating the risks.

GONERIL

That's better than exaggerating our trust. It's always better to get rid of what you're scared of than to be afraid. I know how his mind works. I've written to my sister telling her everything he's said. If she welcomes him and his hundred knights after I've shown how inappropriately he's behaved—

OSWALD *enters.*

OSWALD

Here, ma'am.

GONERIL

Well, Oswald? Have you written that letter to my sister yet?

OSWALD

Yes, ma'am.

GONERIL

Take some men and horses and go to her. Tell her everything that worries me. Add details of your own to back up what I'm saying. Now go, and hurry back.

OSWALD *exits.*

No, no, my husband, I'm not angry that you urge me to deal more gently with my father. But you're showing a lack of wisdom that that is much more noticeable than your tenderness toward him.

ALBANY

Maybe you know more than I do. But people often screw things up trying to make them better.

GONERIL
Nay, then—

ALBANY
Well, well, th' event.

Exeunt

GONERIL

No, not at all—

ALBANY

All right, all right. Time will tell.

They exit.

ACT 1, SCENE 5

Enter LEAR, KENT *disguised, and* FOOL

LEAR

(to KENT, *giving him letters)* Go you before to Gloucester
with these letters. Acquaint my daughter no further with
anything you know than comes from her demand out of the
letter. If your diligence be not speedy, I shall be there afore
5   you.

KENT

I will not sleep, my lord, till I have delivered your letter.

Exit KENT

FOOL

If a man's brains were in 's heels, were 't not in danger of
kibes?

LEAR

Ay, boy.

FOOL

10   Then, I prithee, be merry. Thy wit shall ne'er go slipshod.

LEAR

Ha, ha, ha!

FOOL

Shalt see thy other daughter will use thee kindly. For
though she's as like this as a crab's like an apple, yet I can tell
what I can tell.

LEAR

15   Why, what canst thou tell, my boy?

FOOL

She will taste as like this as a crab does to a crab. Thou canst
tell why one's nose stands i' th' middle on 's face?

ACT 1, SCENE 5

LEAR enters with KENT in disguise, and the FOOL.

LEAR

(to KENT, giving him letters) Go ahead of us and deliver these letters to the Earl of Gloucester. Answer my daughter's questions about the letter, but don't tell her anything else you know. If you're not quick enough, I'll get there before you.

KENT

I won't sleep until I've delivered your letter, my lord.

KENT exits.

FOOL

If a man's brain were in his feet, wouldn't it be susceptible to frostbite?

LEAR

Yes, boy.

FOOL

In that case, cheer up. Your brains won't need slippers to protect them from frostbite, since your brains aren't in your feet—if they were you wouldn't take this useless journey to see Regan.

LEAR

Ha, ha, ha!

FOOL

Your other daughter Regan will treat you kindly, you'll see. Even though she's as similar to Goneril as one crabapple is like another, still . . . I know what I know.

LEAR

And what do you know, boy?

FOOL

I know that Regan will taste just like Goneril—both of them sour crabapples. Do you know why the nose is in the middle of a person's face?

LEAR

No.

FOOL

Why, to keep one's eyes of either side 's nose, that what a
20   man cannot smell out, he may spy into.

LEAR

I did her wrong—

FOOL

Canst tell how an oyster makes his shell?

LEAR

No.

FOOL

Nor I neither. But I can tell why a snail has a house.

LEAR

25   Why?

FOOL

Why, to put 's head in—not to give it away to his daughters
and leave his horns without a case.

LEAR

I will forget my nature. So kind a father!—Be my horses
ready?

FOOL

30   Thy asses are gone about 'em. The reason why the seven
stars are no more than seven is a pretty reason.

LEAR

Because they are not eight?

FOOL

Yes indeed. Thou wouldst make a good fool.

LEAR

To take 't again perforce— Monster ingratitude!

LEAR

No.

FOOL

Why, to keep the eyes on the sides, so that you can see anything that you can't sniff out.

LEAR

I was wrong to her—

FOOL

Do you know how an oyster makes its shell?

LEAR

No.

FOOL

Me neither. But I know why a snail carries its house on its back.

LEAR

Why?

FOOL

So that he always has a roof over his head. He can't give his house away to his daughters, leaving himself without shelter.

LEAR

I want to forget what I am. Such a kind father!—Are my horses ready?

FOOL

Your attendant asses are getting the horses ready. There's a nice reason why the constellation Pleiades has only seven stars in it.

LEAR

Because it doesn't have eight?

FOOL

That's right. You'd make a good fool.

LEAR

I could take back my crown by force—What outrageous ingratitude!

FOOL

35 If thou wert my fool, nuncle, I'd have thee beaten for being
old before thy time.

LEAR

How's that?

FOOL

Thou shouldst not have been old till thou hadst been wise.

LEAR

O, let me not be mad, not mad, sweet heaven!
40 I would not be mad.
Keep me in temper. I would not be mad.

Enter a GENTLEMAN

How now? Are the horses ready?

GENTLEMAN

Ready, my lord.

LEAR

Come, boy.

Exeunt LEAR *and* GENTLEMAN

FOOL

45 She that's a maid now and laughs at my departure,
Shall not be a maid long unless things be cut shorter.

Exit

FOOL

If you were my fool, uncle, I'd have you beaten for getting old before your time.

LEAR

How's that?

FOOL

You're not supposed to get old until you're wise.

LEAR

Oh, dear God, don't let me go mad! Keep me balanced and sane. I don't want to go mad.

A **GENTLEMAN** *enters.*

So, are the horses ready?

GENTLEMAN

They're ready, my lord.

LEAR

Come on, boy.

LEAR *and the* **GENTLEMAN** *exit.*

FOOL

(speaking to the audience) Any girl who laughs because I'm going with the king is too foolish to remain a virgin very long.

He exits.

ACT TWO

SCENE 1

Enter EDMUND *the bastard and* CURAN, *severally*

EDMUND
Save thee, Curan.

CURAN
And you, sir. I have been with your father and given him
notice that the Duke of Cornwall and Regan his duchess
will be here with him this night.

EDMUND
5   How comes that?

CURAN
Nay, I know not. You have heard of the news abroad?—
I mean the whispered ones, for they are yet but ear-kissing
arguments.

EDMUND
Not I. Pray you, what are they?

CURAN
10   Have you heard of no likely wars toward 'twixt the two
Dukes of Cornwall and Albany?

EDMUND
Not a word.

CURAN
You may do then in time. Fare you well, sir.

Exit CURAN

EDMUND
The duke be here tonight? The better—best!
15   This weaves itself perforce into my business.
My father hath set guard to take my brother.
And I have one thing, of a queasy question,
Which I must act. Briefness and fortune, work!—
Brother, a word. Descend, brother, I say.

ACT TWO
SCENE 1

EDMUND *and* CURAN *enter from different directions.*

EDMUND

Hello, Curan.

CURAN

Hello, sir. I just saw your father the Lord Gloucester and notified him that the Duke of Cornwall and his wife Regan will stay with him here tonight.

EDMUND

Why is that?

CURAN

I don't know. Have you heard the latest news?—I mean the whispered rumors, since that's all they are at this point.

EDMUND

No, I haven't. What's going on?

CURAN

You haven't heard of the war brewing between the Dukes of Cornwall and Albany?

EDMUND

Not a word.

CURAN

You may hear about it soon. Goodbye, sir.

CURAN *exits.*

EDMUND

The duke will be here tonight? All the better—in fact it's the best that could happen. His arrival fits perfectly into my plan. My father's ready to arrest my brother, and I have one risky thing to do. Fast work and a little luck are all I need.—Brother, could I have a word with you? Come down, brother.

Enter EDGAR

20 My father watches. O sir, fly this place.
Intelligence is given where you are hid.
You have now the good advantage of the night.
Have you not spoken 'gainst the Duke of Cornwall aught?
He's coming hither—now, i' th' night, i' th' haste,
25 And Regan with him. Have you nothing said
Upon his party 'gainst the Duke of Albany?
Advise yourself.

EDGAR
                                    I am sure on 't, not a word.

EDMUND
I hear my father coming. Pardon me.
In cunning I must draw my sword upon you.
30 Draw. Seem to defend yourself. Now quit you well.—
(loudly) Yield! Come before my father. Light, ho! Here!
(aside to EDGAR*)* Fly, brother, fly.
(loudly)
                                    Torches, torches!
(aside to EDGAR*)* So, farewell.

                                    Exit EDGAR

Some blood drawn on me would beget opinion.
35 Of my more fierce endeavor.
(cuts his own arm)
                                    I have seen drunkards
35 Do more than this in sport.—Father, father!—
Stop, stop!—No help?

Enter GLOUCESTER *and servants with torches*

GLOUCESTER
Now Edmund, where's the villain?

EDGAR *enters.*

Father is on the lookout. Get out of here quickly! It has leaked out that you're hiding here. If you leave now, you can take advantage of the darkness and sneak away. You haven't said anything against the Duke of Cornwall, have you? He's rushing on his way here right now, and Regan's with him. Have you said anything against Cornwall or Albany? Think about it.

EDGAR

I'm sure of it. I haven't said a word.

EDMUND

I hear my father coming. Forgive me. I have to pretend to threaten you with my sword. Draw your sword too, as if you're defending yourself. Be convincing. *(loudly)* Give up! Go see my father.—Bring in some light!*(speaking so that only* EDGAR *can hear)* Run, brother. *(loudly)* Torches, bring in the torches! *(speaking so that only* EDGAR *can hear)* Goodbye, then.

EDGAR *exits.*

If I had some blood on me it would look like I'd fought more fiercely. *(he cuts his own arm)* I've seen drunk men do worse than this just fooling around.—Father, father!—Stop, stop!—Won't anyone help me?

GLOUCESTER *enters along with servants carrying torches.*

GLOUCESTER

Edmund, where's your wicked brother?

EDMUND
Here stood he in the dark, his sharp sword out,
Mumbling of wicked charms, conjuring the moon
40   To stand 's auspicious mistress—

GLOUCESTER
But where is he?

EDMUND
Look, sir, I bleed.

GLOUCESTER
                              Where is the villain, Edmund?

EDMUND
Fled this way, sir, when by no means he could—

GLOUCESTER
Pursue him, ho! Go after.

                                        Exeunt some servants

                              "By no means" what?

EDMUND
45   Persuade me to the murder of your lordship,
But that I told him the revenging gods
'Gainst parricides did all the thunder bend,
Spoke with how manifold and strong a bond
The child was bound to th' father. Sir, in fine,
50   Seeing how loathly opposite I stood
To his unnatural purpose, in fell motion,
With his preparèd sword he charges home
My unprovided body, latched mine arm.
And when he saw my best alarumed spirits,
55   Bold in the quarrel's right, roused to the encounter,
Or whether ghasted by the noise I made,
Full suddenly he fled.

GLOUCESTER
                              Let him fly far.
Not in this land shall he remain uncaught.
And found—dispatch. The noble duke my master,
60   My worthy arch and patron, comes tonight.

EDMUND

He was standing here in the dark with his sword pointing at me. He was mumbling some black magic spells, appealing to the moon to help him in his evil plans—

GLOUCESTER

But where is he?

EDMUND

Look, sir, I'm bleeding.

GLOUCESTER

Where is the villain, Edmund?

EDMUND

He ran out that way, sir, when he couldn't—

GLOUCESTER

Follow him, now! Go.

Some servants exit.

When he couldn't what?

EDMUND

When he couldn't persuade me to kill you. I told him that the gods hate men who kill their fathers and unleash all their thunder on them, and that the bond between father and child was sacred. In short, when I told him how firmly opposed I was to his hideous plan, he pulled out his sword and lunged at my defenseless body, cutting my arm. Bolstered by righteousness, I prepared to fight, and when he saw my excitement—or perhaps because my shouting scared him—he ran away suddenly.

GLOUCESTER

Let him run far away. If he stays in this country he'll be found. And if he's caught, he'll be executed. The Duke of Cornwall, my master and patron, is arriving tonight. On his authority I'll proclaim that whoever

By his authority I will proclaim it
That he which finds him shall deserve our thanks,
Bringing the murderous coward to the stake.
He that conceals him, death.

EDMUND

65   When I dissuaded him from his intent,
And found him pight to do it, with cursed speech
I threatened to discover him. He replied,
"Thou unpossessing bastard! Dost thou think
If I would stand against thee, would the reposal
70   Of any trust, virtue, or worth in thee
Make thy words faithed? No. What I should deny—
As this I would, ay, though thou didst produce
My very character—I'd turn it all
To thy suggestion, plot, and damnèd practice.
75   And thou must make a dullard of the world,
If they not thought the profits of my death
Were very pregnant and potential spirits
To make thee seek it."

Tucket within

GLOUCESTER
                          O strange and fastened villain!
Would he deny his letter, said he? I never got him.—
80   Hark, the duke's trumpets. I know not why he comes.
All ports I'll bar. The villain shall not 'scape.
The duke must grant me that. Besides, his picture
I will send far and near, that all the kingdom
May have the due note of him.—And of my land,
85   Loyal and natural boy, I'll work the means
To make thee capable.

Enter the Duke of CORNWALL, REGAN, *and attendants*

CORNWALL
How now, my noble friend? Since I came hither,
Which I can call but now, I have heard strange news.

finds Edgar and helps bring the murderous coward to justice will be rewarded. Whoever helps Edgar hide will die.

EDMUND

After I urged him not to kill you, I saw that he was still determined to do it. Enraged, I threatened to expose him. He answered, "You penniless bastard! Do you really think that if it came down to my word against yours, anyone would believe you? No. I'd deny whatever evidence you had against me—even if it were in my own handwriting—and turn it all into evidence against you and your plans for treachery. And you must think people are stupid if you believe they wouldn't realize all the motives you have for trying to kill me."

Trumpets play offstage.

GLOUCESTER

Oh, how monstrously evil! He said he would deny that he wrote his letter? He cannot truly be my son.— Listen. The duke's trumpets. I don't know why he's come here. I'll forbid all ships from leaving our harbors. The villain won't escape. The duke will agree with me on that. And I'll send his picture everywhere so that the whole kingdom will know what he looks like.—And as for you, my loyal and true son, I'll find some way to make you my heir.

The Duke of CORNWALL *enters with* REGAN *and attendants.*

CORNWALL

How are you, my friend? Ever since I arrived here, just now, I've been hearing strange rumors.

REGAN
　　If it be true, all vengeance comes too short
90　　Which can pursue th' offender. How dost, my lord?

GLOUCESTER
　　O madam, my old heart is cracked, it's cracked.

REGAN
　　What, did my father's godson seek your life?—
　　He whom my father named, your Edgar?

GLOUCESTER
　　O, lady, lady, shame would have it hid.

REGAN
95　　Was he not companion with the riotous knights
　　That tend upon my father?

GLOUCESTER
　　I know not, madam. 'Tis too bad, too bad.

EDMUND
　　Yes, madam, he was of that consort.

REGAN
　　No marvel then, though he were ill affected.
100　　'Tis they have put him on the old man's death,
　　To have th' expense and spoil of his revenues.
　　I have this present evening from my sister
　　Been well informed of them—and with such cautions
　　That if they come to sojourn at my house
105　　I'll not be there.

CORNWALL
　　　　　　　　Nor I, assure thee, Regan.—
　　Edmund, I hear that you have shown your father
　　A childlike office.

EDMUND
　　　　　　　　It was my duty, sir.

GLOUCESTER
　　He did bewray his practice, and received
　　This hurt you see striving to apprehend him.

CORNWALL
110　　Is he pursued?

REGAN

If they're true, no punishment is harsh enough for the criminal. How are you, my lord?

GLOUCESTER

Oh, madam, my old heart is broken, broken.

REGAN

Did my father's godson try to kill you? The one whom my father named, your son Edgar?

GLOUCESTER

Oh, my lady, I'm ashamed to admit it.

REGAN

Wasn't he friends with all those brawling knights who serve my father?

GLOUCESTER

I don't know, madam. Oh, it's too terrible.

EDMUND

To answer your question, ma'am—yes, he was friendly with those knights.

REGAN

Then it's no surprise they had a bad influence on him. They probably put him up to killing old man Gloucester to get his money. Tonight I received a letter from my sister telling me all about them—and warning me not be at home in case they come to stay at my house.

CORNWALL

And I won't be there either.—Edmund, I'm told you've acted like a true son to your father.

EDMUND

I just did my duty, sir.

GLOUCESTER

He exposed Edgar's murderous plot, and was wounded, as you see there, when trying to apprehend him.

CORNWALL

Are your men searching for him?

GLOUCESTER
Ay, my good lord.

CORNWALL
If he be taken, he shall never more
Be feared of doing harm. Make your own purpose
How in my strength you please.—For you, Edmund,
Whose virtue and obedience doth this instant
115   So much commend itself, you shall be ours.
Natures of such deep trust we shall much need.
You we first seize on.

EDMUND
I shall serve you, sir,
Truly, however else.

GLOUCESTER
(to CORNWALL*)* For him I thank your grace.

CORNWALL
120   You know not why we came to visit you—

REGAN
Thus out of season, threading dark-eyed night.
Occasions, noble Gloucester, of some poise,
Wherein we must have use of your advice:
Our father he hath writ, so hath our sister,
125   Of differences, which I least thought it fit
To answer from our home. The several messengers
From hence attend dispatch. Our good old friend,
Lay comforts to your bosom, and bestow
Your needful counsel to our business,
130   Which craves the instant use.

GLOUCESTER
I serve you, madam.
Your graces are right welcome.

Flourish. Exeunt

GLOUCESTER

Yes, my lord.

CORNWALL

If he's caught, he'll never make trouble for anyone again. Feel free to use my authority however you wish in order to apprehend him.—As for you, Edmund, you've been so loyal and virtuous throughout this whole business. I'd like you to work for me. I need people as trustworthy as you.

EDMUND

I'll always be loyal to you, sir.

GLOUCESTER

(to CORNWALL*)* Thank you, my lord, for your kindness to Edmund.

CORNWALL

You don't know why we came to visit you—

REGAN

Yes, and so unexpectedly, at night. There are some important matters we need your advice on, Gloucester. My father and my sister have both recently written to me about arguments between them. I realized it would be inconvenient to answer them from home, especially since the king may be on his way there. Their messengers are ready, waiting to deliver our response in these matters. So please, old friend, give us some good advice. We need it desperately and immediately.

GLOUCESTER

I'm at your service, madam. Both of you are very welcome here.

Trumpets play. They all exit.

ACT 2, SCENE 2

Enter KENT *disguised and* OSWALD *the steward, severally*

OSWALD
Good dawning to thee, friend. Art of this house?

KENT
Ay.

OSWALD
Where may we set our horses?

KENT
I' th' mire.

OSWALD
5   Prithee, if thou lovest me, tell me.

KENT
I love thee not.

OSWALD
Why, then, I care not for thee.

KENT
If I had thee in Lipsbury pinfold, I would make thee care
for me.

OSWALD
10   Why dost thou use me thus? I know thee not.

KENT
Fellow, I know thee.

OSWALD
What dost thou know me for?

KENT
A knave, a rascal, an eater of broken meats; a base, proud,
shallow, beggarly, three-suited, hundred-pound, filthy,
15   worsted-stocking knave; a lily-livered, action-taking knave;
a whoreson, glass-gazing, super-serviceable finical rogue;
one-trunk-inheriting slave; one that wouldst be a bawd in
way of good service; and art nothing but the composition of
a knave, beggar, coward, pander, and the son and heir of a
20   mongrel bitch; one whom I will beat into clamorous whining
if thou deniest the least syllable of thy addition.

ACT 2, SCENE 2

KENT enters in disguise. OSWALD enters from elsewhere.

OSWALD

Good morning to you, friend. Do you work in this house?

KENT

Yes, I do.

OSWALD

Where should we stable our horses?

KENT

In the mud.

OSWALD

Please, sir, be kind to me and tell me.

KENT

I won't be kind to you.

OSWALD

In that case, I don't much care for you either.

KENT

If I could get my hands on you, I'd make you care.

OSWALD

Why are you talking to me like this? I don't even know you.

KENT

Ah, but I know you.

OSWALD

Who am I then?

KENT

You're a lowlife, a rascal who eats leftover scraps. You're an ignoble, arrogant, shallow, vulgar, pretentious, conceited, filthy third-rate servant who thinks he's something special. You're a cowardly lawyer-loving bastard; a vain, brown-nosing, prissy scoundrel who'd pimp himself out to advance his career; a bag lady. You're nothing but a lowlife, a beggar, a coward, and a pimp, the son and heir of a mutt bitch. I'll beat you until you whine and cry if you deny the least bit of this.

OSWALD
Why, what a monstrous fellow art thou, thus to rail on one
that is neither known of thee nor knows thee!

KENT
25   What a brazen-faced varlet art thou to deny thou knowest
me! Is it two days ago since I tripped up thy heels and beat
thee before the king? Draw, you rogue, for though it be
night yet the moon shines. I'll make a sop o' th' moonshine
of you. *(draws his sword)* Draw, you whoreson cullionly
barber-monger, draw!

OSWALD
30   Away! I have nothing to do with thee.

KENT
Draw, you rascal. You come with letters against the king
and take Vanity the puppet's part against the royalty of her
father. Draw, you rogue, or I'll so carbonado your shanks.
Draw, you rascal! Come your ways.

OSWALD
35   Help, ho! Murder! Help!

KENT
Strike, you slave. Stand, rogue. Stand, you neat slave,
strike! *(strikes OSWALD)*

OSWALD
Help, ho! Murder, murder!

Enter EDMUND *the bastard with his rapier drawn, the Duke of*
CORNWALL, *the Duchess* REGAN, GLOUCESTER, *and servants*

EDMUND
How now? What's the matter? Part.

KENT
40   *(to* EDMUND*)* With you, goodman boy, if you please. Come,
I'll flesh ye. Come on, young master.

OSWALD

What an ogre you are to slander someone you don't know, and who doesn't know you!

KENT

What a shameless jerk you are to pretend you don't know me! It was just two days ago that I tripped you and beat you up in front of the king. Draw your sword, scoundrel. It may be nighttime, but there's enough moonlight to fight by. I'll make ground beef out of you. *(he draws his sword)* Draw, you affected, preening son of a bitch! Draw your sword!

OSWALD

Get away from me! I've got nothing to do with you.

KENT

Draw your sword, you jerk! You come here with letters against the king, and you take his conceited daughter's side against his royal highness. Draw your sword, scoundrel, or I'll slice your thighs like flank steak. Draw your sword! Come on!

OSWALD

Help! Murderer! Help!

KENT

Fight, peasant. Don't run away, scoundrel. Stand and fight, you overdressed servant, fight! *(he hits* OSWALD*)*

OSWALD

Help! Murder, murder!

EDMUND *enters with his sword drawn, followed by the Duke of* CORNWALL, *the Duchess* REGAN, GLOUCESTER, *and servants.*

EDMUND

What's going on here? Get away from each other.

KENT

(to EDMUND*)* Well, kid, let's see you fight. Come on, I'll show you how.

GLOUCESTER
Weapons, arms? What's the matter here?

CORNWALL
Keep peace, upon your lives.
He dies that strikes again. What is the matter?

REGAN
45   The messengers from our sister and the king.

CORNWALL
What is your difference? Speak.

OSWALD
I am scarce in breath, my lord.

KENT
No marvel, you have so bestirred your valor. You cowardly
rascal, nature disclaims in thee. A tailor made thee.

CORNWALL
50   Thou art a strange fellow. A tailor make a man?

KENT
Ay, a tailor, sir. A stone-cutter or painter could not have
made him so ill though they had been but two years o' th'
trade.

CORNWALL
Speak yet. How grew your quarrel?

OSWALD
55   This ancient ruffian, sir, whose life I have spared at suit of
his gray beard—

KENT
Thou whoreson zed, thou unnecessary letter!—My lord, if
you will give me leave, I will tread this unbolted villain into
mortar and daub the wall of a jakes with him.—Spare my
60   gray beard, you wagtail?

CORNWALL
Peace, sirrah!
You beastly knave, know you no reverence?

KENT
Yes, sir, but anger hath a privilege.

GLOUCESTER

You have weapons? What's going on here?

CORNWALL

Stop it, I order you. The next person to strike again dies. What's going on here?

REGAN

These are the messengers from my sister and the king.

CORNWALL

What are you fighting about? Tell me.

OSWALD

I'm out of breath, sir.

KENT

No wonder, with all your exertions, you cowardly rascal. You're not worth being called a man. The only thing manly about you are your clothes. A tailor made you.

CORNWALL

That's an odd thing to say. How can a tailor make a person?

KENT

Definitely a tailor, sir. A sculptor or a painter couldn't have screwed him up as bad as that, even as an apprentice.

CORNWALL

But tell me what you're fighting about.

OSWALD

This old ruffian here, whom I didn't kill because he's so old—

KENT

You useless bastard—you're like the letter "z," a totally unnecessary addition to the alphabet.—My lord, please let me grind this lumpy lowlife into a powder and use it to plaster up the bathroom walls.—You didn't kill me because I'm so old, you fawning dog?

CORNWALL

Calm down. Don't you have any manners, you savage?

KENT

Yes, sir, but not when I'm enraged.

CORNWALL
Why art thou angry?

KENT
65   That such a slave as this should wear a sword,
Who wears no honesty. Such smiling rogues as these,
Like rats, oft bite the holy cords atwain
Which are too intrinse t' unloose, smooth every passion
That in the natures of their lords rebel,
70   Bring oil to fire, snow to the colder moods;
Renege, affirm, and turn their halcyon beaks
With every gale and vary of their masters,
Knowing naught, like dogs, but following.—
A plague upon your epileptic visage!
75   Smile you my speeches as I were a fool?
Goose, an I had you upon Sarum plain,
I'd drive ye cackling home to Camelot.

CORNWALL
Why, art thou mad, old fellow?

GLOUCESTER
(to **KENT***)*   How fell you out?
Say that.

KENT
80   No contraries hold more antipathy
Than I and such a knave.

CORNWALL
Why dost thou call him "knave"? What's his offense?

KENT
His countenance likes me not.

CORNWALL
No more perchance does mine, nor his, nor hers.

KENT
85   Sir, 'tis my occupation to be plain.
I have seen better faces in my time
Than stands on any shoulder that I see
Before me at this instant.

CORNWALL

Why are you enraged?

KENT

I'm angry that a dishonorable lowlife like this wears a sword like a gentleman. Smiling swindlers such as he undo the sacred bonds that unite people together, and only encourage the unreasonable passions of their masters. They foster both rage and apathy. They say "Yes" and "No," turning their noses whichever way the wind blows without taking a firm stance on anything. They blindly follow their masters' impulses, like dogs.—Damn your ugly stinking face! Are you laughing at what I say, as if I were a fool? If I had my way with you right now, I'd send you to back to where you came from.

CORNWALL

Are you insane, old man?

GLOUCESTER

(to KENT) What did you start quarreling over? Just tell us.

KENT

I couldn't hate that jerk over there any more than I do.

CORNWALL

Why are you calling him a jerk? What did he do to you?

KENT

I don't like his face.

CORNWALL

But maybe you don't like mine, or his, or hers either.

KENT

I'm used to telling the truth, sir, and I have to say that I've seen better faces than those I see here.

CORNWALL
                                        This is some fellow,
Who, having been praised for bluntness, doth affect
90   A saucy roughness and constrains the garb
Quite from his nature. He cannot flatter, he.
An honest mind and plain, he must speak truth.
An they will take it, so. If not, he's plain.
These kind of knaves I know, which in this plainness
95   Harbor more craft and more corrupter ends
Than twenty silly-ducking observants
That stretch their duties nicely.

KENT
Sir, in good faith, or in sincere verity,
Under th' allowance of your great aspect,
100   Whose influence, like the wreath of radiant fire
On flickering Phoebus' front—

CORNWALL
                                        What mean'st by this?

KENT
To go out of my dialect, which you discommend so much.
I know, sir, I am no flatterer. He that beguiled you in a plain
accent was a plain knave, which for my part I will not be,
105   though I should win your displeasure to entreat me to 't.

CORNWALL
(to OSWALD) What was th' offense you gave him?

OSWALD
                                        I never gave him any.
It pleased the king his master very late
To strike at me upon his misconstruction
When he, conjunct and flattering his displeasure,
110   Tripped me behind; being down, insulted, railed,
And put upon him such a deal of man
That worthied him, got praises of the king
For him attempting who was self-subdued.
And in the fleshment of this dread exploit
115   Drew on me here again.

CORNWALL

This is a guy who's been praised for his honest bluntness, and who now insolently pretends to be plainspoken and twists the natural meanings of words. No flattery for him, no sir! He's honest, he's got to speak the truth. If people take what he says, fine. If not, he's got truth on his side! I know his type. He's sneaky behind all his so-called bluntness, sneakier than twenty brown-nosing bootlickers who only tell you what you want to hear.

KENT

Dearest, kindest, most honorable sir, may I say, with your esteemed approval, which is lit up by the illuminating radiance of the sun-god Phoebus, that—

CORNWALL

What do you mean by that?

KENT

I tried to stop speaking plainly, since you dislike plain speech so much. Sir, I know I'm not a flatterer. The guy who tricked you with plain language was just a plain crook—which I'm not, however much I may displease you by not being one.

CORNWALL

(to OSWALD*)* How did you offend him?

OSWALD

I never offended him at all. Recently, the king hit me because of a misunderstanding. This man took sides with the king and tripped me. When I was down on the ground he insulted me, and then started acting tough to seem courageous in front of the king. The king praised him, even though I had never offered any resistance at all. Now he pulled out his sword on me again, still riled up from our first encounter.

KENT
                            None of these rogues and cowards
     But Ajax is their fool.

CORNWALL
                            Fetch forth the stocks, ho!—
     You stubborn ancient knave, you reverend braggart,
     We'll teach you.

KENT
                            Sir, I am too old to learn.
     Call not your stocks for me. I serve the king,
120 On whose employment I was sent to you.
     You shall do small respect, show too bold malice
     Against the grace and person of my master,
     Stocking his messenger.

CORNWALL
                            Fetch forth the stocks!
     As I have life and honor, there shall he sit till noon.

REGAN
125 Till noon? Till night, my lord, and all night too.

KENT
     Why, madam, if I were your father's dog,
     You should not use me so.

REGAN
                            Sir, being his knave, I will.

     Stocks brought out

CORNWALL
     This is a fellow of the selfsame color
     Our sister speaks of.—Come, bring away the stocks!

GLOUCESTER
130 Let me beseech your grace not to do so.
     His fault is much, and the good king his master
     Will check him for 't. Your purposed low correction
     Is such as basest and contemned'st wretches
     For pilferings and most common trespasses
135 Are punished with.

KENT

These cowards manage to make fools of brave men.

CORNWALL

The "stocks" consisted of a wooden frame in which you could lock a criminal's ankles so that he or she couldn't move.

Bring out the stocks!—We'll teach you, you stubborn old bastard, you arrogant show-off.

KENT

Sir, I'm too old to be taught anything. Don't put me in the stocks. I serve the king, who sent me here. If you put me in the stocks you'll insult him both as a king and as a man.

CORNWALL

Bring out the stocks! I swear on my life and honor, he'll sit here in the stocks until noon.

REGAN

Only until noon, my lord? No, the whole day, and all night too.

KENT

Ma'am, you wouldn't treat me like this if I were your father's dog.

REGAN

But since you're his scoundrel servant, I will.

The stocks are brought out.

CORNWALL

This guy is exactly the kind of person your sister warned us about.—Come on, bring in the stocks, now!

GLOUCESTER

I beg you not to do this, my lord. He's done wrong, and his master the king will punish him for it. But the kind of punishment you propose is more suited to petty shoplifters than to royal attendants.

The king his master needs must take it ill,
That he, so slightly valued in his messenger,
Should have him thus restrained.

CORNWALL

I'll answer that.

REGAN

My sister may receive it much more worse
140   To have her gentleman abused, assaulted
For following her affairs.—Put in his legs.

KENT is put in the stocks

CORNWALL

(to GLOUCESTER) Come, my good lord, away.

Exeunt all but GLOUCESTER and KENT

GLOUCESTER

I am sorry for thee, friend. 'Tis the duke's pleasure,
Whose disposition, all the world well knows,
145   Will not be rubbed nor stopped. I'll entreat for thee.

KENT

Pray you do not, sir. I have watched and traveled hard.
Some time I shall sleep out. The rest I'll whistle.
A good man's fortune may grow out at heels.
Give you good morrow.

GLOUCESTER

150   The duke's to blame in this. 'Twill be ill taken.

Exit GLOUCESTER

KENT

Good King, that must approve the common saw,
Thou out of heaven's benediction comest
To the warm sun.

The king will be offended to find out that his messenger is so badly treated.

CORNWALL

I'll take responsibility for that.

REGAN

My sister would be much more offended to have her trusted messenger abused and assaulted just for carrying out her orders.—Put his legs in the stocks.

KENT is put in the stocks.

CORNWALL

(to GLOUCESTER) Let's go, my lord.

Everyone exits except GLOUCESTER and KENT.

GLOUCESTER

I'm sorry, my friend. The duke always gets it his way, and everyone knows you can't budge him once he's made up his mind. I'll try talking to him again.

KENT

Please don't, sir. I've been up for a long time and have done a lot of traveling recently. This punishment will be a good chance to catch up on my sleep. The rest of the time I'll whistle to entertain myself. Even good men have bad luck. Have a good morning.

GLOUCESTER

It's wrong for the duke to do this. The king will be angry with him.

GLOUCESTER exits.

KENT

Oh, good King Lear, you're proving that, just as they say, everything goes from good to bad. *(he takes out a*

(takes out a letter)
155   Approach, thou beacon to this underglobe,
       That by thy comfortable beams I may
       Peruse this letter. Nothing almost sees miracles
       But misery. I know 'tis from Cordelia,
       Who hath most fortunately been informed
160   Of my obscurèd course and *(reads the letter)* "shall find time
       From this enormous state, seeking to give
       Losses their remedies." All weary and o'erwatched,
       Take vantage, heavy eyes, not to behold
       This shameful lodging.
165   Fortune, good night. Smile once more. Turn thy wheel.
       (sleeps)

letter) Rise and shine, sun, so I can read this letter. Only those who are truly miserable see miracles. I know this letter is from Cordelia, who knows that I'm serving the king in disguise. *(looking at the letter)* She says that she will have time, now that she's away from the monstrous conditions here, to find a way to fix things. I'm exhausted. I've been awake too long. This fatigue gives me an excuse to shut my eyes so I can't see myself humiliated in the stocks. Good night, Lady Luck. Smile and spin your wheel of fortune again. *(he sleeps)*

ACT 2, SCENE 3

Enter EDGAR

EDGAR
I heard myself proclaimed,
And by the happy hollow of a tree
Escaped the hunt. No port is free, no place
That guard and most unusual vigilance
5   Does not attend my taking. Whiles I may 'scape,
I will preserve myself, and am bethought
To take the basest and most poorest shape
That ever penury in contempt of man
Brought near to beast. My face I'll grime with filth,
10   Blanket my loins, elf all my hair in knots,
And with presented nakedness outface
The winds and persecutions of the sky.
The country gives me proof and precedent
Of Bedlam beggars, who with roaring voices
15   Strike in their numbed and mortified bare arms
Pins, wooden pricks, nails, sprigs of rosemary,
And with this horrible object from low farms,
Poor pelting villages, sheepcotes, and mills,
Sometime with lunatic bans, sometime with prayers,
20   Enforce their charity. "Poor Turlygod!" "Poor Tom!"—
That's something yet. Edgar I nothing am.

Exit

ACT 2, SCENE 3

EDGAR *enters.*

EDGAR

I heard myself declared an outlaw and escaped capture by hiding in the trunk of a hollow tree. Every town and port is crawling with henchmen on the lookout, waiting to capture me. But I'll survive while I can. I've decided to disguise myself as the lowliest and rattiest beggar that mankind has ever seen. I'll smear my face with filth, put on a loincloth, make my hair matted and tangled, and face the bad weather wearing almost nothing. I've seen beggars out of insane asylums who stick pins and nails into their numb arms. They pray or roar lunatic curses, horrifying farmers and villagers into giving them alms. "Poor crazy Tom!" they call themselves. Well, at least that's something. As Edgar, I'm nothing at all.

He exits.

ACT 2, SCENE 4

KENT *in the stocks*
Enter LEAR, FOOL, *and* GENTLEMAN

LEAR

'Tis strange that they should so depart from home,
And not send back my messenger.

GENTLEMAN

As I learned,
The night before there was no purpose in them
Of this remove.

KENT

(to LEAR)   Hail to thee, noble master!

LEAR

5   Ha! Makest thou this shame thy pastime?

KENT

No, my lord.

FOOL

Ha, ha! Look, he wears cruel garters. Horses are tied by the
heads, dogs and bears by the neck, monkeys by the loins,
and men by the legs . When a man's overlusty at legs, then
he wears wooden nether-stocks.

LEAR

10   *(to KENT)* What's he that hath so much thy place mistook
To set thee here?

KENT

It is both he and she:
Your son and daughter.

LEAR

No.

KENT

Yes.

LEAR

No, I say.

KENT

I say "Yea."

ACT 2, SCENE 4

KENT *is in the stocks.* LEAR *enters with the* FOOL *and the* GENTLEMAN.

LEAR

It's strange that Regan and her husband left their house without sending back my messenger.

GENTLEMAN

According to what I heard, they had no travel plans as of last night.

KENT

(to LEAR*)* Hail, noble master!

LEAR

What's this? Are you sitting around in this humiliation to amuse yourself?

KENT

No, my lord.

FOOL

Ha, ha! That's a nasty garter belt. You tie up horses by their heads, dogs and bears by their necks, monkeys by their waists, and humans by their legs. When a person's prone to wanderlust, he has to wear wooden socks, like a chastity belt around his ankles.

LEAR

(to KENT*)* Who could have misunderstood your assigment so completely as to lock you up like this?

KENT

Your daughter and son-in-law.

LEAR

No.

KENT

Yes.

LEAR

I'm telling you "No."

KENT

And I'm telling you "Yes."

LEAR
> No, no, they would not.

KENT
>   Yes, they have.

LEAR
By Jupiter, I swear "No."

KENT
15 By Juno, I swear "Ay."

LEAR
>   They durst not do 't.
They could not, would not do 't. 'Tis worse than murder
To do upon respect such violent outrage.
Resolve me with all modest haste which way
Thou mightst deserve or they impose this usage,
20 Coming from us.

KENT
>   My lord, when at their home
I did commend your highness' letters to them.
Ere I was risen from the place that showed
My duty kneeling, came there a reeking post,
Stewed in his haste, half breathless, panting forth
25 From Goneril his mistress salutations,
Delivered letters spite of intermission,
Which presently they read, on whose contents
They summoned up their meiny, straight took horse,
Commanded me to follow and attend
30 The leisure of their answer, gave me cold looks.
And meeting here the other messenger,
Whose welcome I perceived had poisoned mine—
Being the very fellow which of late
Displayed so saucily against your highness—
35 Having more man than wit about me, drew.
He raised the house with loud and coward cries.
Your son and daughter found this trespass worth
The shame which here it suffers.

LEAR

No, no, they wouldn't.

KENT

Yes, they have.

LEAR

By the god Jupiter above, I swear "No."

KENT

By Jupiter's wife Juno, I swear "Yes."

LEAR

They wouldn't dare. They couldn't, they wouldn't. It's worse than murder to humiliate a king's messenger like this. Tell me as quickly and clearly as you can what you did to deserve this punishment, or what made them think they could inflict it on you.

KENT

My lord, when I arrived at their home I gave them your letter. Before I had a chance to get up from my respectful kneeling position, Goneril's messenger arrived, stinky, sweaty, and out of breath. He interrupted me, spouted out greetings from her, and delivered her letter, which they opened immediately. After reading it, they gathered their entourage together and got on their horses to go. They glared at me and ordered me to follow them and wait for their answer. After we arrived here, I ran into that other messenger who made them give me the cold shoulder—the very same guy who was so rude to you, King. I admit it was foolish to draw my sword on him, but I had to act like a man. He woke up the whole house with his loud and cowardly screams. That's why your daughter and son-in-law are punishing me shamefully.

FOOL

Winter's not gone yet, if the wild geese fly that way.

40 Fathers that wear rags
Do make their children blind.
But fathers that bear bags
Shall see their children kind.
Fortune, that arrant whore,
45 Ne'er turns the key to th' poor.
But for all this thou shalt have as many dolors for thy
daughters as thou canst tell in a year.

LEAR

O, how this mother swells up toward my heart!
Hysterica passio, down, thou climbing sorrow.
50 Thy element's below.—Where is this daughter?

KENT

With the earl, sir, here within.

LEAR

Follow me not. Stay here.

Exit LEAR

GENTLEMAN

Made you no more offense but what you speak of?

KENT

None.
55 How chance the king comes with so small a train?

FOOL

An thou hadst been set i' th' stocks for that question,
thou'dst well deserved it.

KENT

Why, Fool?

FOOL

We'll set thee to school to an ant to teach thee there's no
60 laboring i' th' winter. All that follow their noses are led by
their eyes but blind men, and there's not a nose among
twenty but can smell him that's stinking. Let go thy hold
when a great wheel runs down a hill, lest it break thy neck

FOOL

This story bodes more stormy weather.
Fathers who wear rags
Make their children neglect them.
But fathers who are rich
Make their children kind.
Lady Luck is a fickle whore
And never gives the poor a break.
But despite all this, your daughters will give you a lot
of money—or do I mean pain?—in the coming year.

LEAR

I'm getting hysterical. I feel my stomach squeezing up
against my heart. Calm down, you belong lower
down!—Where is this daughter of mine?

KENT

Inside, sir, with the earl.

LEAR

Don't follow me. Stay here.

He exits.

GENTLEMAN

You didn't do anything else to earn this punishment?

KENT

Nothing. Tell me, why did the king arrive with such a
small entourage?

FOOL

If they'd put you in the stocks for asking that question,
you would've deserved it.

KENT

Why, Fool?

FOOL

You need to learn what ants know well about winter—
there's no point in slaving away if there's no hope for
profit. Serving the king will get you nowhere. Everyone can see that, and even blind men can smell the
stench of his misery now. When you see a huge wheel

with following it. But the great one that goes up the hill, let
65 him draw thee after. When a wise man gives thee better
counsel, give me mine again. I would have none but knaves
follow it since a fool gives it.
That sir which serves and seeks for gain,
And follows but for form,
70 Will pack when it begins to rain
And leave thee in the storm.
But I will tarry. The fool will stay.
And let the wise man fly.
The knave turns fool that runs away;
75 The fool, no knave, perdie.

KENT
Where learned you this, Fool?

FOOL
Not i' th' stocks, fool.

Enter LEAR *and* GLOUCESTER

LEAR
Deny to speak with me? They are sick? They are weary?
They have traveled all the night?—mere fetches, ay!
80 The images of revolt and flying off.
Fetch me a better answer.

GLOUCESTER
                                    My dear lord,
You know the fiery quality of the duke,
How unremoveable and fixed he is
In his own course.

LEAR
                              Vengeance, plague, death, confusion!
85 "Fiery"? What "quality"? Why, Gloucester, Gloucester,
I'd speak with the Duke of Cornwall and his wife.

GLOUCESTER
Well, my good lord, I have informed them so.

rolling down a hill, you shouldn't try to hold on to it or it'll break your neck. But if you see a wheel going uphill, latch on for the ride. And when a wise man gives you better advice than I just did, give me my advice back again. I only want idiots following my advice, the advice of a fool.

The gentleman who serves you only for profit
And is only superficially loyal to you
Will take off when it starts to rain
And leave you alone in the storm.
But I'll linger. The fool will stay.
And let the wise man run away.
The servant who runs away is a fool.
But this fool is no scoundrel, by God.

KENT

Where did you learn that song, Fool?

FOOL

Not in the stocks, fool.

LEAR *and* GLOUCESTER *enter.*

LEAR

How can they refuse to speak with me? How can they say that they're sick or exhausted or that they have traveled all night!? They're playing with me. These are tricks. This is rebellion. Go ask them again and make them see me this time.

GLOUCESTER

My dear lord, you know how passionately stubborn the duke is. He never changes his mind.

LEAR

Hell! Damn it all to hell! "Passionately"? What "passion"? Gloucester, Gloucester, I want to speak with the Duke of Cornwall and his wife.

GLOUCESTER

My lord, I informed them as much.

LEAR
"Informed them"? Dost thou understand me, man?

GLOUCESTER
Ay, my good lord.

LEAR
90 The king would speak with Cornwall. The dear father
Would with his daughter speak, commands, tends service.
Are they "informed" of this? My breath and blood!
"Fiery"? The "fiery" duke? Tell the hot duke that Lear—
No, but not yet. Maybe he is not well.
95 Infirmity doth still neglect all office
Whereto our health is bound. We are not ourselves
When nature, being oppressed, commands the mind
To suffer with the body. I'll forbear,
And am fallen out with my more headier will
100 To take the indisposed and sickly fit
For the sound man.
(notices KENT *again)*
                              Death on my state! Wherefore
Should he sit here? This act persuades me
That this remotion of the duke and her
Is practice only. Give me my servant forth.
105 Go tell the duke and 's wife I'd speak with them—
Now, presently. Bid them come forth and hear me,
Or at their chamber door I'll beat the drum
Till it cry sleep to death.

GLOUCESTER
                              I would have all well betwixt you.

                                        Exit GLOUCESTER

LEAR
O me, my heart, my rising heart! But down.

LEAR

"Informed them"? Do you understand what I'm saying, man?

GLOUCESTER

Yes, my lord.

LEAR

The king wants to speak with Cornwall. The father wants to speak with his daughter. He orders them—he begs them. Did you inform them of that? This is unbelievable! "Passionate"? The "passionate" duke? Tell the hot-headed duke that I... But no, not yet. Maybe he's not feeling well. When we're ill we can't carry out our duties as well as when we're healthy. When our bodies are out of order, our minds can't function properly. I'll hold off, and subdue my impulsive temper, which makes me judge a sick man as if he were well. *(he notices* KENT *again)* A curse on my royal power! Why should he sit here like this? The fact that they punished him convinces me that Regan and the duke are avoiding me on purpose. I want my servant released. Go tell the duke and his wife I'll speak to them right now, at once. Tell them to come here and hear me out, or else I'll beat a drum at their bedroom door until they can't sleep any more.

GLOUCESTER

I just want everything to be all right between you.

GLOUCESTER *exits.*

LEAR

Oh, my heart, my heart is rising into my throat! Stay down, heart.

FOOL

110   Cry to it, nuncle, as the cockney did to the eels when she put
      'em i' th' paste alive. She knapped 'em o' th' coxcombs with
      a stick and cried, "Down, wantons, down!" 'Twas her
      brother that, in pure kindness to his horse, buttered his hay.

Enter the Duke of **CORNWALL,** **REGAN,** **GLOUCESTER,** *and
servants*

LEAR

      Good morrow to you both.

CORNWALL

115   Hail to your grace.

KENT *here set at liberty*

REGAN

      I am glad to see your highness.

LEAR

      Regan, I think you are. I know what reason
      I have to think so: if thou shouldst not be glad,
      I would divorce me from thy mother's tomb,
120   Sepulchring an adultress.
      (to **KENT***)*   Oh, are you free?
      Some other time for that.

                                        Exit **KENT**

                  Belovèd Regan,
      Thy sister's naught. O Regan, she hath tied
      Sharp-toothed unkindness, like a vulture, here.
      (indicates his heart)

FOOL

The point of the story is that the housewife acts too late. She should have killed the eels before putting them into the pie.

Horses won't eat greasy hay, so buttering hay is another example of foolishness.

That's right, uncle, talk to your heart, like the housewife who yelled at the eels she was putting in her pie. She hit 'em on the head with a stick and shouted, "Down, you naughty things, down!" That was the woman whose brother wanted to be nice to his horse, and buttered its hay.

The Duke of CORNWALL, REGAN, *and* GLOUCESTER *enter with their servants.*

LEAR

Good morning to you both.

CORNWALL

Hail to your majesty.

KENT *is set free.*

REGAN

I'm glad to see your highness.

LEAR

I believe you are, Regan. You know why I think so? Because if you weren't glad, I'd divorce your dead mother, because I'd know she cheated on me. Any true daughter of mine would definitely be glad to see me. *(to* KENT*)* Oh, are you free? We'll talk about it later.

KENT *exits.*

My dear Regan, your sister's not worth anything. Oh, Regan, she's torn me apart with unkindness, like a vulture, right here. *(points to his heart)* I can hardly

I can scarce speak to thee. Thou'lt not believe
125   With how depraved a quality— O Regan!

REGAN
I pray you, sir, take patience. I have hope
You less know how to value her desert
Than she to scant her duty.

LEAR
                    Say, how is that?

REGAN
I cannot think my sister in the least
130   Would fail her obligation. If, sir, perchance
She have restrained the riots of your followers,
'Tis on such ground and to such wholesome end
As clears her from all blame.

LEAR
My curses on her!

REGAN
135   O sir, you are old.
Nature in you stands on the very verge
Of his confine. You should be ruled and led
By some discretion that discerns your state
Better than you yourself. Therefore I pray you
140   That to our sister you do make return.
Say you have wronged her, sir.

LEAR
                  Ask her forgiveness?
Do you but mark how this becomes the house?—
(kneels) "Dear daughter, I confess that I am old.
Age is unnecessary. On my knees I beg
145   That you'll vouchsafe me raiment, bed, and food."

REGAN
Good sir, no more. These are unsightly tricks.
Return you to my sister.

REGAN

LEAR

speak. You'll never believe how monstrously—oh, Regan!

Calm down, sir, please. I hope there's been a misunderstanding. It's more likely that you don't know how to appreciate her than that she'd ever fail in her duties as a daughter.

LEAR

How do you mean?

REGAN

I can't believe my sister would neglect her obligations in any way. If she restrained your rowdy knights, she had such a good reason that you can't blame her for it.

LEAR

I curse her.

REGAN

Sir, you're old. Your life is stretched to its limit. You should let others take care of you and submit to people who know better than you do what's good for you. Please go back to Goneril's house. Admit you were wrong.

LEAR

Apologize? Do you think this kind of thing is appropriate for the royal family? *(he kneels)* "Dear daughter, I admit I'm old. Old people are useless. I'm begging you, on my knees, to give me food, clothes, and a bed."

REGAN

No more, please. These are ugly antics. Go back to my sister's.

LEAR
(rising)   Never, Regan.
She hath abated me of half my train,
Looked black upon me, struck me with her tongue,
150   Most serpentlike, upon the very heart.
All the stored vengeances of heaven fall
On her ingrateful top! Strike her young bones,
You taking airs, with lameness!

CORNWALL
                                        Fie, sir, fie!

LEAR
You nimble lightnings, dart your blinding flames
155   Into her scornful eyes! Infect her beauty,
You fen-sucked fogs drawn by the powerful sun,
To fall and blister!

REGAN
                        O the blessed gods!
So will you wish on me when the rash mood is on.

LEAR
No, Regan, thou shalt never have my curse.
160   Thy tender-hafted nature shall not give
Thee o'er to harshness. Her eyes are fierce, but thine
Do comfort and not burn. 'Tis not in thee
To grudge my pleasures, to cut off my train,
To bandy hasty words, to scant my sizes,
165   And in conclusion to oppose the bolt
Against my coming in. Thou better know'st
The offices of nature, bond of childhood,
Effects of courtesy, dues of gratitude.
Thy half o' th' kingdom hast thou not forgot,
170   Wherein I thee endowed.

REGAN
                            Good sir, to the purpose.

LEAR
Who put my man i' th' stocks?

LEAR

(*getting up*) Never, Regan. She's sent away half my knights, glared at me, and aimed her venomous insults straight at my heart. She and her ingratitude can go to hell! I hope she gets sick and becomes lame!

CORNWALL

Shush, sir, please!

LEAR

I hope lightning strikes her in the eyes! I hope poisonous swampy fog covers her face and ruins her complexion!

REGAN

Oh, dear gods! That's how you'll talk about me when you're in this mood.

LEAR

No, Regan. I'll never curse you. You're so gentle, you'd never be harsh like her. Her eyes are vicious, but yours are comforting. You'd never deny me my pleasures, downsize my entourage, insult me thoughtlessly, reduce my allowance, or lock me out of the house. You know better than she does how important the duties of a child to a parent are, and the responsibilities that come from gratitude. You haven't forgotten the half of a kingdom I gave you.

REGAN

Sir, let's get to the point.

LEAR

Who put my messenger in the stocks?

Tucket within

CORNWALL

What trumpet's that?

Enter OSWALD *the steward*

REGAN

I know 't—my sister's. This approves her letter
That she would soon be here. *(to* OSWALD*)*
Is your lady come?

LEAR

175   This is a slave whose easy borrowed pride
Dwells in the fickle grace of her he follows.—
Out, varlet, from my sight!

CORNWALL

What means your grace?

Enter GONERIL

LEAR

Who stocked my servant? Regan, I have good hope
Thou didst not know on 't.—Who comes here? O heavens,
180   If you do love old men, if your sweet sway
Allow obedience, if yourselves are old,
Make it your cause. Send down, and take my part!
(to GONERIL*)* Art not ashamed to look upon this beard?—
O Regan, wilt thou take her by the hand?

GONERIL

185   Why not by th' hand, sir? How have I offended?
All's not offense that indiscretion finds
And dotage terms so.

LEAR

O sides, you are too tough.
Will you yet hold?—How came my man i' th' stocks?

Trumpets play offstage.

CORNWALL

What's that trumpet?

OSWALD enters.

REGAN

I know it. It's my sister's. She'll be here soon, just like her letter said. *(to OSWALD)* Has my sister arrived?

LEAR

This is a lowlife who basks in the reflection of the fading glory of the woman he works for.—Get out of my sight, scoundrel!

CORNWALL

What do you mean, your highness?

GONERIL enters.

LEAR

Who put my servant in the stocks? Regan, I hope you didn't know anything about that.—Ah, who's this? Dear gods, if you love old men like me, if you believe in obedience, if you yourselves are old, then please send me down some help! *(to GONERIL)* Aren't you ashamed to look at me after the way you've treated me in my old age?—Oh, Regan, are you taking her by the hand?

GONERIL

Why shouldn't she take my hand, father? How exactly have I offended you? Just because a senile man with poor judgment calls something an insult doesn't necessarily mean it is one.

LEAR

Oh, how can the sides of my body hold in my grieving heart?—How did my messenger wind up in the stocks?

CORNWALL
I set him there, sir, but his own disorders
190 Deserved much less advancement.

LEAR
                                        You! Did you?

REGAN
I pray you, father, being weak, seem so.
If till the expiration of your month,
You will return and sojourn with my sister,
Dismissing half your train, come then to me.
195 I am now from home, and out of that provision
Which shall be needful for your entertainment.

LEAR
Return to her, and fifty men dismissed?
No, rather I abjure all roofs, and choose
To be a comrade with the wolf and owl—
200 To wage against the enmity o' th' air—
Necessity's sharp pinch! Return with her?
Why, the hot-blooded France that dowerless took
Our youngest born—I could as well be brought
To knee his throne, and, squirelike, pension beg
205 To keep base life afoot. Return with her?
Persuade me rather to be slave and sumpter
To this detested groom. *(indicates* OSWALD*)*

GONERIL
                              At your choice, sir.

LEAR
Now, I prithee, daughter, do not make me mad.
I will not trouble thee, my child. Farewell.
210 We'll no more meet, no more see one another.
But yet thou art my flesh, my blood, my daughter—
Or rather a disease that's in my flesh,
Which I must needs call mine. Thou art a boil,
A plague-sore or embossèd carbuncle
215 In my corrupted blood. But I'll not chide thee.
Let shame come when it will. I do not call it.

CORNWALL

I sent him there, sir, but his crimes deserved a worse punishment.

LEAR

You! You did it?

REGAN

Please, father, since you're weak, act like it. Get rid of half your knights and go back to spend the rest of your month with my sister. Afterward, you can stay with me. Right now I'm away from home and I can't provide you with proper care.

LEAR

Go back with her? Send away fifty of my knights? No. I'd rather renounce living in a house, and wander in the open air in the hardships of poverty, as a friend of the wolf and the owl. Go back with her? I might as well go before the King of France, who took my youngest daughter without a dowry, kneel before his throne, and beg him to give me a tiny pension to stay alive. Go back with her? I'd rather be a slave or a packhorse for this hateful stablehand here. *(he points to* OSWALD*)*

GONERIL

As you wish, sir.

LEAR

I beg you, daughter, don't make me crazy. I won't bother you. We'll never see each other again. But you're still my child, my flesh and blood—or rather you're a disease in my flesh, a disease I still have to call my own. You're a pustule, a sore, a tumor digesting my bloodline. But I'll stop rebuking you. You'll feel shame when the time is right, and I don't urge you to be ashamed now. I won't beg the gods to punish you, or caution you to fear their judgment. Become a better

I do not bid the thunder-bearer shoot,
Nor tell tales of thee to high-judging Jove.
Mend when thou canst. Be better at thy leisure.
220 I can be patient. I can stay with Regan,
I and my hundred knights.

REGAN

                              Not altogether so, sir.
I looked not for you yet, nor am provided
For your fit welcome. Give ear, sir, to my sister.
For those that mingle reason with your passion
225 Must be content to think you old, and so—
But she knows what she does.

LEAR

                              Is this well spoken now?

REGAN

I dare avouch it, sir. What, fifty followers?
Is it not well? What should you need of more—
Yea, or so many—sith that both charge and danger
230 Speak 'gainst so great a number? How, in one house,
Should many people under two commands
Hold amity? 'Tis hard; almost impossible.

GONERIL

Why might not you, my lord, receive attendance
From those that she calls servants, or from mine?

REGAN

235 Why not, my lord? If then they chanced to slack you,
We could control them. If you will come to me—
For now I spy a danger—I entreat you
To bring but five and twenty. To no more
Will I give place or notice.

LEAR

240 I gave you all—

REGAN

And in good time you gave it.

person when you're ready, if you're inclined. I'll wait patiently. Meanwhile I'll stay with Regan with my hundred knights.

REGAN

It's not quite that simple. I wasn't expecting you, and I'm not ready to receive you. Please hear what Goneril is saying. We're trying to be reasonable while you're so upset, and we understand that you're old, and… But Goneril knows what she's doing.

LEAR

Do you mean what you've just said?

REGAN

Yes, I do. Isn't fifty knights enough for you? Why would you need more than that? Or even that many. Fifty knights are expensive to maintain, and there's always a risk they'll rebel. How could so many people, under two masters, get along under one roof? It would be hard, almost impossible.

GONERIL

Why couldn't you be attended by my servants, or by Regan's?

REGAN

Yes, why not, my lord? Then if they're negligent, we could control them. Now that I think about the danger of these knights, if you come to stay with me, please bring no more than twenty-five of them with you. I won't lodge any more than that under my roof.

LEAR

I gave you everything—

REGAN

And it was about time too.

LEAR
Made you my guardians, my depositaries,
But kept a reservation to be followed
With such a number. What, must I come to you
245   With five and twenty, Regan? Said you so?

REGAN
And speak 't again, my lord. No more with me.

LEAR
Those wicked creatures yet do look well favored
When others are more wicked. Not being the worst
Stands in some rank of praise. *(to* GONERIL*)* I'll go with thee.
250   Thy fifty yet doth double five and twenty,
And thou art twice her love.

GONERIL
                                          Hear me, my lord.
What need you five and twenty, ten, or five
To follow in a house where twice so many
Have a command to tend you?

REGAN
                                          What need one?

LEAR
255   O, reason not the need! Our basest beggars
Are in the poorest thing superfluous.
Allow not nature more than nature needs,
Man's life's as cheap as beast's. Thou art a lady.
If only to go warm were gorgeous,
260   Why, nature needs not what thou gorgeous wear'st,
Which scarcely keeps thee warm. But, for true need—
You heavens, give me that patience, patience I need.
You see me here, you gods, a poor old man,
As full of grief as age, wretched in both.
265   If it be you that stir these daughters' hearts
Against their father, fool me not so much
To bear it tamely. Touch me with noble anger.
And let not women's weapons, water drops,
Stain my man's cheeks! No, you unnatural hags,

LEAR

I made you de facto rulers of my kingdom on condition that I could keep a hundred knights of my own. Why should I now have to make do with only twenty-five? Regan, is that what you said?

REGAN

Yes, I'll say it again, my lord. No more than twenty-five.

LEAR

Bad people start to look better in comparison with worse people. Not being the worst daughter deserves some praise, I guess. *(to* GONERIL*)* I'll go stay with you, then. Your fifty is twice her twenty-five, so you must love me twice as much as she does.

GONERIL

Hear me out, my lord. Why do you need twenty-five knights, or ten, or even five, when you're staying in a house with a staff of double that at your service?

REGAN

Why do you need even one?

LEAR

Oh, don't ask me why I "need" them! Even the poorest beggars have some meager possessions they don't really "need." If you allow people no more than what they absolutely need to survive, then a human life is no better than an animal's. You're a well-dressed lady. If you dressed only to stay warm, you wouldn't need these gorgeous clothes you're wearing—which don't keep you warm at all. If you want to talk about true needs, what I really need is patience. Oh, gods, give me patience! You see me here, gods, a grieving old man, as wretched in his grief as he is in his old age. If you're the ones setting my daughters against me, don't let me be foolish enough to take it lying down. Give me noble anger, and don't let any womanly tears

270   I will have such revenges on you both
      That all the world shall—I will do such things—
      What they are yet I know not, but they shall be
      The terrors of the earth. You think I'll weep?
      No, I'll not weep.

      Storm and tempest

275   I have full cause of weeping, but this heart
      Shall break into a hundred thousand flaws,
      Or ere I'll weep.—O Fool, I shall go mad!

      Exeunt LEAR, GENTLEMAN, FOOL, *and* GLOUCESTER

CORNWALL
      Let us withdraw. 'Twill be a storm.
REGAN
      This house is little. The old man and his people
280   Cannot be well bestowed.
GONERIL
      'Tis his own blame. Hath put himself from rest,
      And must needs taste his folly.
REGAN
      For his particular I'll receive him gladly,
      But not one follower.
GONERIL
                          So am I purposed.
285   Where is my lord of Gloucester?
CORNWALL
      Followed the old man forth. He is returned.

      Enter GLOUCESTER

GLOUCESTER
      The king is in high rage.

fall down my man's cheeks. No, you monstrous hags, I'll get revenge on you both that will make the whole world… I will do such things—I don't know what I'll do exactly, but it'll be devastating. You expect me to cry? Well, I won't.

A storm breaks out.

I have a good reason to cry, but my heart will splinter into a hundred thousand pieces before I let myself cry.—Oh, Fool, I'll go mad!

King LEAR, *the* GENTLEMAN, *and the* FOOL *exit with* GLOUCESTER.

CORNWALL
Let's go inside. There's going to be a storm.

REGAN
This is a small house. There's no room for the old man and his followers.

GONERIL
It's his fault that he's all worked up like this. He has to pay the price for his foolish actions.

REGAN
I'll be happy to keep him in my house, but not a single knight.

GONERIL
That's what I intend to do too. Where is Gloucester?

CORNWALL
He followed the old man. Here he comes back.

GLOUCESTER *returns.*

GLOUCESTER
The king is enraged.

CORNWALL
                              Whither is he going?

GLOUCESTER
  He calls to horse, but will I know not whither.

CORNWALL
  'Tis best to give him way. He leads himself.

GONERIL
290   *(to* GLOUCESTER*)* My lord, entreat him by no means to stay.

GLOUCESTER
  Alack, the night comes on, and the high winds
  Do sorely ruffle. For many miles about
  There's scarce a bush.

REGAN
                              O sir, to wilful men,
  The injuries that they themselves procure
295   Must be their schoolmasters. Shut up your doors.
  He is attended with a desperate train.
  And what they may incense him to, being apt
  To have his ear abused, wisdom bids fear.

CORNWALL
  Shut up your doors, my lord. 'Tis a wild night.
300   My Regan counsels well. Come out o' th' storm.

                                        Exeunt

CORNWALL

Where's he going?

GLOUCESTER

He has called for his horse, but I don't know where he's headed.

CORNWALL

It's best just to let him go. He won't listen to anyone's advice.

GONERIL

(to GLOUCESTER*)* My lord, don't try to persuade him to stay.

GLOUCESTER

Ah, but it's getting dark, and the winds are strong and stormy. There's hardly a bush for miles around. He'll have no shelter.

REGAN

Oh, sir, impetuous people learn their lessons from the consequences of their foolish actions. Lock the doors. His attendants are desperate, violent men. I'm afraid of what they might encourage him to do, considering the state he's in.

CORNWALL

Lock the doors, my lord. It's a wild night. Regan gives good advice. Come in out of the storm.

They all exit.

ACT THREE

SCENE 1

Storm still
Enter KENT *disguised and* GENTLEMAN, *severally*

KENT
Who's there, besides foul weather?

GENTLEMAN
One minded like the weather, most unquietly.

KENT
I know you. Where's the king?

GENTLEMAN
Contending with the fretful elements.
5   Bids the winds blow the earth into the sea
Or swell the curlèd water 'bove the main,
That things might change or cease. Tears his white hair,
Which the impetuous blasts, with eyeless rage,
Catch in their fury and make nothing of.
10 Strives in his little world of man to outscorn
The to-and-fro–conflicting wind and rain.
This night—wherein the cub-drawn bear would couch,
The lion and the belly-pinchèd wolf
Keep their fur dry—unbonneted he runs,
15 And bids what will take all.

KENT
                                                But who is with him?

GENTLEMAN
None but the fool, who labors to outjest
His heart-struck injuries.

ACT THREE
SCENE 1

The storm continues to rage. KENT *enters in disguise.*
The GENTLEMAN *enters from a different direction.*

KENT

Who's there, aside from this foul weather?

GENTLEMAN

Someone whose mood is as foul as the weather, very troubled.

KENT

I know you. Where's the king?

GENTLEMAN

Struggling with the wind and rain. He's shouting at the wind to blow the earth into the sea, or make the sea flood the earth—he wants to see the world return to primal chaos. He keeps tearing out his white hair, which the blindly raging winds catch up and blow away into nothingness. Small but brave in his surroundings, he's trying to stand up against the wind and rain blowing back and forth. He's running bareheaded, calling for the end of the world, out there on a night like this, when even savage animals ravenous with hunger crawl under cover and hide.

KENT

But who's with him?

GENTLEMAN

Nobody but the fool, who's trying to soothe the wounds in the king's heart with jokes.

KENT
                                          Sir, I do know you,
And dare upon the warrant of my note
Commend a dear thing to you. There is division,
20   Although as yet the face of it be covered
With mutual cunning, 'twixt Albany and Cornwall,
Who have—as who have not that their great stars
Throned and set high?—servants, who seem no less,
Which are to France the spies and speculations
25   Intelligent of our state. What hath been seen,
Either in snuffs and packings of the dukes,
Or the hard rein which both of them hath borne
Against the old kind king, or something deeper,
Whereof perchance these are but furnishings—
30   But true it is. From France there comes a power
Into this scattered kingdom, who already,
Wise in our negligence, have secret feet
In some of our best ports and are at point
To show their open banner. Now to you.
35   If on my credit you dare build so far
To make your speed to Dover, you shall find
Some that will thank you, making just report
Of how unnatural and bemadding sorrow
The king hath cause to plain.
40   I am a gentleman of blood and breeding,
And from some knowledge and assurance offer
This office to you.

GENTLEMAN
I will talk further with you.

KENT

Sir, I know you, and I trust you enough to share something very important with you. There's a feud between Albany and Cornwall, although they've been clever enough to hide it thus far. Like other powerful rulers, they have servants who are actually French spies in disguise. These spies have noticed something, perhaps in the squabbles between Albany and Cornwall, or in the tough line both of them have taken against the good old king, or perhaps in some deeper matter at the root of both of these problems— The point is that the King of France has sent troops into our divided kingdom. Some French agents are already at work in our main ports and are on the verge of declaring open war. Now this is where you come in. If you trust me enough to hurry to Dover, you'll earn the gratitude of many people when you fairly report the monstrous and maddening extent of the king's suffering. I'm a nobleman, and I know what I'm doing in assigning this job to you.

GENTLEMAN

Let's discuss it some more.

KENT

> *(giving* GENTLEMAN *a purse and a ring)*
>
>   No, do not.
> For confirmation that I am much more
> Than my outwall, open this purse and take
> What it contains. If you shall see Cordelia—
> As fear not but you shall—show her this ring.
> And she will tell you who that fellow is
> That yet you do not know. Fie on this storm!
> I will go seek the king.

GENTLEMAN

> Give me your hand. Have you no more to say?

KENT

> Few words, but to effect more than all yet:
> That when we have found the king—in which your pain
> That way; I'll this—he that first lights on him
> Holla the other.

>   *Exeunt severally*

KENT

(giving the GENTLEMAN a purse and a ring) No, there's no need. To assure you that I am a nobleman in disguise, here is some money. If you see Cordelia—as I'm sure you will—show her this ring. She'll tell you who I am. Damn this storm! I'll go find the king.

GENTLEMAN

Let me shake your hand. Do you have anything else to tell me?

KENT

Only a few more words, but they're the most important. Let me go this way, and you go that way. When one of us finds the king, he'll call out to the other one.

They exit in opposite directions.

ACT 3, SCENE 2

Storm still
Enter LEAR *and* FOOL

LEAR

Blow, winds, and crack your cheeks! Rage, blow!
You cataracts and hurricanoes, spout
Till you have drenched our steeples, drowned the cocks!
You sulfurous and thought-executing fires,
5   Vaunt-couriers of oak-cleaving thunderbolts,
Singe my white head! And thou, all-shaking thunder,
Smite flat the thick rotundity o' th' world,
Crack nature's molds, all germens spill at once
That make ingrateful man!

FOOL

10   O nuncle, court holy water in a dry house is better than this
rainwater out o' door. Good nuncle, in, and ask thy
daughters blessing. Here's a night pities neither wise man
nor fool.

LEAR

Rumble thy bellyful! Spit, fire! Spout, rain!
15   Nor rain, wind, thunder, fire are my daughters.
I tax not you, you elements, with unkindness.
I never gave you kingdom, called you children.
You owe me no subscription. Why then, let fall
Your horrible pleasure. Here I stand, your slave—
20   A poor, infirm, weak, and despised old man.
But yet I call you servile ministers,
That will with two pernicious daughters joined
Your high engendered battles 'gainst a head
So old and white as this. Oh, ho! 'Tis foul.

FOOL

25   He that has a house to put 's head in has a good headpiece.
The codpiece that will house

ACT 3, SCENE 2

The storm continues. LEAR *and the* FOOL *enter.*

LEAR

Blow, winds! Blow until your cheeks crack! Rage on, blow! Let tornadoes spew water until the steeples of our churches and the weathervanes are all drowned. Let quick sulfurous lightning, strong enough to split enormous trees, singe the white hair on my head. Let thunder flatten the spherical world, crack open all the molds from which nature forms human beings, and spill all the seeds from which ungrateful humans grow!

FOOL

Oh, uncle, it's better to smile and flatter indoors where it's dry than get soaked out here. Please, uncle, let's go in and ask your daughters to forgive you. This storm has no pity for either wise men or fools.

LEAR

Let thunder rumble! Let lightning spit fire! Let the rain spray! The rain, the wind, the thunder and lightning are not my daughters. Nature, I don't accuse your weather of unkindness. I never gave you a kingdom or raised you as my child, and you don't owe me any obedience. So go ahead and have your terrifying fun. Here I am, your slave—a poor, sick, weak, hated old man. But I can still accuse you of kowtowing, taking my daughters' side against me, ancient as I am. Oh, it's foul!

FOOL

Anyone who has a house to cover his head has a good head on his shoulders.
The guy who finds a place to put his penis

Before the head has any—
The head and he shall louse.
So beggars marry many.
30 The man that makes his toe
What he his heart should make
Shall of a corn cry woe,
And turn his sleep to wake.
For there was never yet fair woman but she made mouths
        in a glass.

Enter KENT *disguised*

LEAR
35 No, I will be the pattern of all patience.
I will say nothing.

KENT
Who's there?

FOOL
Marry, here's grace and a codpiece—that's a wise man and
a fool.

KENT
40 *(to* LEAR*)* Alas, sir, are you here? Things that love night
Love not such nights as these. The wrathful skies
Gallow the very wanderers of the dark
And make them keep their caves. Since I was man,
Such sheets of fire, such bursts of horrid thunder,
45 Such groans of roaring wind and rain I never
Remember to have heard. Man's nature cannot carry
Th' affliction nor the fear.

LEAR
                                    Let the great gods
That keep this dreadful pudder o'er our heads
Find out their enemies now. Tremble, thou wretch
50 That hast within thee undivulgèd crimes
Unwhipped of justice. Hide thee, thou bloody hand,
Thou perjured, and thou simular man of virtue

Before he has a house of his own
Will wind up dirt poor and covered with lice
With a crowd of slut daughters to add to the slut wife.
The man who kicks away
The person he should love
Will bring himself pain
And sleepless nights.
For there never was a pretty woman who didn't like to
preen in the mirror.

KENT enters in disguise.

LEAR

No, I'll be patient. I won't say a word.

KENT

Who's there?

FOOL

A wise man and a fool.

KENT

(to LEAR) Ah, sir, you're here? Even creatures of the
night aren't out tonight in this storm. The angry skies
terrify the animals that usually prowl in the dark,
making them stay in their caves. Never in my life have
I heard such horrible blasts of thunder, such a roaring
downpour, such groaning winds. It's too trying and
terrifying for humans to bear.

LEAR

Let the gods who stirred up this dreadful storm bring
their enemies to light. Any wretched person who has
committed secret crimes and escaped justice should
tremble in fear now. Better hide now, you murderers,
you perjurers, you incest-practicing people who pretend to be virtuous. Tremble and shake, villain, for

That art incestuous. Caitiff, to pieces shake,
That under covert and convenient seeming
55   Hast practiced on man's life. Close pent-up guilts,
Rive your concealing continents and cry
These dreadful summoners grace. I am a man
More sinned against than sinning.

KENT

                                      Alack, bareheaded?
Gracious my lord, hard by here is a hovel.
60   Some friendship will it lend you 'gainst the tempest.
Repose you there, while I to this hard house—
More harder than the stones whereof 'tis raised,
Which even but now, demanding after you,
Denied me to come in—return, and force
65   Their scanted courtesy.

LEAR

                                      My wits begin to turn.—
(to **FOOL***)*
Come on, my boy. How dost, my boy? Art cold?
I am cold myself.
(to **KENT***)*
                        Where is this straw, my fellow?
The art of our necessities is strange
That can make vile things precious. Come, your hovel.
Poor fool and knave, I have one part in my heart
70   That's sorry yet for thee.

FOOL

(sings)
        He that has and a little tiny wit—
        With heigh-ho, the wind and the rain—
        Must make content with his fortunes fit,
        For the rain it raineth every day.

LEAR
75   True, my good boy.—Come, bring us to this hovel.

                              Exeunt **LEAR** *and* **KENT**

secretly plotting against human lives. Let all your bottled-up crimes come flooding out at last, as you beg for mercy from the gods who summon these terrifying winds and thunderbolts. Other people have sinned against me more than I have sinned against them.

KENT

Why, you're not even wearing a hat? My lord, there's a hut nearby. It will give you some protection from this storm. Rest there while I go back to the unfriendly house where your sisters are staying, and ask them for help. They are harder than the stones the house is made of. Just now, when I asked them if they knew where you were, they wouldn't let me in. But I'll go back and force them to be polite.

LEAR

I'm starting to lose my mind. *(to the* FOOL*)* Come on, my boy. How are you? Are you cold? I'm cold myself. *(to* KENT*)* Where's this hut, man? Odd how when you're desperate, even shoddy things like this hut can seem precious. Show me where that hut is. Poor fool, part of me still feels sorry for you.

FOOL

(singing)
> *The stupid man—*
> *Hey-hoy, the wind and the rain—*
> *Must take what he can get,*
> *Since the rain comes every day.*

LEAR

That's true, my good boy.—Come on, take us to that hut.

LEAR *and* KENT *exit.*

FOOL
This is a brave night to cool a courtesan.
I'll speak a prophecy ere I go.
When priests are more in word than matter,
When brewers mar their malt with water,
80   When nobles are their tailors' tutors,
No heretics burned but wenches' suitors,
When every case in law is right,
No squire in debt nor no poor knight,
When slanders do not live in tongues,
85   Nor cutpurses come not to throngs,
When usurers tell their gold i' th' field,
And bawds and whores do churches build—
Then shall the realm of Albion
Come to great confusion.
90   Then comes the time, who lives to see 't,
That going shall be used with feet.
This prophecy Merlin shall make, for I live before his time.

Exit

FOOL

This would be a great night to satisfy a whore's lust.
I'll recite a prophecy before I go.
One day, when priests don't practice what they preach,
When brewers dilute their beer with water,
When noblemen teach their tailors how to sew,
When instead of heretics being burned at the stake,
lovers are burned by syphilis,
When every law case is tried fairly,
When no gentleman is in debt,
When no one slanders anyone else,
And thieves don't snatch wallets in crowds,
When moneylenders count their gold in the open air,
And pimps and whores build fine churches—
Then the kingdom of England
Will come to ruin.
And whoever lives to see that day
Will walk with his feet.
This is the prophecy that the wizard Merlin will make
one day. I'm a little ahead of my time in saying it now.

He exits.

According to legend, Merlin was the wizard at the court of King Arthur and the Round Table and predicted the end of the world in rhymes that are similar to the fool's prophecy. However, King Lear takes place centuries before the time the mythical Merlin is supposed to have existed.

ACT 3, SCENE 3

Enter GLOUCESTER *and* EDMUND *the bastard, with lights*

GLOUCESTER
Alack, alack, Edmund, I like not this unnatural dealing.
When I desire their leave that I might pity him, they took
from me the use of mine own house, charged me on pain of
their perpetual displeasure neither to speak of him, entreat
5   for him, nor any way sustain him.

EDMUND
Most savage and unnatural!

GLOUCESTER
Go to, say you nothing. There's a division betwixt the
dukes. And a worse matter than that: I have received a letter
this night. 'Tis dangerous to be spoken. I have locked the
10   letter in my closet. These injuries the king now bears will be
revenged home. There's part of a power already footed. We
must incline to the king. I will look him and privily relieve
him. Go you and maintain talk with the duke, that my
charity be not of him perceived. If he ask for me, I am ill and
15   gone to bed. Though I die for it—as no less is threatened
me—the king my old master must be relieved. There is
some strange thing toward, Edmund. Pray you, be careful.

Exit GLOUCESTER

EDMUND
This courtesy, forbid thee, shall the duke
Instantly know, and of that letter too.
20   This seems a fair deserving, and must draw me
That which my father loses—no less than all.
The younger rises when the old doth fall.

Exit

ACT 3, SCENE 3

GLOUCESTER *and* EDMUND *enter with torches.*

GLOUCESTER

Oh, oh, Edmund, I don't like this monstrous business. When asked the Duke and Duchess of Cornwall if I could take pity on the king and shelter him from the storm, they took my house away from me and ordered me never to talk about him, lobby for him, or support him in any way.

EDMUND

That's uncivilized and unnatural!

GLOUCESTER

Oh, be quiet. There's a feud between the two dukes. And there's something even worse than that. I got a letter tonight. It's dangerous to talk about it. I've locked it up in my room. The humiliation that the king is suffering now will be revenged thoroughly. Armed forces have already landed. We have to take the king's side. I'll look for him and secretly help him. You go and talk to the duke so he won't notice I'm helping the king. If he asks to see me, tell him I'm sick and went to bed. Even if I have to die—as they threaten—I have to help the king. Strange things are about to happen, Edmund. Please be careful.

GLOUCESTER *exits.*

EDMUND

I'll tell the duke right away that you're going to see the king, which is forbidden. And I'll tell him about the letter too. You'll get what you deserve, and I'll be rewarded with everything you lose—in other words, all your lands. The young generation rises while the old one falls.

He exits.

ACT 3, SCENE 4

Enter LEAR, KENT *disguised, and* FOOL

KENT

Here is the place, my lord. Good my lord, enter.
The tyranny of the open night's too rough
For nature to endure.

Storm still

LEAR

Let me alone.

KENT

Good my lord, enter here.

LEAR

Wilt break my heart?

KENT

5   I had rather break mine own. Good my lord, enter.

LEAR

Thou think'st 'tis much that this contentious storm
Invades us to the skin. So 'tis to thee.
But where the greater malady is fixed
The lesser is scarce felt. Thou'dst shun a bear,
10 But if thy flight lay toward the raging sea
Thou'dst meet the bear i' th' mouth. When the mind's free,
The body's delicate. The tempest in my mind
Doth from my senses take all feeling else
Save what beats there—filial ingratitude.
15 Is it not as this mouth should tear this hand
For lifting food to 't? But I will punish home.
No, I will weep no more. In such a night
To shut me out! Pour on, I will endure.
In such a night as this! O Regan, Goneril,
20 Your old kind father, whose frank heart gave all—
Oh, that way madness lies. Let me shun that.
No more of that.

ACT 3, SCENE 4

LEAR enters with KENT in disguise and the FOOL.

KENT

Here's the hut, my lord. Please go inside. The night's too rough for humans to bear.

The storm continues.

LEAR

Leave me for a bit.

KENT

My lord, here is the entrance.

LEAR

Will you break my heart?

KENT

I'd rather break my own heart. Now please go in.

LEAR

You think it's a big deal that this fierce storm is soaking me to the skin. It's a big deal to you. But whenever you feel a larger pain, the smaller one disappears. You would run away from a bear, but if the only way to run was into the stormy ocean, you'd turn around and confront the bear. When your mind is at peace, your body is sensitive to the elements. But this storm in my mind keeps me from feeling anything except what's tormenting me—how ungrateful my children are! Isn't their ingratitude like the mouth biting the hand that feeds it? But I'll punish them thoroughly. No, I won't cry any more. Imagine them locking me out on a night like this! But let it rain; I'll survive. On a night like this! Oh, Regan, Goneril, your kind old father whose generous heart gave you everything—Oh, if I think about that I'll go mad. I want to avoid that. No more of these thoughts.

KENT

Good my lord, enter here.

LEAR

Prithee, go in thyself. Seek thine own ease.
This tempest will not give me leave to ponder
On things would hurt me more. But I'll go in.
(to FOOL) In, boy. Go first. You houseless poverty—
Nay, get thee in. I'll pray, and then I'll sleep.

Exit FOOL

Poor naked wretches, whereso'er you are,
That bide the pelting of this pitiless storm,
How shall your houseless heads and unfed sides,
Your looped and windowed raggedness, defend you
From seasons such as these? Oh, I have ta'en
Too little care of this! Take physic, pomp.
Expose thyself to feel what wretches feel,
That thou mayst shake the superflux to them
And show the heavens more just.

EDGAR

(within) Fathom and half, fathom and half! Poor Tom!
Enter FOOL

FOOL

Come not in here, nuncle. Here's a spirit. Help me, help me!

KENT

Give me thy hand. Who's there?

FOOL

A spirit, a spirit. He says his name's Poor Tom.

KENT

What art thou that dost grumble there i' th' straw?
Come forth.

Enter EDGAR disguised

KENT

My lord, please go inside here.

LEAR

Go inside yourself. Make yourself comfortable. This storm protects me from thoughts that would hurt me more. But I'll go in. *(to* FOOL*)* You go in first, boy. Oh, you suffering homeless people—No, you go in. I'll pray first, then I'll sleep.

The FOOL *exits.*

Poor homeless creatures suffering this storm, wherever you are, how will you survive a night like this with no roof over your heads, no fat on your sides to keep you warm, and only rags for clothes? When I was king I didn't do enough to help you. Powerful men, take your medicine by learning about hardship. Go out and feel what the impoverished feel. Then you can give them your extra wealth and make the world more fair.

EDGAR

(from inside) The water in here is nine feet deep! Poor Tom!

FOOL *enters.*

FOOL

Don't come in here, uncle! There's a spirit in here! Help me, help me!

KENT

Give me your hand. Who's there?

FOOL

A ghost, a ghost! He says his name's Poor Tom.

KENT

Who are you, moaning in the hut like that? Come out.

EDGAR *enters disguised.*

EDGAR

Away! The foul fiend follows me! Through the sharp
hawthorn blows the cold wind. Hum! Go to thy cold bed
45   and warm thee.

LEAR

Didst thou give all to thy two daughters, and art thou come
to this?

EDGAR

Who gives any thing to Poor Tom, whom the foul fiend
hath led through fire and through flame, through ford and
50   whirlipool, o'er bog and quagmire; that hath laid knives
under his pillow and halters in his pew, set ratsbane by his
porridge, made him proud of heart to ride on a bay trotting-
horse over four-inched bridges to course his own shadow
for a traitor? Bless thy five wits. Tom's a-cold. Oh, do-de,
55   do-de, do-de. Bless thee from whirlwinds, star-blasting,
and taking! Do Poor Tom some charity, whom the foul
fiend vexes. There could I have him now—and there—and
there again—and there.

Storm still

LEAR

What, has his daughters brought him to this pass?—
60   Couldst thou save nothing? Wouldst thou give 'em all?

FOOL

Nay, he reserved a blanket, else we had been all shamed.

LEAR

Now all the plagues that in the pendulous air
Hang fated o'er men's faults light on thy daughters!

KENT

He hath no daughters, sir.

EDGAR

Go away! The devil's after me! The cold wind blows through the hawthorn trees. Ha! Get into your cold beds and warm yourselves up.

LEAR

Did you give everything to your two daughters and end up like this?

EDGAR

Whoever gave a thing to Poor Tom? The devil has chased him through fires, across rivers and whirlpools, and over swamps. The devil has put knives under Tom's pillow and hangman's ropes in his church pew, encouraging him to kill himself. The devil has put rat poison next to Poor Tom's oatmeal and made him gallop his horse over narrow bridges, chasing his own shadow as if it were a traitor. Bless your five senses! Tom's chilly. Oh do-de, do-de, do-de. God protect you from tornadoes, evil stars, and diseases! Take pity on Poor Tom, who is persecuted by the devil. I can almost catch him. There!… And over there!… And over there!
The storm continues.

LEAR

Have his daughters made him crazy like this?— Couldn't you have kept something for yourself? Did you have to give them everything?

FOOL

No, he kept a blanket to cover himself with. If he hadn't, we'd all be embarrassed to look at him.

LEAR

Then may your daughters be cursed with all the horrible fates that await sinners!

KENT

He doesn't have any daughters, sir.

LEAR

65   Death, traitor! Nothing could have subdued nature
To such a lowness but his unkind daughters.
Is it the fashion that discarded fathers
Should have thus little mercy on their flesh?
Judicious punishment! 'Twas this flesh begot
70   Those pelican daughters.

EDGAR

Pillicock sat on Pillicock hill. Alow, alow, loo, loo!

FOOL

This cold night will turn us all to fools and madmen.

EDGAR

Take heed o' th' foul fiend. Obey thy parents, keep thy
word's justice, swear not, commit not with man's sworn
75   spouse, set not thy sweet heart on proud array. Tom's a-
cold.

LEAR

What hast thou been?

EDGAR

A servingman, proud in heart and mind, that curled my
hair, wore gloves in my cap, served the lust of my mistress'
80.   heart and did the act of darkness with her, swore as many
oaths as I spake words and broke them in the sweet face of
heaven—one that slept in the contriving of lust and waked
to do it. Wine loved I deeply, dice dearly, and in woman
outparamoured the Turk. False of heart, light of ear, bloody
85.   of hand—hog in sloth, fox in stealth, wolf in greediness,
dog in madness, lion in prey. Let not the creaking of shoes
nor the rustling of silks betray thy poor heart to woman.
Keep thy foot out of brothels, thy hand out of plackets, thy
pen from lenders' books, and defy the foul fiend. Still
90.   through the hawthorn blows the cold wind, says, "Suum,
mun, nonny." Dauphin my boy, my boy, cessez. Let him
trot by.

Storm still

LEAR

Like hell! Nothing but cruel daughters could have degraded him like this. Is it fashionable now for neglected fathers to get so little pity? That's a fair punishment! I'm the one who fathered those bloodsucking daughters.

EDGAR

"pillicock" = penis; "pillicock hill" = vulva

Pillicock sat on Pillicock hill. La, la, la, la!

FOOL

This stormy night will turn us all into fools and madmen.

EDGAR

Beware of the devil. Obey your parents, keep your word, don't swear, don't sleep with another man's wife, and don't covet flashy clothes. Tom's chilly.

LEAR

What were you before this?

EDGAR

I used to be an honorable devoted servant who curled his hair, wore his mistress's glove in his hat as a token of her affection, and slept with his mistress whenever she wanted. I swore oaths with every other word out of my mouth, and broke the oaths shamelessly. I used to dream of having sex and wake up to do it. I loved wine and gambling, and had more women than a Turkish sultan keeps in his harem. I was disloyal and violent. I eavesdropped. I was as lazy as a hog, as sneaky as a fox, as greedy as a wolf, as mad as a dog, and as ruthless as a lion. Don't ever let a woman know what you're thinking. Stay away from whores, don't chase skirts, don't borrow money, and resist the devil. The cold wind's still blowing through the hawthorn tree. *(speaking to an imaginary horse)* Dauphin, my boy, stop that.—Let the horse go by.

The storm continues.

LEAR

Why, thou wert better in thy grave than to answer with thy
uncovered body this extremity of the skies.—Is man no
95   more than this? Consider him well.—Thou owest the
worm no silk, the beast no hide, the sheep no wool, the cat
no perfume. Ha! Here's three on 's are sophisticated.
Thou art the thing itself.
Unaccommodated man is no more but such a poor, bare,
100   forked animal as thou art.—
Off, off, you lendings! Come. Unbutton here.
(tears at his clothes)

Enter GLOUCESTER *with a torch*

FOOL

Prithee, nuncle, be contented. 'Tis a naughty night to swim
in. Now a little fire in a wild field were like an old lecher's
heart—a small spark, all the rest on 's body cold. Look, here
105   comes a walking fire.

EDGAR

This is the foul fiend Flibbertigibbet. He begins at curfew
and walks till the first cock. He gives the web and the pin,
squints the eye and makes the harelip, mildews the white
wheat and hurts the poor creature of earth.
110   Swithold footed thrice the 'old.
He met the nightmare and her ninefold,
Bid her alight,
And her troth plight.
And aroint thee, witch, aroint thee!

KENT

115   How fares your grace?

LEAR

(indicating GLOUCESTER*)* What's he?

KENT

Who's there? What is 't you seek?

LEAR

You'd be better off dead than facing the storm as naked as you are. Is this all a human being is? Look at him. *(to* EDGAR*)* You are not indebted to animals for your clothes since don't wear silk, leather, or wool— not even perfume. Ha! The three of us are sophisticated compared to you. You're the real thing. The human being unburdened by the trappings of civilization is no more than a poor, naked, two-legged animal like you. Off with these clothes borrowed from animals! Let me unbutton this. *(he tears at his clothes)*

Perfume can be made from the secretions of a civet cat.

GLOUCESTER *enters with a torch.*

FOOL

Please calm down, uncle. This is a nasty night to go swimming. On a night like this a campfire in an empty field would be like the heart of a dirty old man—a tiny spark in a cold body. Look, here comes a walking fire.

EDGAR

This is the devil Flibbertigibbet. He gets up at nightfall and wanders around till dawn. He can make your eyes squint and film over and give you a harelip. He rots ripened wheat and hurts the poor creatures of the earth. Saint Withold crossed the field three times, He met a she-demon and her nine kids, He told her to promise To stop doing harm. And go away, witch, go away.

KENT

How are you, your highness?

LEAR

(pointing at GLOUCESTER*)* Who's that?

KENT

Who are you? What do you want?

GLOUCESTER
What are you there? Your names?

EDGAR
120   Poor Tom, that eats the swimming frog, the toad, the
tadpole, the wall newt, and the water; that in the fury of his
heart, when the foul fiend rages, eats cow dung for salads,
swallows the old rat and the ditch-dog, drinks the green
mantle of the standing pool; who is whipped from tithing to
tithing and stocked, punished and imprisoned; who hath
125   had three suits to his back, six shirts to his body,
Horse to ride and weapon to wear.
But mice and rats and such small deer
Have been Tom's food for seven long year.
Beware my follower. Peace, Smulkin. Peace, thou fiend!

GLOUCESTER
130   *(to* LEAR *)* What, hath your grace no better company?

EDGAR
The Prince of Darkness is a gentleman. Modo he's called,
and Mahu.

GLOUCESTER
(to LEAR *)* Our flesh and blood, my lord, is grown so vile
That it doth hate what gets it.

EDGAR
135   Poor Tom's a-cold.

GLOUCESTER
Go in with me. My duty cannot suffer
To obey in all your daughters' hard commands.
Though their injunction be to bar my doors
And let this tyrannous night take hold upon you,
140   Yet have I ventured to come seek you out
And bring you where both fire and food is ready.

LEAR
First let me talk with this philosopher.—
(to EDGAR *)* What is the cause of thunder?

GLOUCESTER

Who are you? What are your names?

EDGAR

Poor Tom, who eats frogs, toads, tadpoles, lizards, and newts. When the devil tells me to, I eat cow dung for salads, I swallow old rats and dead dogs, I drink pond scum. In every village I'm whipped and put in the stocks, punished and imprisoned. But I used to be a respectable servant, with three suits and six shirts. Once I had a horse to ride and a sword to wear, but now poor Tom's been eating rats and mice for seven long years. Beware of the devil who follows me around. Calm down, Smulkin, you fiend!

GLOUCESTER

(to LEAR*)* Don't you have anyone more respectable with you, your highness?

EDGAR

Oh, the devil is quite a gentleman. He's called Modo and Mahu.

GLOUCESTER

(to LEAR*)* My lord, our children have become so beastly that they hate their own parents.

EDGAR

Poor Tom's chilly.

GLOUCESTER

Come back to my house with me. I couldn't bear to obey all of your daughters' harsh orders. They commanded me to lock my doors and leave you out in this merciless storm, but I've come out here to find you and take you where there's warmth and food.

LEAR

First let me talk with this philosopher here.—*(to* EDGAR*)* What causes thunder?

KENT

(to LEAR) Good my lord, take his offer. Go into the house.

LEAR

145   I'll talk a word with this same learnèd Theban.—
       What is your study?

EDGAR

How to prevent the fiend and to kill vermin.

LEAR

Let me ask you one word in private.

LEAR *and* EDGAR *talk aside*

KENT

(aside to GLOUCESTER)
Importune him once more to go, my lord.
150   His wits begin t' unsettle.

GLOUCESTER

                              Canst thou blame him?

Storm still

His daughters seek his death. Ah, that good Kent—
He said it would be thus, poor banished man.
Thou say'st the king grows mad. I'll tell thee, friend,
I am almost mad myself. I had a son,
155   Now outlawed from my blood. He sought my life,
But lately, very late. I loved him, friend—
No father his son dearer. Truth to tell thee,

KENT

(to LEAR*)* Sir, please take him up on his offer and go back with him.

LEAR

In Shakespeare's time the Greeks were associated with wisdom and education, especially in philosophy. Important Greek works in philosophy and the sciences had been recently rediscovered after centuries of oblivion.

I want to chat a bit with this wise Greek man.—What kind of philosophy do you study?

EDGAR

How to keep the devil away and kill rats.

LEAR

Let me ask you something in private.
LEAR and EDGAR talk privately.

KENT

(speaking so that only GLOUCESTER *can hear)* Ask him again to return with you, my lord. He's beginning to lose his mind.

GLOUCESTER

Can you blame him?

The storm continues.

His daughters want to kill him. Ah, good old Kent said this would happen—that poor, banished man. You say the king is losing his mind. Let me tell you, my friend, I'm almost insane myself. I had a son, whom I've legally disowned. He tried to kill me recently, very recently. I loved him, as much as any father ever loved his son. To tell you the truth, I'm

The grief hath crazed my wits. What a night's this!
(to LEAR*)* I do beseech your grace—

LEAR

                              O, cry your mercy, sir.—
160   *(to* EDGAR*)* Noble philosopher, your company.

EDGAR

                                        Tom's a-cold.

GLOUCESTER
In, fellow. There, into th' hovel. Keep thee warm.

LEAR
Come let's in all.

KENT
                    This way, my lord.

LEAR
(indicating EDGAR*)*

                                        With him!
I will keep still with my philosopher.

KENT
(to GLOUCESTER*)*
165   Good my lord, soothe him. Let him take the fellow.

GLOUCESTER
Take him you on.

KENT
(to EDGAR*)* Sirrah, come on. Go along with us.

LEAR
Come, good Athenian.

GLOUCESTER
                        No words, no words. Hush.

EDGAR
Child Roland to the dark tower came,
170   His word was still "Fie, foh, and fum,
I smell the blood of a British man."

                                        Exeunt

crazed with grief. What a storm! *(to* LEAR*)* Your highness, please, I'm begging you—

LEAR

Excuse me, sir.—*(to* EDGAR*)* Noble philosopher,
come talk to me.

EDGAR

Tom's chilly.

GLOUCESTER

Get into the hut, man. Stay warm.

LEAR

Come on, let's all go inside.

KENT

This way, my lord.

LEAR

(pointing to EDGAR*)* I'll go with him. I want to stay with
my philosopher.

KENT

(to GLOUCESTER*)* My lord, calm him down. Let him
take that guy inside too.

GLOUCESTER

All right, bring him along.

KENT

(to EDGAR*)* Boy, come along with us.

LEAR

Come on, my dear Greek philosopher.

GLOUCESTER

Hush, don't talk.

EDGAR

The young knight Roland came to the dark tower.
He said, "Fee, fie, fo, fum,
I smell the blood of an Englishman."

They all exit.

ACT 3, SCENE 5

Enter CORNWALL *and* EDMUND

CORNWALL
I will have my revenge ere I depart his house.

EDMUND
How, my lord, I may be censured, that nature thus gives
way to loyalty, something fears me to think of.

CORNWALL
I now perceive it was not altogether your brother's evil
5   disposition made him seek his death, but a provoking merit
set awork by a reprovable badness in himself.

EDMUND
How malicious is my fortune, that I must repent to be just!
(giving CORNWALL *a letter)* This is the letter which he spoke
of, which approves him an intelligent party to the
10   advantages of France. O heavens, that this treason were
not, or not I the detector!

CORNWALL
Go with me to the duchess.

EDMUND
If the matter of this paper be certain, you have mighty
business in hand.

CORNWALL
15   True or false, it hath made thee Earl of Gloucester. Seek out
where thy father is, that he may be ready for our
apprehension.

EDMUND
(aside) If I find him comforting the king, it will stuff his
suspicion more fully.*(to* CORNWALL*)*
20   I will persevere in my course of loyalty, though the conflict
be sore between that and my blood.

CORNWALL
I will lay trust upon thee, and thou shalt find a dearer father
in my love.

Exeunt

ACT 3, SCENE 5

CORNWALL *enters with* EDMUND.

CORNWALL

I'll get my revenge before I leave this house.

EDMUND

I'm afraid to think how I'll be criticized for letting my natural affection for my father give way to my loyalty to you.

CORNWALL

Now I realize your brother tried to kill your father not just because your brother is an evil man, but because your father deserved it by being wicked himself.

EDMUND

How unlucky am I, having to apologize for doing the right thing! *(giving* CORNWALL *a letter)* This is the letter he was talking about, and it confirms he was a spy for France. Oh God, I wish he had never betrayed us, or that I hadn't been the one to discover his treason.

CORNWALL

Come with me to see the duchess.

EDMUND

If this letter's right, you've got a lot to deal with.

CORNWALL

Right or not, it's made you the Earl of Gloucester. Go find your father and let him know we're going to arrest him.

EDMUND

(to himself) If I catch my father helping the king, he'll seem even more guily. *(to* CORNWALL*)* I'll do what I must loyally, even though it pains me to take action against my father.

CORNWALL

I put my trust in you. You'll see that I'm a better father to you than Gloucester.

They exit.

ACT 3, SCENE 6

Enter GLOUCESTER, LEAR, KENT *disguised,* FOOL, *and*
EDGAR *disguised*

GLOUCESTER
Here is better than the open air. Take it thankfully. I will
piece out the comfort with what addition I can. I will not be
long from you.

KENT
All the power of his wits have given way to his impatience.
5   The gods reward your kindness!

Exit GLOUCESTER

EDGAR
Frateretto calls me and tells me Nero is an angler in the lake
of darkness. Pray, innocent, and beware the foul fiend.

FOOL
Prithee, nuncle, tell me whether a madman be a gentleman
or a yeoman?

LEAR
10   A king, a king!

FOOL
No, he's a yeoman that has a gentleman to his son, for he's
a mad yeoman that sees his son a gentleman before him.

LEAR
To have a thousand with red burning spits
Come hissing in upon 'em!

EDGAR
15   The foul fiend bites my back.

ACT 3, SCENE 6

GLOUCESTER *enters with* LEAR, *the* FOOL, *and* KENT *and*
EDGAR, *both in disguise.*

GLOUCESTER

It's better here than outside. Be happy about it. I'll do what I can to make you even more comfortable. I won't be gone long.

KENT

He can't bear his grief and so he's losing his mind. May God reward you for your kindness!

GLOUCESTER *exits.*

EDGAR

Nero was a first-century A.D. Roman emperor who, according to legend, played the fiddle while Rome burned.

The devil Frateretto is telling me that the diabolical Roman emperor Nero likes to go fishing in hell. Pray to the gods, you fool, and beware the foul devil.

FOOL

Here's a riddle, uncle. Is the lunatic a gentleman or an ordinary guy?

LEAR

He's a king, a king!

FOOL

No, he's an ordinary guy who's got a gentleman for a son, since someone would have to be crazy to let his son become a gentleman before he's achieved that distinction himself.

LEAR

I see Regan and Goneril in hell—A thousand hissing devils with sizzling red pitchforks come up to them!

EDGAR

The nasty devil's biting my butt.

FOOL

    He's mad that trusts in the tameness of a wolf, a horse's
    health, a boy's love, or a whore's oath.

LEAR

    It shall be done. I will arraign them straight.
    (to EDGAR*)* Come, sit thou here, most learnèd justicer.
    (to FOOL*)*
20   Thou, sapient sir, sit here.—Now, you she-foxes—

EDGAR

    Look, where he stands and glares!—Want'st thou eyes at
    trial, madam?
    (sings)
    Come o'er the bourn, Bessy, to me—

FOOL

    (sings)
    Her boat hath a leak,
25   *And she must not speak*
    Why she dares not come over to thee.

EDGAR

    The foul fiend haunts Poor Tom in the voice of a
    nightingale. Hoppedance cries in Tom's belly for two white
    herring. Croak not, black angel. I have no food for thee.

KENT

30   *(to* LEAR*)* How do you, sir? Stand you not so amazed.
    Will you lie down and rest upon the cushions?

LEAR

    I'll see their trial first. Bring in the evidence.
    (to EDGAR*)* Thou robèd man of justice, take thy place.
    (to FOOL*)* And thou, his yoke-fellow of equity,
35   Bench by his side.
    (to KENT*)*
                You are o' th' commission.
    Sit you too.

EDGAR

    Let us deal justly.

FOOL

You've got to be crazy to trust a wolf that pretends to be tame, a horse that seems healthy, a teenager in love, or a whore who swears she'll be faithful.

LEAR

Lear begins a mock trial of Goneril and Regan.

I'll do it. I'll put them on trial right now. *(to EDGAR)* Come sit here, our able judge. *(to FOOL)* And you sit here, wise sir.—Now, you she-foxes—

EDGAR

There he is, standing and glaring at me!—Hey, lady, can't you see how the judge is?
(sings)
> *Come over the stream to me, dear Bessy—*

FOOL

(sings)
> *She's getting her period,*
> *And she won't tell you*
> *Why she won't come see you.*

EDGAR

The devil sings like a nightingale to haunt Poor Tom. The demon Hoppedance is in Tom's belly, crying for some fish to eat. Stop whining, devil. I've got no food to give you.

KENT

(to LEAR) How are you, sir? Please don't stand there in a daze. Wouldn't you like to lie down on the pillows?

LEAR

No, I want to see their trial first. Let's have the evidence. *(to EDGAR)* Take your place, honorable judge. *(to FOOL)* And you, his fellow justice of the peace, sit next to him. *(to KENT)* You can also be a judge. Sit down as well.

EDGAR

Let's give a fair verdict.

(sings)
Sleepest or wakest thou, jolly shepherd?
Thy sheep be in the corn.
40   *And for one blast of thy minikin mouth,*
Thy sheep shall take no harm.
Purr! The cat is gray.

LEAR

Arraign her first. 'Tis Goneril. I here take my oath before
this honorable assembly, she kicked the poor king her
45   father.

FOOL

Come hither, mistress. Is your name Goneril?

LEAR

She cannot deny it.

FOOL

Cry you mercy, I took you for a joint-stool.

LEAR

And here's another, whose warped looks proclaim
50   What store her heart is made on. Stop her there!
Arms, arms, sword, fire, corruption in the place!
False justicer, why hast thou let her 'scape?

EDGAR

Bless thy five wits.

KENT

(to LEAR*)* O pity! Sir, where is the patience now,
55   That thou so oft have boasted to retain?

EDGAR

(aside) My tears begin to take his part so much,
They'll mar my counterfeiting.

LEAR

                                    The little dogs and all,
Tray, Blanch, and Sweetheart—see, they bark at me.

EDGAR

Tom will throw his head at them.—Avaunt, you curs!
60   Tooth that poisons if it bite,
Mastiff, greyhound, mongrel grim,

(sings)

> Are you asleep or awake, happy shepherd?
> Your sheep are running around the cornfield.
> But if you blow your cute little horn,
> Your sheep will be fine.
> Purr! The devil-cat is gray.

LEAR

Let's put Goneril on trial first. There she is. I hereby swear before this honored assembly that she kicked her father when he was down.

FOOL

Come here, ma'am. Is your name Goneril?

LEAR

She can't deny it.

FOOL

I'm so sorry, ma'am, I thought you were a good person, a well-made chair instead of a crude stool.

LEAR

And here's Regan, whose grotesque face betrays her twisted heart. Stop her! Guards, guards, use your weapons. Fire! The courtroom is in chaos. You corrupt judge, why did you let her escape?

EDGAR

Bless your heart.

KENT

(to LEAR) How sorrowful! Sir, where's the self-control you used to be so proud of?

EDGAR

(to himself) I feel so sorry for him that my tears are starting to ruin my disguise.

LEAR

Look at the three little dogs, Tray, Blanch, and Sweetheart—all barking at me.

EDGAR

Tom will chase them off.—Go away, you mongrels! Whether your mouth is black or white,

Hound or spaniel, brach or him,
Bobtail tyke or trundle-tail—
Tom will make them weep and wail.
65   For with throwing thus my head,
Dogs leap the hatch, and all are fled.
Be thy mouth or black or white,
Do-de, de-de. Cessez! Come, march to wakes and fairs and
market towns. Poor Tom, thy horn is dry.

LEAR

70   Then let them anatomize Regan. See what breeds about her
heart. Is there any cause in nature that makes these hard
hearts? *(to* EDGAR*)* You, sir, I entertain you for one of my
hundred. Only I do not like the fashion of your garments.
You will say they are Persian attire, but let them be
75   changed.

KENT

Now, good my lord, lie here and rest awhile.

LEAR

Make no noise, make no noise. Draw the curtains—so, so,
so. We'll go to supper i' th' morning. So, so, so. *(sleeps)*

FOOL

And I'll go to bed at noon.

Enter GLOUCESTER

GLOUCESTER

80   *(to* KENT*)* Come hither, friend. Where is the king my
master?

KENT

Here, sir, but trouble him not. His wits are gone.

GLOUCESTER

Good friend, I prithee, take him in thy arms.
I have o'erheard a plot of death upon him.

Whether you bite to kill,
Mastiff, greyhound, or ugly mutt,
Hound or spaniel, bitch or dog,
Whether your tail is short or curly—
Tom will make you cry and wail.
With one little toss of his head,
He can scare you off for good.
Do-dee, dee-dee da. Stop! Run off, go visit fairs and
festivals! Poor Tom, your cup is empty.

LEAR

Now let them dissect Regan and her hard heart. Is
there any natural cause for hardening of the heart? *(to
EDGAR)* Sir, you can serve me as one of my hundred
knights. But I don't like your style of clothes. I'm sure
you'll tell me they're fabulous, but I think you should
change them anyway.

KENT

Please lie down and rest a while, my lord.

LEAR

Be quiet, be quiet. Draw the curtains, just like that.
We'll have supper in the morning. That's right.
(he falls asleep)

FOOL

And I'll go to bed at noon.

GLOUCESTER *enters.*

GLOUCESTER

(to KENT) Come here, my friend. Where's my master
the king?

KENT

He's here, sir, but please don't bother him. He's out of
his right mind.

GLOUCESTER

Please get him, my friend, I beg you. I've overheard
people plotting to kill him. I have a carriage ready. Put

85   There is a litter ready. Lay him in 't
      And drive towards Dover, friend, where thou shalt meet
      Both welcome and protection. Take up thy master.
      If thou shouldst dally half an hour, his life,
      With thine and all that offer to defend him,
90   Stand in assurèd loss. Take up, take up,
      And follow me, that will to some provision
      Give thee quick conduct.

KENT
                              Oppressèd nature sleeps.—
      This rest might yet have balmed thy broken sinews,
      Which, if convenience will not allow,
95   Stand in hard cure.
      (to **FOOL***)*
                              Come, help to bear thy master.
      Thou must not stay behind.

GLOUCESTER
                              Come, come, away.

                              Exeunt all but **EDGAR**

EDGAR
      When we our betters see bearing our woes,
      We scarcely think our miseries our foes.
      Who alone suffers, suffers most i' th' mind,
100   Leaving free things and happy shows behind.
      But then the mind much sufferance doth o'erskip
      When grief hath mates and bearing fellowship.
      How light and portable my pain seems now
      When that which makes me bend makes the king bow.
105   He childed as I fathered. Tom, away!
      Mark the high noises and thyself bewray
      When false opinion, whose wrong thought defiles thee,
      In thy just proof repeals and reconciles thee.
      What will hap more tonight, safe 'scape the king!
110   Lurk, lurk.
                                              Exit

him inside and take him to Dover, where you'll find
people who'll welcome and protect him. Carry your
master out. If you waste even half an hour, he'll be
killed, along with you and everyone else helping him.
Bring him here, carry him and follow me. I'll quickly
take you to where you can find supplies.

KENT

Lear's suffering has finally put him to sleep. *(to the
sleeping* **LEAR***)* This rest might have calmed your shat-
tered nerves. It will be difficult for you to get better
now that rest is impossible. *(to* **FOOL***)* Come on, help
me carry your master. You can't stay here.

GLOUCESTER

Come on, come on.

Everyone exits except **EDGAR***.*

EDGAR

When we see that our betters have the same problems
we do, we can almost forget our own misery. The person who suffers alone suffers the most. Companions
in sorrow alleviate our grief. My troubles seem so easy
to bear now that I see the king collapsing under a similar sorrow. His children have done the same to him as
my father has to me. Let's go, Tom. We'll pay atten-
tion to the political situation, and you'll be able to
reveal your true identity when you're proven innocent. Whatever else happens tonight, I hope the king
escapes safely! Lurk out of sight.

He exits.

ACT 3, SCENE 7

Enter CORNWALL, *and* REGAN, *and* GONERIL, *and* EDMUND
the bastard, and servants

CORNWALL
(*to* GONERIL) Post speedily to my lord your husband. Show
him this letter. The army of France is landed.
—Seek out the traitor Gloucester.

Exeunt some servants

REGAN
Hang him instantly.

GONERIL
Pluck out his eyes.

CORNWALL
5   Leave him to my displeasure.—Edmund, keep you our
sister company. The revenges we are bound to take upon
your traitorous father are not fit for your beholding. Advise
the duke where you are going, to a most festinate
preparation. We are bound to the like. Our posts shall be
10   swift and intelligent betwixt us.—Farewell, dear sister.
(*to* EDMUND) Farewell, my lord of Gloucester.

Enter OSWALD *the steward*

How now? Where's the king?

OSWALD
My lord of Gloucester hath conveyed him hence.
Some five or six and thirty of his knights,
15   Hot questrists after him, met him at gate,
Who with some other of the lord's dependants
Are gone with him towards Dover, where they boast
To have well-armèd friends.

ACT 3, SCENE 7

CORNWALL *enters with* REGAN, GONERIL, EDMUND, *and servants.*

CORNWALL

(to GONERIL*)* Hurry to your husband. Show him this letter. The French army has landed.—Find the traitor Gloucester.

Some servants exit.

REGAN

Hang him immediately.

GONERIL

Gouge out his eyes!

CORNWALL

Leave him to my wrath.—Edmund, go with my sister-in-law. You shouldn't have to see the punishment we inflict on your father. Tell the Duke of Albany to prepare for war immediately. We will do the same. We'll keep the lines of communication open between us. *(to* GONERIL*)* Goodbye, my dear sister-in-law. *(to* EDMUND*)* Goodbye, lord Gloucester.

OSWALD *enters.*

Hello. Where's the king?

OSWALD

Lord Gloucester has helped him leave. Thirty-five or thirty-six of his knights met him at the gate, and together with some others they've set off for Dover, where they claim to have powerful friends.

CORNWALL
Get horses for your mistress.

Exit OSWALD

GONERIL
20   Farewell, sweet lord, and sister.

CORNWALL
Edmund, farewell.

Exeunt GONERIL *and* EDMUND *the bastard*

Go seek the traitor Gloucester.
Pinion him like a thief, bring him before us.

Exeunt some servants

Though well we may not pass upon his life
Without the form of justice, yet our power
25   Shall do a courtesy to our wrath, which men
May blame, but not control.—Who's there? The traitor?

Enter GLOUCESTER, *brought in by two or three servants*

REGAN
Ingrateful fox, 'tis he.

CORNWALL
Bind fast his corky arms.

GLOUCESTER
What mean your graces? Good my friends, consider
You are my guests. Do me no foul play, friends.

CORNWALL
30   Bind him, I say.

Servants bind GLOUCESTER

CORNWALL

Prepare the horses for your lady.

OSWALD exits.

GONERIL

Goodbye, my sweet lord.—Goodbye, my sister.

CORNWALL

Goodbye, Edmund.

GONERIL and EDMUND exit.

Go find the traitor Gloucester. Tie him up like a thief and bring him here to me.

Some servants exit.

I can't condemn him to death without a formal trial, but I'm powerful enough that I can still do *something* to express my anger. Some men may blame me for doing this, but they won't be able to do anything about it.—Who's there? Is that the traitor?

Two or three servants bring in GLOUCESTER.

REGAN

Ungrateful traitor! That's him.

CORNWALL

Tie up his withered old arms.

GLOUCESTER

What are you doing? My friends, remember that you're my guests here. Don't play any nasty tricks on me.

CORNWALL

Tie him up, I tell you.

Servants tie up GLOUCESTER.

REGAN

                    Hard, hard.—O filthy traitor!

GLOUCESTER

    Unmerciful lady as you are, I'm none.

CORNWALL

    To this chair bind him.—Villain, thou shalt find—

    REGAN *plucks* GLOUCESTER*'s beard*

GLOUCESTER

    By the kind gods, 'tis most ignobly done
    To pluck me by the beard.

REGAN

35 So white, and such a traitor?

GLOUCESTER

    Naughty lady,
    These hairs which thou dost ravish from my chin
    Will quicken and accuse thee. I am your host.
    With robbers' hands my hospitable favors
40 You should not ruffle thus. What will you do?

CORNWALL

    Come, sir, what letters had you late from France?

REGAN

    Be simple-answered, for we know the truth.

CORNWALL

    And what confederacy have you with the traitors
    Late footed in the kingdom?

REGAN

                            To whose hands
45 You have sent the lunatic king. Speak.

GLOUCESTER

    I have a letter guessingly set down,
    Which came from one that's of a neutral heart,
    And not from one opposed.

CORNWALL

                            Cunning.

REGAN

Tie him up harder.—You filthy traitor!

GLOUCESTER

I'm not a traitor, unfair lady.

CORNWALL

Tie him to this chair.—You'll see, criminal—

REGAN pulls GLOUCESTER'S beard.

GLOUCESTER

By the gods, it's disgraceful for you to pull my beard.

REGAN

As old and white-haired as you are, and you're such a traitor?

GLOUCESTER

Wicked woman, these white hairs you're pulling off my chin will come to life and accuse you of wrong-doing. You are my guests. This is no way to treat a host who has welcomed you into his house. What do you think you're doing?

CORNWALL

Tell us about the letters that you got from France.

REGAN

Get to the point, since we already know the truth.

CORNWALL

And what's your connection with the traitors who landed in our kingdom recently?

REGAN

The ones you've sent our lunatic king to. Tell us.

GLOUCESTER

I got a letter that made some guesses about what was going on, without any proof. It came from a neutral party, not from someone opposed to you.

CORNWALL

How clever of you.

REGAN
                                                    And false.

CORNWALL
     Where hast thou sent the king?

GLOUCESTER
                                                    To Dover.

REGAN
50   Wherefore to Dover? Wast thou not charged at peril—

CORNWALL
     Wherefore to Dover?—Let him first answer that.

GLOUCESTER
     I am tied to th' stake, and I must stand the course.

REGAN
     Wherefore to Dover, sir?

GLOUCESTER
     Because I would not see thy cruèl nails
55   Pluck out his poor old eyes, nor thy fierce sister
     In his anointed flesh stick boarish fangs.
     The sea, with such a storm as his bare head
     In hell-black night endured, would have buoyed up,
     And quenched the stellèd fires.
60   Yet poor old heart, he holp the heavens to rain.
     If wolves had at thy gate howled that stern time,
     Thou shouldst have said, "Good porter, turn the key,"
     All cruèls else subscribed. But I shall see
     The wingèd vengeance overtake such children.

CORNWALL
65   "See" 't shalt thou never.—Fellows, hold the chair.—
     Upon these eyes of thine I'll set my foot.

GLOUCESTER
     He that will think to live till he be old,
     Give me some help!

     CORNWALL *plucks out one of* GLOUCESTER's *eyes*
     and stamps on it

REGAN

Clever lies.

CORNWALL

Where have you sent the king?

GLOUCESTER

To Dover.

REGAN

Why Dover? Weren't you ordered, on penalty of—

CORNWALL

Why Dover?—Let him answer that question first.

GLOUCESTER

I'm backed into a corner with nowhere to run.

REGAN

Why Dover?

GLOUCESTER

Because I didn't want to watch while you gouged out his poor old eyes with your cruel fingernails, or while your vicious sister sank her fangs into his sacred flesh. You left him out in the storm in the black night, bareheaded, a storm so terrible that if it had happened at sea, the waters would have risen up and extinguished the fire burning in the stars. And the poor old man just wept, mixing his tears with the rain. If wolves had been howling outside your gate at the heart of that storm, you would've told your doorman to let them in, despite all the cruelties you inflict on the world. But soon I'll see the gods punish you for your lack of respect to your father.

CORNWALL

You won't be seeing anything.—Hold his chair still, men.—I'm going to put my foot on his eyes.

GLOUCESTER

Oh, help me, anyone who wants to live long!

CORNWALL gouges out one of GLOUCESTER's eyes and steps on it.

O cruel! O you gods!

REGAN
70   One side will mock another—th' other too.

CORNWALL
If you see vengeance—

FIRST SERVANT
Hold your hand, my lord!
I have served you ever since I was a child.
But better service have I never done you
75   Than now to bid you hold.

REGAN
How now, you dog?

FIRST SERVANT
If you did wear a beard upon your chin,
I'd shake it on this quarrel. What do you mean?

CORNWALL
My villein!

FIRST SERVANT
Nay then, come on, and take the chance of anger.

FIRST SERVANT and CORNWALL draw and fight
CORNWALL is wounded

REGAN
(to another servant)
80   Give me thy sword.—A peasant stand up thus?
(takes a sword, runs at FIRST SERVANT behind, and kills him)

FIRST SERVANT
Oh, I am slain!—My lord, you have one eye left
To see some mischief on him. Oh!
(dies)

CORNWALL
Lest it see more, prevent it.—Out, vile jelly!

Oh, so cruel! Oh dear gods!

REGAN

Now he's a little crooked. Gouge out the other eye too.

CORNWALL

If you see vengeance—

FIRST SERVANT

Stop, my lord! I've served you since childhood, but I've never done you a better service than telling you to stop.

REGAN

What's this, you dog?

FIRST SERVANT

I am willing to fight you if I must. What do you mean by all this?

CORNWALL

My peasant, acting like this?

FIRST SERVANT

Come on then. Over my dead body.

The **FIRST SERVANT** *and* **CORNWALL** *draw swords and fight.* **CORNWALL** *is wounded.*

REGAN

(to another servant) Give me your sword.—A lowly peasant defying his lord like this?

She takes a sword and stabs the **FIRST SERVANT** *from behind, killing him.*

FIRST SERVANT

I am dying!—My lord, you still have one eye left to see Cornwall punished. Oh!
(he dies)

CORNWALL

We'll just have to stop him from seeing ever again. Out, vile jelly, pop out of your eye sockets!

(plucks out GLOUCESTER*'s other eye)*
Where is thy luster now?

GLOUCESTER
85   All dark and comfortless. Where's my son Edmund?
Edmund, enkindle all the sparks of nature
To quit this horrid act.

REGAN
                                  Out, treacherous villain!
Thou call'st on him that hates thee. It was he
That made the overture of thy treasons to us,
90   Who is too good to pity thee.

GLOUCESTER
       O my follies! Then Edgar was abused.
Kind gods, forgive me that, and prosper him!

REGAN
       Go thrust him out at gates, and let him smell
His way to Dover.
               Exeunt some servants with GLOUCESTER

95   *(to* CORNWALL*)* How is 't, my lord? How look you?

CORNWALL
       I have received a hurt. Follow me, lady.—
Turn out that eyeless villain. Throw this slave
Upon the dunghill.—Regan, I bleed apace.
Untimely comes this hurt. Give me your arm.

                   Exit CORNWALL *with* REGAN

SECOND SERVANT
100   I'll never care what wickedness I do,
If this man come to good.

THIRD SERVANT
       If she live long,
And in the end meet the old course of death,
Women will all turn monsters.

(he gouges out GLOUCESTER*'s other eye)*
Where's your sparkle now?

GLOUCESTER

Nothing but darkness and horror. Where's my son
Edmund? Edmund, let your love for me ignite your
bloodlust to avenge this horrible crime!

REGAN

Wrong, evil traitor. You're appealing to a son who
hates you. He was the one who revealed your treason
to us. He's too good to have any compassion for you.

GLOUCESTER

What a fool I've been! This means I've mistreated
Edgar. Dear God, forgive me. Let him be well!

REGAN

Kick him out of the gate. He can sniff his way to
Dover.

Some servants exit with GLOUCESTER.

(to CORNWALL*)* What is it, my lord? Why do you look
like that?

CORNWALL

I'm wounded. Follow me, madam.—Throw the blind
traitor outside. And throw this dead peasant into the
manure pit.—Regan, I'm bleeding. It's a bad time for
such an injury. Give me your arm.

CORNWALL *and* REGAN *exit.*

SECOND SERVANT

If our criminal master gets off free, I won't care what
happens to me anymore.

THIRD SERVANT

If she lives a long and happy life, then all women may
as well turn into monsters.

SECOND SERVANT
105   Let's follow the old earl, and get the Bedlam
        To lead him where he would. His roguish madness
        Allows itself to any thing.

THIRD SERVANT
        Go thou. I'll fetch some flax and whites of eggs
        To apply to his bleeding face. Now heaven help him!

Exeunt severally

SECOND SERVANT

> Let's follow the old earl, and get that crazy Tom to take him wherever he wants to go. As a wandering lunatic, he can do whatever he wants.

THIRD SERVANT

> Go ahead. I'll get some cloth and egg whites to bandage his bleeding face. Heaven help him!

They exit in different directions.

ACT FOUR
SCENE 1

Enter EDGAR *diguised*

EDGAR
Yet better thus, and known to be contemned,
Than still contemned and flattered. To be worst,
The lowest and most dejected thing of fortune
Stands still in esperance, lives not in fear.
The lamentable change is from the best;
The worst returns to laughter. Welcome, then,
Thou unsubstantial air that I embrace!
The wretch that thou hast blown unto the worst
Owes nothing to thy blasts.

Enter GLOUCESTER *led by an* OLD MAN

But who comes here?
My father, poorly led? World, world, O world!
But that thy strange mutations make us hate thee,
Life would not yield to age.

OLD MAN
(to GLOUCESTER*)*
O my good lord,
I have been your tenant and your father's tenant
these fourscore years.

GLOUCESTER
Away, get thee away. Good friend, be gone.
Thy comforts can do me no good at all.
Thee they may hurt.

OLD MAN
Alack, sir, you cannot see your way.

GLOUCESTER
I have no way, and therefore want no eyes.

ACT FOUR

SCENE 1

EDGAR *enters in disguise.*

EDGAR

Still, I'm better off now, as a beggar who is openly hated, than when I was flattered to my face hated in secret. The lowliest and most dejected creatures live without fear and still harbor hope. The worst kind of change is when good fortune turns sour. At the bottom, any change is for the better. So I welcome this wind freely. I've sunk as far down as I can go, so I've got nothing more to fear from the weather.

GLOUCESTER *enters, led by an* OLD MAN.

But who is this? My father, led by a poor peasant? Oh, life is full of surprises! We age and die because they wear us out.

OLD MAN

(to GLOUCESTER*)* My good lord, I've rented land from you and your father for eighty years.

GLOUCESTER

Away, get out of here. Leave me, my friend. There's nothing you can do to help me now, and being with me puts your life in danger.

OLD MAN

But you can't see where you're going, sir.

GLOUCESTER

I don't have anywhere to go, so I don't need to see. When I could see, I didn't always see clearly. I made

I stumbled when I saw. Full oft 'tis seen,
Our means secure us and our mere defects
Prove our commodities. O dear son Edgar,
25   The food of thy abusèd father's wrath,
Might I but live to see thee in my touch,
I'd say I had eyes again!

OLD MAN
                                How now? Who's there?

EDGAR
        (aside) O gods! Who is 't can say "I am at the worst"?
I am worse than e'er I was.

OLD MAN
        (to GLOUCESTER*)*
                                'Tis poor mad Tom.

EDGAR
        (aside) And worse I may be yet. The worst is not
30   So long as we can say "This is the worst."

OLD MAN
        (to EDGAR*)* Fellow, where goest?

GLOUCESTER
        Is it a beggarman?

OLD MAN
        Madman and beggar too.

GLOUCESTER
        He has some reason, else he could not beg.
35   I' th' last night's storm I such a fellow saw,
Which made me think a man a worm. My son
Came then into my mind, and yet my mind
Was then scarce friends with him. I have heard more since.
As flies to wanton boys are we to th' gods.
40   They kill us for their sport.

mistakes, I stumbled and fell. It's often the case that having something makes us spoiled, while not having it turns out to be advantageous. So may it be with my eyesight. Oh, my dear son Edgar,
how enraged I was at you when I was deceived. If I live long enough to touch you again, that would be as good as having my eyesight back.

OLD MAN

Who's that? Who's there?

EDGAR

(to himself) Oh, gods! Who can ever say, "This is as bad as it can get"? I'm worse off now than ever before.

OLD MAN

(to GLOUCESTER) It's poor crazy Tom.

EDGAR

(to himself) And my life could still be worse. If you have the presence of mind to say, "This is the worst," then it's not the worst yet.

OLD MAN

(to EDGAR) Where are you going, man?

GLOUCESTER

Is it a beggar?

OLD MAN

Yes, he's both crazy and a beggar.

GLOUCESTER

Well, he can't be completely crazy, or he wouldn't be able to beg. Last night during the storm I saw a man who was both poor and crazy. He made me think that men are as weak and insignificant as worms. I was reminded of my son, even though I despised my son at that time. Now I know better. The gods play around with us as cruelly as schoolboys who pull the wings off flies.

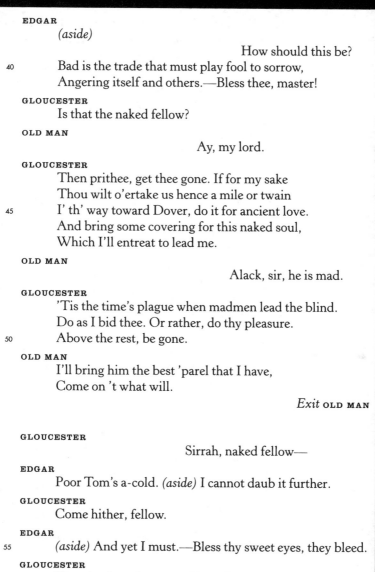

EDGAR
(aside)

How should this be?
40 Bad is the trade that must play fool to sorrow,
Angering itself and others.—Bless thee, master!

GLOUCESTER
Is that the naked fellow?

OLD MAN
Ay, my lord.

GLOUCESTER
Then prithee, get thee gone. If for my sake
Thou wilt o'ertake us hence a mile or twain
45 I' th' way toward Dover, do it for ancient love.
And bring some covering for this naked soul,
Which I'll entreat to lead me.

OLD MAN
Alack, sir, he is mad.

GLOUCESTER
'Tis the time's plague when madmen lead the blind.
Do as I bid thee. Or rather, do thy pleasure.
50 Above the rest, be gone.

OLD MAN
I'll bring him the best 'parel that I have,
Come on 't what will.

Exit OLD MAN

GLOUCESTER
Sirrah, naked fellow—

EDGAR
Poor Tom's a-cold. *(aside)* I cannot daub it further.

GLOUCESTER
Come hither, fellow.

EDGAR
55 *(aside)* And yet I must.—Bless thy sweet eyes, they bleed.

GLOUCESTER
Know'st thou the way to Dover?

EDGAR

(to himself) What's going on? I hate pretending I'm a wandering beggar when all I want to do now is comfort my poor father.—Bless you, master.

GLOUCESTER

Is that the naked guy?

OLD MAN

Yes, my lord.

GLOUCESTER

(to the OLD MAN) Then please go. If you're willing to do me a favor, as an old friend, then catch up to us a mile or two further on the way to Dover, and bring some clothes for this poor beggar. I'll ask him to be my guide.

OLD MAN

But sir, he's crazy.

GLOUCESTER

It's the tragedy of our times that lunatics must lead the blind. Do as I asked you. Or rather, do what you feel like doing. But above all, get out of here.

OLD MAN

I'll bring the crazy beggar the best clothes I have, no matter what happens.

He exits.

GLOUCESTER

Hey, naked guy—

EDGAR

Poor Tom's chilly. *(to himself)* I can't play this role any longer.

GLOUCESTER

Come here, man.

EDGAR

(to himself) But I must.—Bless you, sir. Your dear eyes are bleeding.

GLOUCESTER

Do you know the way to Dover?

EDGAR

Both stile and gate, horseway and footpath. Poor Tom hath
been scared out of his good wits. Bless thee, goodman's son,
from the foul fiend! Five fiends have been in poor Tom at
60   once: of lust, as Obidicut; Hobbididence, prince of
dumbness; Mahu, of stealing; Modo, of murder;
Flibbertigibbet, of mopping and mowing, who since
possesses chambermaids and waiting-women. So bless
thee, master.

GLOUCESTER

(giving EDGAR *a purse)*
65   Here, take this purse, thou whom the heavens' plagues
Have humbled to all strokes. That I am wretched
Makes thee the happier. Heavens, deal so still.
Let the superfluous and lust-dieted man,
That slaves your ordinance, that will not see
70   Because he doth not feel, feel your power quickly.
So distribution should undo excess,
And each man have enough. Dost thou know Dover?

EDGAR

Ay, master.

GLOUCESTER

There is a cliff, whose high and bending head
75   Looks fearfully in the confinèd deep.
Bring me but to the very brim of it,
And I'll repair the misery thou dost bear
With something rich about me. From that place
I shall no leading need.

EDGAR

80   Give me thy arm.
Poor Tom shall lead thee.

Exeunt

EDGAR

I know it like the back of my hand, every step of the way. Poor Tom has been scared out of his mind. Bless you, good man, and stay away from the devil. Five devils haunted Poor Tom at the same time: Obidicut, the devil of lust; Hobbididence, the devil of mutes; Mahu, the devil of stealing; Modo, the devil of murder; and Flibbertigibbet, the devil of mockery, who causes chambermaids to make silly faces. Bless you, master.

GLOUCESTER

(giving EDGAR *a purse)* Here, take some money. The torments of heaven have brought you down to this humble state. My misery makes you more fortunate in comparison. It should always work like that. The spoiled man who has everything, who can't see the misery around him because he doesn't feel it himself, should be made to feel agony so he can learn to share his wealth. That way wealth would be redistributed until everyone has enough to survive. Are you familiar with Dover?

EDGAR

Yes, sir.

GLOUCESTER

There's a cliff there that leans precariously over the deep sea. Take me to the edge of it, and I'll reward all your troubles with something valuable. Once I'm there, I won't need a guide anymore.

EDGAR

Give me your arm. Poor Tom will take you there.

They exit.

ACT 4, SCENE 2

Enter GONERIL *and* EDMUND *the bastard*

GONERIL
Welcome, my lord. I marvel our mild husband
Not met us on the way.

Enter OSWALD

                              Now, where's your master?

OSWALD
Madam, within—but never man so changed.
I told him of the army that was landed.
5   He smiled at it. I told him you were coming.
His answer was "The worse." Of Gloucester's treachery
And of the loyal service of his son,
When I informed him, then he called me "sot,"
And told me I had turned the wrong side out.
10   What most he should dislike seems pleasant to him;
What like, offensive.

GONERIL
(to EDMUND*)*

                              Then shall you go no further.
It is the cowish terror of his spirit
That dares not undertake. He'll not feel wrongs
Which tie him to an answer. Our wishes on the way
May prove effects. Back, Edmund, to my brother.
15   Hasten his musters and conduct his powers.
I must change names at home, and give the distaff
Into my husband's hands. This trusty servant
Shall pass between us. Ere long you are like to hear—
If you dare venture in your own behalf—
20   A mistress's command. Wear this. Spare speech.
Decline your head. This kiss, if it durst speak,
Would stretch thy spirits up into the air.
(kisses EDMUND*)* Conceive, and fare thee well.

ACT 4, SCENE 2

GONERIL *enters with* EDMUND.

GONERIL

Welcome, my lord. I'm surprised my bland husband didn't meet me on the way here.

OSWALD *enters.*

Where's your master?

OSWALD

He's inside, ma'am, but he has changed dramatically since you last saw him. When I told him that the invading army has landed, he just smiled at me. When I told him you were on your way, he replied, "Too bad." When I told him about Gloucester's betrayal and his son Edmund's loyal service, he called me an idiot and said I had it all wrong. He was delighted by the bad news and disgusted by the good news.

GONERIL

(to EDMUND*)* Then don't come in with me. He's a coward and can't commit himself to doing anything risky. He chooses not to be insulted rather than challenge those who offend him. But what we talked about with longing on the way may soon come true. Edmund, go back to see my brother-in-law. Gather his soldiers and organize his troops. I plan to take charge of my household. From now on I will wear the pants, and my husband can play the housewife. We can trust Oswald to carry messages between us. If you act boldly, you will soon obey me as your true mistress. Take this as a token of my esteem. Don't speak. Lean down. This kiss should encourage you. *(she kisses* EDMUND*)* I hope you understand me. Goodbye, and good luck.

Goneril may be referring to the beginnings of a romance between her and Edmund.

Goneril's words suggest both that she will take charge and that she will become Edmund's lover. In many productions, Goneril gives Edmund a chain that she puts around his neck.

EDMUND
Yours in the ranks of death.

GONERIL
25   My most dear Gloucester!

Exit EDMUND

Oh, the difference of man and man!
To thee a woman's services are due.
My fool usurps my body.

OSWALD
Madam, here comes my lord.

Exit OSWALD

Enter ALBANY

GONERIL
I have been worth the whistle.

ALBANY
O Goneril,
30   You are not worth the dust which the rude wind
Blows in your face. I fear your disposition.
That nature, which contemns its origin
Cannot be bordered certain in itself.
She that herself will sliver and disbranch
35   From her material sap perforce must wither
And come to deadly use.

GONERIL
No more. The text is foolish.

ALBANY
Wisdom and goodness to the vile seem vile.
Filths savor but themselves. What have you done?
Tigers, not daughters, what have you performed?
40   A father, and a gracious agèd man,
Whose reverence even the head-lugged bear would lick,
Most barbarous, most degenerate, have you madded.

EDMUND

I'm at your service until death.

GONERIL

My dear Gloucester!

EDMUND exits.

What a man!—especially compared to my husband. Edmund, you deserve me to be your woman. There's a fool sharing my bed now.

OSWALD

Ma'am, my master's coming.

He exits.

ALBANY enters.

GONERIL

So you finally find me worthy of your attentions.

ALBANY

Goneril, you aren't worth the dust the wind blows in your face. I don't trust you. You can't trust anyone who abuses her own father, her flesh and blood. A woman who breaks off relations with her bloodline is like a branch that tries to break away from the tree. She will wither and come to a bad end.

GONERIL

Oh, shut up. Your words are idiotic.

ALBANY

Bad people can't appreciate wisdom or goodness. They only like things as bad as themselves. What have you two sisters done? You're tigers, not daughters. Barbaric degenerates, you've driven insane a kindly old father, whom even an angry bear would treat gently. Could my good brother-in-law—a man to whom

Could my good brother suffer you to do it—
A man, a prince by him so benefited?
45 If that the heavens do not their visible spirits
Send quickly down to tame these vile offenses,
It will come:
Humanity must perforce prey on itself
Like monsters of the deep.

GONERIL
                                    Milk-livered man
50 That bear'st a cheek for blows, a head for wrongs—
Who hast not in thy brows an eye discerning
Thine honor from thy suffering; that not know'st
Fools do those villains pity who are punished
Ere they have done their mischief. Where's thy drum?
55 France spreads his banners in our noiseless land,
With plumèd helm thy state begins to threat,
Whiles thou, a moral fool, sits still and cries,
"Alack, why does he so?"

ALBANY
                                    See thyself, devil!
Proper deformity shows not in the fiend
60 So horrid as in woman.

GONERIL
                                    O vain fool!

ALBANY
Thou changèd and self-covered thing, for shame!
Bemonster not thy feature. Were 't my fitness
To let these hands obey my blood,
They are apt enough to dislocate and tear
65 Thy flesh and bones. Howe'er thou art a fiend,
A woman's shape doth shield thee.

GONERIL
Marry, your manhood, mew!

Enter FIRST MESSENGER

the king gave half his kingdom—have allowed you to do it? If the heavens don't punish these crimes immediately, the end will come. Human beings will become cannibals, like ravenous sea fishes.

GONERIL

Coward! You take everything lying down, you just turn the other cheek—you can't even see the difference between being honored and being taken advantage of! If we punish criminals before they have a chance to commit their crimes, you're a fool to pity them. Why aren't you preparing for war? The French have invaded our peaceful country. Your territory is at risk, and all you can do is sit around like a preachy fool and whine, "Ah, why is he doing that?"

By "criminals," Goneril may be referring to Gloucester, Lear, Cordelia, or all three.

ALBANY

Look at yourself, devilish shrew! A woman deformed by hatred and rage is more horrifying than the devil!—at least the devil is *supposed* to look that way.

GONERIL

You useless fool!

ALBANY

Shame on you, warped hag! Your true demonic features are distorting your body. If I let myself do what I yearn to, I'd rip the flesh off your bones. But I won't attack a woman, even if she is a demon.

GONERIL

I sneeze on your manhood. Ha!

The **FIRST MESSENGER** *enters.*

ALBANY
What news?

FIRST MESSENGER
O my good lord, the Duke of Cornwall's dead,
70 Slain by his servant, going to put out
The other eye of Gloucester.

ALBANY
Gloucester's eyes?

FIRST MESSENGER
A servant that he bred, thrilled with remorse,
Opposed against the act, bending his sword
To his great master; who thereat enraged
75 Flew on him and amongst them felled him dead—
But not without that harmful stroke, which since
Hath plucked him after.

ALBANY
This shows you are above,
You justicers, that these our nether crimes
So speedily can venge! But oh, poor Gloucester—
80 Lost he his other eye?

FIRST MESSENGER
Both, both, my lord.—
This letter, madam, craves a speedy answer.
'Tis from your sister.

GONERIL
(aside)
One way I like this well.
But being widow, and my Gloucester with her,
May all the building in my fancy pluck
Upon my hateful life. Another way
85 The news is not so tart.—I'll read and answer.

Exit GONERIL

ALBANY

What news do you bring?

FIRST MESSENGER

Oh my lord, the Duke of Cornwall's dead. He was killed by his servant as he about to gouge out Gloucester's other eye.

ALBANY

Gloucester's eyes?

FIRST MESSENGER

A servant Gloucester had raised in his house, full of compunction, opposed the blinding and turned his sword on the Duke of Cornwall. Enraged, Cornwall attacked and killed the servant, but not without receiving his own wound, of which he later died.

ALBANY

There's justice in heaven after all! That these crimes are punished so quickly is proof. But oh, poor Gloucester! Did he lose his other eye?

FIRST MESSENGER

He lost both, my lord.—Ma'am, this letter is from your sister, and needs an immediate answer.

GONERIL

(to herself) In a way I'm glad to hear that Cornwall is dead. But on the other hand, Edmund is traveling with Regan, who is now a widow. If something happens between them on the road, it would shatter my hopes of having Edmund for myself and escaping this hateful life. Still, there are benefits to having Cornwall out of the way.—I'll read this letter and answer it.

She exits.

ALBANY
Where was his son when they did take his eyes?

FIRST MESSENGER
Come with my lady hither.

ALBANY
                                    He is not here.

FIRST MESSENGER
No, my good lord. I met him back again.

ALBANY
Knows he the wickedness?

FIRST MESSENGER
90   Ay, my good lord. 'Twas he informed against him,
And quit the house on purpose that their punishment
Might have the freer course.

ALBANY
                                    Gloucester, I live
To thank thee for the love thou showed'st the king,
And to revenge thine eyes.—Come hither, friend.
95   Tell me what more thou know'st.

Exeunt

ALBANY

Where was Gloucester's son Edmund when they gouged his eyes out?

FIRST MESSENGER

He was on his way here with your wife.

ALBANY

But he isn't here now.

FIRST MESSENGER

No, my lord. I met him going back again.

ALBANY

Does he know about this wicked crime?

FIRST MESSENGER

Yes, my lord. He was the one who denounced his father. He then left the house specifically so that the punishment might be carried out without concern for their father-son bond.

ALBANY

Gloucester, I'll thank you forever for the love you've shown the king. I'll get revenge for what they did to your eyes.—Come here, my friend. What else you do know?

They exit.

ACT 4, SCENE 3

Enter KENT *disguised and* GENTLEMAN

KENT
Why the King of France is so suddenly gone back know you
the reason?

GENTLEMAN
Something he left imperfect in the state which, since his
coming forth, is thought of; which imports to the kingdom
5   so much fear and danger that his personal return was most
required and necessary.

KENT
Who hath he left behind him general?

GENTLEMAN
The Marshal of France, Monsieur la Far.

KENT
Did your letters pierce the queen to any demonstration of
10   grief?

GENTLEMAN
Ay, sir. She took them, read them in my presence,
And now and then an ample tear trilled down
Her delicate cheek. It seemed she was a queen
Over her passion, who, most rebel-like,
15   Sought to be king o'er her.

KENT
                               O, then it moved her?

GENTLEMAN
Not to a rage. Patience and sorrow strove
Who should express her goodliest. You have seen
Sunshine and rain at once—her smiles and tears
Were like a better way. Those happy smilets
20   That played on her ripe lip seemed not to know
What guests were in her eyes, which parted thence
As pearls from diamonds dropped. In brief,
Sorrow would be a rarity most beloved
If all could so become it.

ACT 4, SCENE 3

KENT enters in disguise, along with the GENTLEMAN.

KENT

Do you know why the King of France suddenly went back home?

GENTLEMAN

He'd left some unfinished business, which he remembered after arriving here. It was urgent and important enough to require his personal presence.

KENT

Whom did he leave in charge here?

GENTLEMAN

The marshal of France, Monsieur la Far.

KENT

Was Queen Cordelia aggrieved by the letters you delivered?

GENTLEMAN

Yes, sir. She took the letters and read them in front of me. Now and then a large tear trickled down her delicate cheek. She seemed to be trying to control her emotions, which were overwhelming her.

KENT

So she was moved by it?

GENTLEMAN

There were no outbursts. She was struggling between emotion and self-control. You've seen how it can rain while the sun shines? That's how she was, smiling and crying at once, only more lovely. The little smile on her full lips didn't seem aware of the tears that were dropping like diamonds from her pearly eyes. If everyone looked so lovely in their sorrow, then sorrow would be highly prized.

KENT
                          Made she no verbal question?

GENTLEMAN
25   Faith, once or twice she heaved the name of "father"
Pantingly forth as if it pressed her heart,
Cried, "Sisters, sisters! Shame of ladies, sisters!
Kent, father, sisters! What, i' th' storm, i' th' night?
Let pity not be believed." There she shook
30   The holy water from her heavenly eyes,
And clamor moistened. Then away she started
To deal with grief alone.

KENT
                          It is the stars,
The stars above us, govern our conditions.
Else one self mate and mate could not beget
35   Such different issues. You spoke not with her since?

GENTLEMAN
No.

KENT
Was this before the king returned?

GENTLEMAN
                              No, since.

KENT
Well, sir, the poor distressèd Lear's i' th' town,
Who sometime in his better tune remembers
40   What we are come about, and by no means
Will yield to see his daughter.

GENTLEMAN
                         Why, good sir?

KENT
A sovereign shame so elbows him. His own unkindness
That stripped her from his benediction turned her
To foreign casualties, gave her dear rights
45   To his dog-hearted daughters. These things sting
His mind so venomously that burning shame
Detains him from Cordelia.

KENT

She didn't ask anything?

GENTLEMAN

Actually, once or twice she sighed and said, "father," as if the word were pressing on her chest. Once she exclaimed, "Sisters, sisters, shame on you! Kent, father, sisters! What, out in a storm in the middle of the night? I can't believe it." The tears fell from her eyes like holy water. Then she ran away to grieve alone.

KENT

It must be fate that makes us who we are—otherwise someone as good as Cordelia could not possibly be related to those two witches. Have you not spoken to her since then?

GENTLEMAN

No.

KENT

Did this happen before the King of France returned home?

GENTLEMAN

No, afterward.

KENT

Well, sir, poor delirious Lear is in town. Sometimes when he's lucid he remembers why we're here, and absolutely refuses to see his daughter.

GENTLEMAN

Why, good sir?

KENT

He's too overwhelmed with shame. He remembers how unkind he was to her, how he disowned her and sent her abroad, how he gave her rightful inheritance to her two dog-hearted sisters. All those memories pain his mind so deeply that guilt and shame keep him away from Cordelia.

GENTLEMAN

Alack, poor gentleman!

KENT

Of Albany's and Cornwall's powers you heard not?

GENTLEMAN

'Tis so. They are afoot.

KENT

50 Well, sir, I'll bring you to our master Lear
And leave you to attend him. Some dear cause
Will in concealment wrap me up awhile.
When I am known aright you shall not grieve
Lending me this acquaintance. I pray you, go
55 Along with me.

Exeunt

GENTLEMAN

Oh, the poor man!

KENT

Have you heard about Albany's and Cornwall's troops?

GENTLEMAN

I have. They're on the march.

KENT

Well, sir, I'll take you to Lear and have you stay with him a while. I have important business that requires me to remain in disguise a while longer. When I've revealed my true identity, you'll be glad you took the time to help me out. Please come with me.

They exit.

ACT 4, SCENE 4

Enter, with drum and colors, CORDELIA, DOCTOR, *and soldiers*

CORDELIA
Alack, 'tis he. Why, he was met even now
As mad as the vexed sea, singing aloud,
Crowned with rank fumiter and furrow-weeds,
With burdocks, hemlock, nettles, cuckoo-flowers,
5 Darnel, and all the idle weeds that grow
In our sustaining corn.—A century send forth.
Search every acre in the high-grown field,
And bring him to our eye.

Exit some soldiers

What can man's wisdom
In the restoring his bereavèd sense?
10 He that helps him take all my outward worth.

DOCTOR
There is means, madam.
Our foster nurse of nature is repose,
The which he lacks—that to provoke in him
Are many simples operative, whose power
15 Will close the eye of anguish.

CORDELIA
All blessed secrets,
All you unpublished virtues of the earth,
Spring with my tears. Be aidant and remediate
In the good man's distress. Seek, seek for him,
Lest his ungoverned rage dissolve the life
20 That wants the means to lead it.

Enter SECOND MESSENGER

ACT 4, SCENE 4

CORDELIA *enters with a* DOCTOR *and soldiers carrying drums and banners.*

CORDELIA

Sadly, it's the king that's missing. They saw him just now as mad and deranged as the stormy sea, singing loudly, wearing a crown of nettles, thorns, hemlock, and all the other weeds that grow in our cornfields.— Send out a hundred soldiers to find him. Search high and low, in every acre of the fields, and bring him here for me to see him.

Some soldiers exit.

What can human knowledge do to make him sane again? I'd give all my wealth to whoever can help him.

DOCTOR

There is a way, ma'am. Nature heals people with rest, which Lear hasn't had. But there are many herbs that will help him rest and take his mind off his anguish for a while.

CORDELIA

Then I'll water all those precious herbs with my tears to make them grow. May they relieve a sick old man's suffering. Go find those herbs for him, before his madness puts his life in danger.

The SECOND MESSENGER *enters.*

SECOND MESSENGER
                                    News, madam.
The British powers are marching hitherward.

CORDELIA
'Tis known before. Our preparation stands
In expectation of them. O dear father,
It is thy business that I go about.
25   Therefore great France
My mourning and importuned tears hath pitied.
No blown ambition doth our arms incite,
But love—dear love!—and our aged father's right.
Soon may I hear and see him.

                                              Exeunt

SECOND MESSENGER
> I have news, ma'am. The British forces are on their way here.

CORDELIA
> We already knew that. Our forces are ready for them. Oh, father, I'm taking care of your business. That's why the King of France listened to my pleas and tears. We're not invading England out of ambition or greed, but out of love—dear love!—and my father's right to his kingdom. I hope I see him and hear him again soon.

They all exit.

ACT 4, SCENE 5

Enter REGAN *and the steward* OSWALD

REGAN
But are my brother's powers set forth?

OSWALD
                                        Ay, madam.

REGAN
Himself in person there?

OSWALD
Madam, with much ado.
Your sister is the better soldier.

REGAN
5   Lord Edmund spake not with your lord at home?

OSWALD
No, madam.

REGAN
What might import my sister's letter to him?

OSWALD
I know not, lady.

REGAN
Faith, he is posted hence on serious matter.
10   It was great ignorance, Gloucester's eyes being out,
To let him live. Where he arrives he moves
All hearts against us. Edmund I think is gone
In pity of his misery to dispatch
His nighted life; moreover to descry
15   The strength o' th' enemy.

OSWALD
I must needs after him, madam, with my letter.

REGAN
Our troops set forth tomorrow. Stay with us.
The ways are dangerous.

ACT 4, SCENE 5

REGAN *enters with* OSWALD.

REGAN

Have my brother-in-law's troops been mobilized?

OSWALD

Yes, ma'am.

REGAN

Is he there in person?

OSWALD

Yes, making a big fuss. Your sister's the better soldier of the two.

REGAN

Lord Edmund didn't speak to your master at home?

OSWALD

No, ma'am.

REGAN

What could my sister's letter to him say?

OSWALD

I don't know, ma'am.

REGAN

He rushed away on serious business. It was a huge mistake to let old Gloucester live after we blinded him. Wherever he goes, he inspires compassion and people turn against us. I think Edmund went off to kill him, to put him out of his blind misery. And also to find out the size of the enemy army.

OSWALD

I have to follow him and give him the letter.

REGAN

Our troops are deployed tomorrow. Stay with us tonight. It's dangerous out there.

OSWALD
                              I may not, madam.
My lady charged my duty in this business.

REGAN
20   Why should she write to Edmund? Might not you
Transport her purposes by word? Belike
Some things—I know not what. I'll love thee much.
Let me unseal the letter.

OSWALD
                              Madam, I had rather—

REGAN
I know your lady does not love her husband.
25   I am sure of that. And at her late being here
She gave strange oeillades and most speaking looks
To noble Edmund. I know you are of her bosom.

OSWALD
I, madam?

REGAN
I speak in understanding. Y' are. I know 't.
30   Therefore I do advise you, take this note.
My lord is dead. Edmund and I have talked,
And more convenient is he for my hand
Than for your lady's. You may gather more.
If you do find him, pray you give him this.
35   And when your mistress hears thus much from you,
I pray desire her call her wisdom to her.
So fare you well.
If you do chance to hear of that blind traitor,
Preferment falls on him that cuts him off.

OSWALD
40   Would I could meet him, madam, I should show
What party I do follow.

REGAN
                              Fare thee well.

                              Exeunt severally

OSWALD

I can't, ma'am. My lady ordered me to deliver her letter.

REGAN

Why would she write to Edmund? Couldn't you just deliver the message orally? It probably has something to do with . . . I don't know. I'll be so grateful to you if you let me open that letter.

OSWALD

Ma'am, I'd rather—

REGAN

I know your lady Goneril doesn't love her husband. I'm sure of that. And when she was here recently she flirted with Edmund and gave him significant glances. I know she trusts you and tells you everything.

OSWALD

Me, ma'am?

REGAN

I know what I'm talking about. You're close to her, I know it. So I recommend you take note of what I'm about to say. My husband is dead. Edmund and I have talked, and it makes more sense for him to marry me than Goneril. You can figure out the rest. If you find him, please give him this. And when your mistress hears about all this, please tell her to use her head next time. So goodbye. If you happen to hear anything about that blind traitor Gloucester, I'll reward anyone who snuffs him out.

Regan probably hands something to Oswald here, such as a letter or a love token.

OSWALD

If I could run into him, ma'am, I'd prove which side I'm on.

REGAN

Goodbye.

They exit in opposite directions.

ACT 4, SCENE 6

Enter GLOUCESTER, *and* EDGAR *disguised in peasant clothing*

GLOUCESTER
When shall we come to th' top of that same hill?

EDGAR
You do climb up it now. Look how we labor.

GLOUCESTER
Methinks the ground is even.

EDGAR
                                        Horrible steep.
Hark, do you hear the sea?

GLOUCESTER
                                        No, truly.

EDGAR
5   Why then, your other senses grow imperfect
By your eyes' anguish.

GLOUCESTER
                        So may it be indeed.
Methinks thy voice is altered, and thou speak'st
In better phrase and matter than thou didst.

EDGAR
You're much deceived. In nothing am I changed
10   But in my garments.

GLOUCESTER
                        Methinks you're better spoken.

EDGAR
Come on, sir. Here's the place. Stand still. How fearful
And dizzy 'tis to cast one's eyes so low!
The crows and choughs that wing the midway air
Show scarce so gross as beetles. Halfway down
15   Hangs one that gathers samphire—dreadful trade!
Methinks he seems no bigger than his head.
The fishermen that walk upon the beach
Appear like mice. And yon tall anchoring bark,

ACT 4, SCENE 6

GLOUCESTER *enters with* EDGAR, *who is dressed as a peasant.*

GLOUCESTER

When will we get to the top of that cliff?

EDGAR

We're walking up to the top right now. See how hard it is to climb?

GLOUCESTER

The ground feels flat to me.

EDGAR

No, it's dreadfully steep. Listen. Do you hear the sea?

GLOUCESTER

No, really, I don't.

EDGAR

Then your other senses must be getting worse because of the trauma of blindness.

GLOUCESTER

It may be so. It seems to me that your voice has changed, and that your speech is more elegant than it used to be.

EDGAR

You're mistaken about all that. The only thing different about me is my clothes.

GLOUCESTER

I think you're more articulate.

EDGAR

Come on, sir. This is the place. Stand still. It's so scary to look down! It makes me dizzy. The crows flying down below look as small as ants. Halfway down the cliff there's somebody clinging to the rock and gathering wild herbs—a risky business! He looks like a dot to me. The fishermen walking along the beach are as small as mice. That big ship over there looks no bigger

Diminished to her cock, her cock a buoy
20   Almost too small for sight. The murmuring surge
That on th' unnumbered idle pebbles chafes
Cannot be heard so high. I'll look no more
Lest my brain turn and the deficient sight
Topple down headlong.

GLOUCESTER
25   Set me where you stand.

EDGAR
Give me your hand. You are now within a foot
Of th' extreme verge. For all beneath the moon
Would I not leap upright.

GLOUCESTER
                                    Let go my hand.
(gives EDGAR *another purse)*
Here, friend, 's another purse, in it a jewel
30   Well worth a poor man's taking. Fairies and gods
Prosper it with thee! Go thou farther off.
Bid me farewell, and let me hear thee going.

EDGAR
Now fare you well, good sir.

GLOUCESTER
                                    With all my heart.
EDGAR *moves aside*

EDGAR
(aside) Why I do trifle thus with his despair
35   Is done to cure it.

GLOUCESTER
                        O you mighty gods, *(kneels)*
This world I do renounce, and in your sights
Shake patiently my great affliction off.
If I could bear it longer and not fall
To quarrel with your great opposeless wills,
40   My snuff and loathèd part of nature should
Burn itself out. If Edgar live, O, bless him!—
Now, fellow, fare thee well. *(falls)*

than its lifeboat, and its lifeboat looks as small as a tiny buoy. Up here you can't even hear the waves crashing against the rocks. I have to stop looking, or my head will start spinning and I'll fall.

GLOUCESTER

Lead me to where you're standing.

EDGAR

Give me your hand. You're now within a foot of the cliff's edge. I wouldn't try to jump up and down here for anything on earth.

GLOUCESTER

Let go of my hand. *(he gives* EDGAR *another purse)* Here's another purse, my friend. Inside it there's a jewel that any poor man would be happy to have. I hope it's only the beginning of future prosperity for you. Now go further away. Say goodbye to me, and let me hear your footsteps as you walk away.

EDGAR

Goodbye, good sir.

GLOUCESTER

With all my heart.

EDGAR *moves aside.*

EDGAR

(to himself) I'm toying with his despair to cure him of it.

GLOUCESTER

Oh, you mighty gods! *(he kneels)* I hereby renounce this world and all my troubles and torments. If I could bear them better, and not fight against your unstoppable decisions, then I would simply wait until I expired naturally. If Edgar's alive, bless him, gods!— Now, man, goodbye. *(he falls)*

EDGAR

                                        Gone, sir. Farewell.
(aside) And yet I know not how conceit may rob
The treasury of life when life itself
45   Yields to the theft. Had he been where he thought,
By this had thought been past. Alive or dead?—
Ho you, sir, friend! Hear you, sir? Speak.—
Thus might he pass indeed. Yet he revives.—
What are you, sir?

GLOUCESTER

                              Away, and let me die.

EDGAR

50   Hadst thou been aught but gossamer, feathers, air,
So many fathom down precipitating,
Thou'dst shivered like an egg. But thou dost breathe,
Hast heavy substance, bleed'st not, speak'st, art sound.
Ten masts at each make not the altitude
55   Which thou hast perpendicularly fell.
Thy life's a miracle. Speak yet again.

GLOUCESTER

But have I fall'n, or no?

EDGAR

From the dread summit of this chalky bourn.
Look up a-height. The shrill-gorged lark so far
60   Cannot be seen or heard. Do but look up.

GLOUCESTER

Alack, I have no eyes.
Is wretchedness deprived that benefit,
To end itself by death? 'Twas yet some comfort
When misery could beguile the tyrant's rage
65   And frustrate his proud will.

EDGAR

                                        Give me your arm.
Up so. How is 't? Feel you your legs? You stand.

GLOUCESTER

Too well, too well.

EDGAR

Gone, sir. Goodbye. *(to himself)* But I still wonder if it's possible for his own imagination to kill him, since he's so willing to die. If he'd been standing on the edge of the cliff as he thought, he'd be dead right now. Is he alive or dead?—Hey, sir, friend! Can you hear me? Answer me.—Maybe he passed away after all. But no, he's stirring.—Who are you, sir?

GLOUCESTER

Go away and let me die.

EDGAR

Even if you were made of feathers and air, you should've been smashed in pieces like an egg after falling as far as you just did. But your flesh is solid, your mind is strong, you're breathing and talking, you're not bleeding. You just fell the height of ten ship masts, straight down. It's a miracle you're alive. Say something again.

GLOUCESTER

But did I fall or not?

EDGAR

You fell from the terrifying top of this chalk cliff. Look for yourself—see the top of the cliff way up there? The lark shrilly singing up there is too far away to be heard. Just look.

GLOUCESTER

I can't. I have no eyes. If you're wretched and desperate, aren't you allowed to kill yourself? It used to be the last ditch comfort of miserable people.

EDGAR

Give me your arm. Get up. There you go. How do you feel? Can you feel your legs? You're standing.

GLOUCESTER

Only too well.

EDGAR
                                This is above all strangeness.
          Upon the crown o' th' cliff, what thing was that
          Which parted from you?

GLOUCESTER
                                A poor unfortunate beggar.

EDGAR
70   As I stood here below, methought his eyes
          Were two full moons. He had a thousand noses,
          Horns whelked and waved like the enragèd sea.
          It was some fiend. Therefore, thou happy father,
          Think that the clearest gods, who make them honors
75   Of men's impossibilities, have preserved thee.

GLOUCESTER
          I do remember now. Henceforth I'll bear
          Affliction till it do cry out itself,
          "Enough, enough," and die. That thing you speak of,
          I took it for a man. Often 'twould say,
80   "The fiend, the fiend!" He led me to that place.

EDGAR
          Bear free and patient thoughts.

          Enter LEAR, *mad*

                                But who comes here?
          The safer sense will ne'er accommodate
          His master thus.

LEAR
          No, they cannot touch me for coining. I am the king himself.

EDGAR
85   *(aside)* O thou side-piercing sight!

LEAR
          Nature's above art in that respect. There's your press-
          money. That fellow handles his bow like a crowkeeper.
          Draw me a clothier's yard. Look, look, a mouse! Peace,

EDGAR

This is beyond weird. What was that thing I saw moving away from you up on the cliff before you fell?

GLOUCESTER

That was a poor unlucky beggar.

EDGAR

From down here, I thought his eyes looked like full moons. He had a thousand noses and twisted horns, like wave crests in a storm at sea. It was some devil. You lucky old man, it seems that the gods have saved your life. They love to perform miracles so that humans will worship them.

GLOUCESTER

I understand now. From now on I'll put up with my anguish until the anguish itself cries out, "Enough, enough!" and disappears. I thought that thing you're talking about was a man. It would often talk about the devil. It took me to that deadly place.

EDGAR

Cheer up and be at peace.

LEAR enters, insane.

But who is that? A sane person would never dress like this.

LEAR

No, they can't accuse me of counterfeiting coins. I'm the king himself.

EDGAR

(to himself) Oh, what a heartbreaking sight!

LEAR

Lear's insane speeches are full of non sequiturs and difficult to follow.

Life's better at breaking hearts than art is.—Hey, a new recruit. Here's your enlistment bonus.—Look how awkwardly he handles his crossbow.—Come on, pull it back farther!—Look, look, a mouse! Calm down,

90 peace, this piece of toasted cheese will do 't. There's my
gauntlet. I'll prove it on a giant. Bring up the brown bills.
O, well flown, bird. I' th' clout, i' th' clout. Hewgh! Give
the word.

EDGAR
Sweet marjoram.

LEAR
Pass.

GLOUCESTER
95 I know that voice.

LEAR
Ha! Goneril with a white beard? Ha, Regan? They flattered
me like a dog and told me I had white hairs in my beard ere
the black ones were there. To say "Ay" and "No" to
everything that I said "Ay" and "No" to was no good
100 divinity. When the rain came to wet me once, and the wind
to make me chatter, when the thunder would not peace at
my bidding—there I found 'em, there I smelt 'em out. Go
to, they are not men o' their words. They told me I was
everything. 'Tis a lie, I am not ague-proof.

GLOUCESTER
105 The trick of that voice I do well remember.
Is 't not the king?

LEAR
Ay, every inch a king.
When I do stare, see how the subject quakes.
I pardon that man's life. What was thy cause?
Adultery? Thou shalt not die. Die for adultery? No. The
110 wren goes to 't, and the small gilded fly does lecher in my
sight. Let copulation thrive, for Gloucester's bastard son
Was kinder to his father than my daughters got 'tween the
lawful sheets. To 't, luxury, pell-mell—for I lack soldiers.

this piece of cheese will get him.—I challenge you to a match. I'll even fight a giant.—Call out the infantry. —Oh, that arrow was well shot. Whoosh! Right in the bull's eye.——What's the password?

EDGAR

Sweet marjoram.

LEAR

That's it!

GLOUCESTER

I know that voice.

LEAR

Ha! Goneril with a white beard? Ha, Regan?—They flattered me and told me how wise I was, wise before my time. To agree to everything I said was not truly devout.—The rain came to drench me, and the wind to make me shiver, and the thunder wouldn't stop roaring when I ordered it to. That's when I learned the truth about them. That's when I sniffed them out. I tell you, they are not honest men. They told me I was everything. It's a lie. I'm not immune to chills.

GLOUCESTER

I recognize something about that voice. Isn't that the king?

LEAR

Yes, every inch a king. My subjects tremble when I look at them. I pardon that man. What are you accused of? Adultery? I'll commute your death sentence. To die for adultery? No. Little birds do it, and dragonflies copulate right in front of me. Let's have more sex in the world, since Gloucester's bastard son was kinder to him than my daughters, conceived in lawful wedlock, have been to me. Get to it, be lustful, sleep around—I need soldiers for my army. Look at that simpering lady over there. From looking at her

Behold yond simpering dame, whose face between her
115   forks presages snow, that minces virtue and does shake the
head to hear of pleasure's name. The fitchew, nor the soiled
horse, goes to 't with a more riotous appetite. Down from
the waist they are centaurs, though women all above. But to
the girdle do the gods inherit; beneath is all the fiends'.
120   There's hell, there's darkness, there's the sulfurous pit—
burning, scalding, stench, consumption! Fie, fie, fie, pah,
pah!—Give me an ounce of civet, good apothecary, to
sweeten my imagination. There's money for thee.

GLOUCESTER
O, let me kiss that hand!

LEAR
125   Let me wipe it first. It smells of mortality.

GLOUCESTER
O ruined piece of nature! This great world
Shall so wear out to naught. Dost thou know me?

LEAR
I remember thine eyes well enough. Dost thou squiny at
me? No, do thy worst, blind Cupid. I'll not love. Read thou
130   this challenge. Mark but the penning of it.

GLOUCESTER
Were all thy letters suns, I could not see one.

EDGAR
(aside) I would not take this from report. It is,
And my heart breaks at it.

LEAR
Read.

GLOUCESTER
135   What, with the case of eyes?

LEAR
Oh ho, are you there with me? No eyes in your head, nor no
money in your purse? Your eyes are in a heavy case, your
purse in a light. Yet you see how this world goes.

face, I'd say she's frigid. She pretends to be virtuous and to disdain the word "sex," but she's hornier than a passel of rabbits. Women are sex machines below the waist, though they're chaste up above. Above the waist they belong to God, but the lower part belongs to the devil. That's where hell is, and darkness, and fires and stench! Death and orgasm! Ah, ah, ah! Give me an aphrodisiac, pharmacist. Let me have sweet dreams. There's money in it for you.

GLOUCESTER

Oh, let me kiss his hand!

LEAR

Let me wipe it off first. It stinks of death.

GLOUCESTER

A ruined man! This is how the whole world will end up, worn away to nothing.—Do you know who I am?

LEAR

Cupid is the blind Greek god of love. He shoots arrows at people to make them fall in love.

I remember your eyes quite well. Are you squinting at me? Go ahead, try to make me fall in love, blind Cupid. I won't ever love again. Read this letter. Just look at the handwriting.

GLOUCESTER

If every letter on that page were a sun, I couldn't see even one of them.

EDGAR

(to himself) I wouldn't believe this if I weren't seeing it with my own eyes. It's real, and it breaks my heart.

LEAR

Read it.

GLOUCESTER

How? With my eye sockets?

LEAR

Oh ho, is that what you're getting at? You want money before you'll read? No eyes in your head til there's money in your wallet? Your eyes are in a bad way, your wallet's empty, but you understand the ways of the world.

GLOUCESTER
I see it feelingly.

LEAR
140 What, art mad? A man may see how this world goes with no
eyes. Look with thine ears. See how yon justice rails upon
yon simple thief. Hark in thine ear: change places and,
handy-dandy, which is the justice, which is the thief? Thou
hast seen a farmer's dog bark at a beggar?

GLOUCESTER
145 Ay, sir.

LEAR
And the creature run from the cur? There thou mightst
behold the great image of authority: a dog's obeyed in office.
Thou rascal beadle, hold thy bloody hand.
Why dost thou lash that whore? Strip thine own back.
150 Thou hotly lust'st to use her in that kind
For which thou whipp'st her. The usurer hangs the cozener.
Through tattered clothes great vices do appear;
Robes and furred gowns hide all. Plate sin with gold,
And the strong lance of justice hurtless breaks.
155 Arm it in rags, a pigmy's straw does pierce it.
None does offend—none, I say, none. I'll able 'em.
Take that of me, my friend, who have the power
To seal th' accuser's lips. Get thee glass eyes,
And like a scurvy politician seem
160 To see the things thou dost not. Now, now, now, now,
Pull off my boots. Harder, harder. So.

EDGAR
(aside) O matter and impertinency mixed! Reason in
madness!

GLOUCESTER

I do understand, by touch.

LEAR

What, are you crazy? You don't need eyes to see how the world works. Look with your ears. Look how the judge yells at a simple thief. Listen. But mix them up, have them switch places, and do you think you'd be able to tell which one is which? Have you seen a farmer's dog bark at a beggar?

GLOUCESTER

Yes, sir.

LEAR

And you saw how the beggar ran from the mutt? That's authority! Even a dog is obeyed sometimes. You stupid cop, stop your violence! Why are you whipping that whore? You should be whipping your-self, since you lust after her and yearn to do the same thing for which you're punishing her. One criminal punishes another. Poor men's sins are much more noticeable than rich men's. Cover up a crime with gold and the arm of justice can't touch it. But dress the crime in rags and it's caught easily. Everyone sins. You can't blame anyone for it anyone, I say. I'll vouch for that. Believe me, my friend, since I have the power to stop the prosecutors. Get yourself some glass eyes, and pretend to see things you can't, like a crooked pol-itician. Now, now, now, now. Pull off my boots. Harder, harder. Like that.

EDGAR

(to himself) Oh, wisdom and absurdity mixed up together! Reason in madness!

LEAR
If thou wilt weep my fortunes, take my eyes.
165   I know thee well enough. Thy name is Gloucester.
Thou must be patient. We came crying hither.
Thou know'st the first time that we smell the air
We wawl and cry. I will preach to thee. Mark me.

GLOUCESTER
Alack, alack the day!

LEAR
170   When we are born, we cry that we are come
To this great stage of fools. This a good block.
It were a delicate stratagem to shoe
A troop of horse with felt. I'll put 't in proof.
And when I have stol'n upon these sons-in-law,
175   Then, kill, kill, kill, kill, kill, kill!

Enter GENTLEMAN *with two others*

GENTLEMAN
Oh, here he is. Lay hand upon him.—Sir,
Your most dear daughter—

LEAR
No rescue? What, a prisoner? I am even
The natural fool of fortune. Use me well.
180   You shall have ransom. Let me have surgeons.
I am cut to th' brains.

GENTLEMAN
                You shall have anything.

LEAR
No seconds? All myself?
Why, this would make a man a man of salt,
To use his eyes for garden water-pots,
185   Ay, and laying autumn's dust.

GENTLEMAN
                Good sir—

LEAR

If you want to cry over my bad luck, I'll give you my eyes. I know you. Your name's Gloucester. You have to be patient with me. I came here crying. The first time we see the world as newborns, we cry and scream. I'll read you a sermon. Listen to this.

GLOUCESTER

Oh, how awful!

LEAR

When we're born, we cry because we've arrived on the stage of life, like all the other fools. That's a nice hat you've got there. How ingenious to make horseshoes out of felt. I'll test it out. And when I've sneaked up on my sons-in-law, then I'll kill, kill, kill, kill, kill, kill!

The GENTLEMAN *enters with two other gentlemen.*

GENTLEMAN

(noticing LEAR*)* Oh, here he is. Grab him.—Sir, your most dear daughter—

LEAR

What, I'm a prisoner? No rescue for me? My luck has always been bad. Treat me well. There's a ransom. I need a doctor. My brains are injured.

GENTLEMAN

You can have anything you want.

LEAR

Will no one back me up? Am I all alone? That would make anyone cry enough to water his garden with his tears.

GENTLEMAN

Good sir—

LEAR
I will die bravely, like a smug bridegroom.
What, I will be jovial. Come, come.
I am a king, my masters, know you that?

GENTLEMAN
You are a royal one, and we obey you.

LEAR
190 Then there's life in 't. Come, an if you get it, you shall get
it by running. Sa, sa, sa, sa.

Exit LEAR *running, followed by two gentlemen*

GENTLEMAN
A sight most pitiful in the meanest wretch,
Past speaking of in a king. Thou hast a daughter
Who redeems nature from the general curse
195 Which twain have brought her to.

EDGAR
Hail, gentle sir.

GENTLEMAN
Sir, speed you. What's your will?

EDGAR
Do you hear aught, sir, of a battle toward?

GENTLEMAN
Most sure and vulgar. Everyone hears that
That can distinguish sound.

EDGAR
200 But, by your favor, how near's the other army?

GENTLEMAN
Near and on speedy foot. The main descry
Stands in the hourly thought.

EDGAR
I thank you, sir. That's all.

LEAR

I'll die courageously, like a well-dressed bridegroom. Okay, I'll be cheery. I'm king. Did you know that, gentlemen?

GENTLEMAN

You're of royal blood, and we obey you.

LEAR

Then there's still a chance. Come and get it! But you'll have to catch me! Catch me if you can! Sa, sa, sa, sa.

LEAR exits running, chased by two gentlemen.

GENTLEMAN

This is a difficult to see even in a beggar. In a king, the sight is unbearable. He has a daughter good enough to cancel out the wickedness of the other two.

EDGAR

Hello, good sir.

GENTLEMAN

How do you do, sir. How can I help you?

EDGAR

Have you heard any news of impending battle?

GENTLEMAN

Certainly. Everyone who can hear has heard about it.

EDGAR

Could you tell me how near the enemy is?

GENTLEMAN

Very near, and approaching fast. The main body of the army is expected here any hour now.

EDGAR

Thank you, sir. That's all I wanted to know.

GENTLEMAN
Though that the queen on special cause is here,
Her army is moved on.

EDGAR
I thank you, sir.

Exit GENTLEMAN

GLOUCESTER
205 You ever gentle gods, take my breath from me.
Let not my worser spirit tempt me again
To die before you please.

EDGAR
Well pray you, father.

GLOUCESTER
Now, good sir, what are you?

EDGAR
210 A most poor man made tame to fortune's blows,
Who by the art of known and feeling sorrows
Am pregnant to good pity. Give me your hand,
I'll lead you to some biding.

GLOUCESTER
Hearty thanks.
The bounty and the benison of heaven
215 To boot and boot.

Enter OSWALD *the steward*

OSWALD
A proclaimed prize! Most happy!
That eyeless head of thine was first framed flesh
To raise my fortunes. Thou old unhappy traitor,
Briefly thyself remember. The sword is out
220 That must destroy thee.

GLOUCESTER
Now let thy friendly hand
Put strength enough to 't.

GENTLEMAN

The queen is here on special business, and her army has moved on.

EDGAR

Thank you, sir.

The GENTLEMAN *exits.*

GLOUCESTER

Gentle gods in heaven, please let me die. Don't tempt me to suicide again.

EDGAR

Pray well, father.

GLOUCESTER

And who are you, good sir?

EDGAR

I'm a poor man who's been humbled by many misfortunes. I've had enough sorrow in my life to feel compassion for others. Give me your hand. I'll lead you to some shelter.

GLOUCESTER

Thank you very much. May heaven bless you.

OSWALD *enters.*

OSWALD

What good luck! I'll get the promised reward. That blind head of yours was created to make me rich. You old traitor, repent all your sins. Prepare to die.

GLOUCESTER

Death is exactly what I want. I hope you're strong enough to do it.

EDGAR *interferes*

OSWALD
                              Wherefore, bold peasant,
Darest thou support a published traitor? Hence,
Lest that th' infection of his fortune take
Like hold on thee. Let go his arm.

EDGAR
225   'Chill not let go, zir, without vurther 'casion.

OSWALD
Let go, slave, or thou diest!

EDGAR
Good gentleman, go your gait, and let poor volk pass. An
'chud ha' bin zwaggered out of my life, 'twould not ha' bin
zo long as 'tis by a vortnight. Nay, come not near th' old
230   man. Keep out, che vor' ye, or I'se try whether your costard
or my ballow be the harder. 'Chill be plain with you.

OSWALD
Out, dunghill!

EDGAR
'Chill pick your teeth, zir. Come, no matter vor your foins.

EDGAR *and* OSWALD *fight*

OSWALD
(falling) Slave, thou hast slain me. Villain, take my purse.
235   If ever thou wilt thrive, bury my body.
And give the letters which thou find'st about me
To Edmund, Earl of Gloucester. Seek him out
Upon the British party. O untimely death! *(dies)*

EDGAR
I know thee well—a serviceable villain,
240   As duteous to the vices of thy mistress
As badness would desire.

GLOUCESTER
                              What, is he dead?

EDGAR *steps in between* GLOUCESTER *and* OSWALD.

OSWALD

Whoa, man, you dare to support someone who's been proclaimed a traitor? Get out of here, before his bad luck infects you too. Let go of his arm.

EDGAR

Edgar speaks with the accent of someone from the west of England here.

Oh no, sir, I won't let him go, sir, not without a good reason.

OSWALD

Let go of him, peasant, or you die!

EDGAR

Get on with your business, sir, and leave the poor people alone. If macho talk like yours could kill me, I'd have died weeks ago. No, don't come near the old man. Keep away, I'm warning you, or I'll find out whether your head is harder than my walking stick. I'm completely serious.

OSWALD

Get out of here, you pile of crap.

EDGAR

I'll knock your teeth out, sir. To hell with your sword.

EDGAR *and* OSWALD *fight.*

OSWALD

(falling) You peasant, you've killed me! Villain, take my money. If you survive, make sure I have a decent burial. Give the letters I'm carrying to Edmund, Earl of Gloucester. He's with the English camp. Oh, early death! *(he dies)*

EDGAR

I know you well. You're a hardworking villain who'd do anything his evil mistress wanted him to.

GLOUCESTER

Is he dead?

EDGAR
Sit you down, father. Rest you.
Let's see these pockets. The letters that he speaks of
May be my friends. He's dead. I am only sorry
245   He had no other death's-man. Let us see.
(takes letters out of oswald's *pocket and opens them)*
Leave, gentle wax, and, manners, blame us not.
To know our enemies' minds, we rip their hearts.
Their papers is more lawful.
(reads)
"Let our reciprocal vows be remembered. You have
250   many opportunities to cut him off. If your will want
not, time and place will be fruitfully offered. There is
nothing done if he return the conqueror. Then am I
the prisoner and his bed my gaol, from the loathed
warmth whereof deliver me, and supply the place for
255   your labor. Your—wife, so I would say—affectionate
servant, and for you her own for venture,
                                        Goneril."
O indistinguished space of woman's will!
A plot upon her virtuous husband's life,
260   And the exchange my brother!—Here in the sands
Thee I'll rake up, the post unsanctified
Of murderous lechers. And in the mature time
With this ungracious paper strike the sight
Of the death-practiced duke. For him 'tis well
265   That of thy death and business I can tell.

GLOUCESTER
The king is mad. How stiff is my vile sense,
That I stand up and have ingenious feeling
Of my huge sorrows. Better I were distract—
So should my thoughts be severed from my griefs,
270   And woes by wrong imaginations lose
The knowledge of themselves.

Drum afar off

EDGAR

Sit down and rest, father. Let's look in his pockets. The letters he spoke of may help me. He's dead. I'm just sorry I had to be the one to kill him. Let's see here. *(takes letters out of* OSWALD*'s pocket and opens them)* Come on, envelope, open up for me. I know it's bad manners, but we kill our enemies to know their secrets. Reading their mail isn't as bad.

(reads)

"Don't forget the vows we made to each other. You have many chances to kill Albany. If you have the strength of will to do it, you'll have many opportunities. If he returns in triumph, then all is lost. I'll be his prisoner, and his bed will be my prison. Help me escape him, and you can take his place. Your—I wish I could say "wife"—loving servant, who is ready to love you,

Goneril."

Is there no limit to women's lust? She's plotting against the life of her virtuous husband, and wants my brother to replace him! *(to the dead* OSWALD*)* I'll bury you here in a shallow grave, you messenger for lustful criminals. In due time I'll show this ugly letter to the duke whose life's at risk. It's a good thing for him that I can tell him about your death and the letter you were carrying.

GLOUCESTER

The king is insane. I hate the fact that I'm sane enough to be aware of my own great suffering. It'd be better to be delirious and unaware of anything. Then my mind would be free of sorrow, and sadness would be forgotten in my hallucinations.

Drums play in the distance.

EDGAR
                                        Give me your hand.
Far off methinks I hear the beaten drum.
Come, father, I'll bestow you with a friend.

Exeunt

EDGAR

Give me your hand. I think I hear the drums far away.
Come, father, I'll leave you at a friend's house.

They exit.

ACT 4, SCENE 7

Enter CORDELIA, KENT *disguised,* GENTLEMAN, *and* DOCTOR

CORDELIA
O thou good Kent, how shall I live and work
To match thy goodness? My life will be too short,
And every measure fail me.

KENT
To be acknowledged, madam, is o'erpaid.
5 All my reports go with the modest truth,
Nor more, nor clipped, but so.

CORDELIA
                              Be better suited.
These weeds are memories of those worser hours.
I prithee, put them off.

KENT
                    Pardon, dear madam.
Yet to be known shortens my made intent.
10 My boon I make it that you know me not
Till time and I think meet.

CORDELIA
                    Then be 't so, my good lord.—
How does the king?

DOCTOR
                Madam, sleeps still.

CORDELIA
                              O you kind gods,
Cure this great breach in his abusèd nature,
Th' untuned and jarring senses, O, wind up,
15 Of this child-changèd father!

DOCTOR
                        So please your majesty
That we may wake the king? He hath slept long.

ACT 4, SCENE 7

CORDELIA *enters with* KENT *in disguise, the*
GENTLEMAN, *and the* DOCTOR.

CORDELIA

Oh, Kent, what could I ever do to become as good as
you are? I won't live long enough, and all my efforts
will fail me.

KENT

Just being thanked is more than enough for me,
madam. I hope all reports about me simply tell the
truth, no more or less.

CORDELIA

Change into better clothes. These rags will just
remind us of those bad times when you had to wear a
disguise. Please take them off.

KENT

I'm sorry, madam, but I can't do that yet. If people
recognize me now, I won't be able to carry out my
plans. I have to ask you, as a favor, not to let on that
you recognize me until the time is right.

CORDELIA

All right, my lord.—How's the king doing?

DOCTOR

He's still sleeping, ma'am.

CORDELIA

Kind gods, heal the wounds that he's wrongly suffered! Restore the sanity of this father whose children
have driven him mad and changed him into a child
again!

DOCTOR

Would you mind if we woke up the king? He's slept a
long time.

CORDELIA
>Be governed by your knowledge, and proceed
>I' th' sway of your own will. Is he arrayed?

Enter LEAR *asleep in a chair carried by servants*

GENTLEMAN
>Ay, madam. In the heaviness of his sleep
20   We put fresh garments on him.

DOCTOR
>Be by, good madam, when we do awake him.
>I doubt not of his temperance.

CORDELIA
>   Very well.

DOCTOR
>Please you, draw near.—Louder the music there!

CORDELIA
>*(kisses* LEAR*)* O my dear father, restoration hang
25   Thy medicine on my lips, and let this kiss
>Repair those violent harms that my two sisters
>Have in thy reverence made!

KENT
>   Kind and dear princess!

CORDELIA
>Had you not been their father, these white flakes
>Did challenge pity of them. Was this a face
30   To be opposed against the warring winds?
>To stand against the deep dread-bolted thunder
>In the most terrible and nimble stroke
>Of quick cross lightning? To watch—poor perdu!—
>With this thin helm? Mine enemy's meanest dog,
35   Though he had bit me, should have stood that night
>Against my fire. And wast thou fain, poor father,
>To hovel thee with swine and rogues forlorn
>In short and musty straw? Alack, alack!
>'Tis wonder that thy life and wits at once
40   Had not concluded all.—He wakes. Speak to him.

CORDELIA

Do whatever you think best. Is he in his royal garments?

Servants carry in LEAR *sleeping in a chair.*

GENTLEMAN

Yes, ma'am. We changed his clothes while he was fast asleep.

DOCTOR

Stay close by when we wake him up, ma'am. I'm sure he will stay under control.

CORDELIA

All right.

DOCTOR

Please come closer.— Make the music louder, please!

CORDELIA

(kisses LEAR*)* Oh, my dear father, please get better. May my kiss heal the wounds inflicted on you by my sisters—who should have respected and cherished you.

KENT

Kind and dear princess!

CORDELIA

If you hadn't been their father, your white hair would have inspired in them only compassion. Is this a face that should have endured the freezing winds or withstood the dreadful thunder or the terrible lightning? To stay awake all night like a guardsman—poor lost soul!—with only your thinning hair for a helmet? I would've let even my enemy's nastiest dog stay inside by the fireplace on that night, even if he had bit me. And were you then happy to find shelter on a bed of hay along with swine and homeless bums? Oh, oh! It's a wonder you didn't lose your life and your mind all at once.—He's waking up. Talk to him.

DOCTOR
Madam, do you. 'Tis fittest.

CORDELIA
How does my royal lord? How fares your majesty?

LEAR
You do me wrong to take me out o' th' grave.
Thou art a soul in bliss, but I am bound
45   Upon a wheel of fire, that mine own tears
Do scald like molten lead.

CORDELIA
Sir, do you know me?

LEAR
You are a spirit, I know. Where did you die?

CORDELIA
(aside to DOCTOR*)* Still, still far wide!

DOCTOR
He's scarce awake. Let him alone awhile.

LEAR
50   Where have I been? Where am I? Fair daylight?
I am mightily abused. I should ev'n die with pity
To see another thus. I know not what to say.
I will not swear these are my hands. Let's see.
I feel this pinprick. Would I were assured
55   Of my condition.

CORDELIA
(kneels)
O, look upon me, sir,
And hold your hands in benediction o'er me.
No, sir, you must not kneel.

LEAR
Pray, do not mock me.
I am a very foolish fond old man,
Fourscore and upward, not an hour more nor less.
60   And to deal plainly
I fear I am not in my perfect mind.
Methinks I should know you, and know this man.

DOCTOR

You talk to him, ma'am. That's most appropriate.

CORDELIA

How are you, my royal lord? How is your majesty doing?

LEAR

You do me wrong by taking me out of the grave. You're a soul in heaven, but I'm tied to the fiery wheel of a torture machine in hell. Even my tears burn me like molten lead.

CORDELIA

Sir, do you know who I am?

LEAR

You're a spirit, I know. Where did you die?

CORDELIA

(whispering to the DOCTOR*)* He's still in outer space.

DOCTOR

He's still half asleep. Let him be for a bit.

LEAR

Where have I been? Where am I? Is it daytime? I've been tricked. I would die of pity to see someone else in my condition. I don't know what to say. I can't even be sure these are my hands. Let's see. I feel this pinprick. I wish I knew what is happening.

CORDELIA

(kneeling) Look at me, sir, and give me your blessing. No, sir, don't kneel.

LEAR

Please don't make fun of me. I'm a foolish, senile old man, eighty-something years old, not an hour more or less. To put it plainly, I'm afraid I'm not quite sane. I feel I should recognize you and that man *(he points to* KENT*)*,

Yet I am doubtful, for I am mainly ignorant
What place this is, and all the skill I have
65 Remembers not these garments. Nor I know not
Where I did lodge last night. Do not laugh at me,
For as I am a man, I think this lady
To be my child Cordelia.

CORDELIA
                              And so I am, I am.

LEAR
Be your tears wet? Yes, faith. I pray, weep not.
70 If you have poison for me, I will drink it.
I know you do not love me, for your sisters
Have, as I do remember, done me wrong.
You have some cause; they have not.

CORDELIA
                                    No cause, no cause.

LEAR
Am I in France?

KENT
75 In your own kingdom, sir.

LEAR
Do not abuse me.

DOCTOR
Be comforted, good madam. The great rage,
You see, is killed in him. And yet it is danger
To make him even o'er the time he has lost.
80 Desire him to go in. Trouble him no more
Till further settling.

CORDELIA
Will 't please your highness walk?

LEAR
You must bear with me.
Pray you now, forget and forgive.
85 I am old and foolish.

                                    Exeunt
                              Manent **KENT** *and* **GENTLEMAN**

but I'm not sure. I don't know where I am. I don't remember these clothes. I can't recall where I slept last night. Don't laugh at me, but I swear I think this lady is my child Cordelia.

CORDELIA

And I am, I am.

LEAR

Are your tears wet? Yes, indeed they are. Please don't cry. If you have poison for me, I'll drink it. I know you don't love me. If I remember, your sisters did me wrong for no reason. But you didn't, even though you had every reason.

CORDELIA

I had no reason, no reason.

LEAR

Am I in France?

KENT

You're in your own kingdom, sir.

LEAR

Don't deceive me.

DOCTOR

You can relax, ma'am. His insane period is over. But it's dangerous to make him try to make sense of the time he lost. Ask him to go in. Don't trouble him further until his mind is more settled.

CORDELIA

Would your highness like to take a walk?

LEAR

You'll have to bear with me. Please forgive and forget. I'm old and foolish.

They exit.
KENT *and the* **GENTLEMAN** *remain.*

GENTLEMAN

Holds it true, sir, that the Duke
of Cornwall was so slain?

KENT

Most certain, sir.

GENTLEMAN

Who is conductor of his people?

KENT

As 'tis said, the bastard son of Gloucester.

GENTLEMAN

They say Edgar, his banished son, is with the Earl of Kent
90   in Germany.

KENT

Report is changeable. 'Tis time to look about. The powers of
the kingdom approach apace.

GENTLEMAN

The arbitrament is like to be bloody. Fare you well, sir.

Exit GENTLEMAN

KENT

My point and period will be throughly wrought,
95   Or well or ill, as this day's battle's fought.

Exit

GENTLEMAN

Is it true, sir, that the Duke of Cornwall was killed as they say?

KENT

Yes, it's true, sir.

GENTLEMAN

Who is leading his men?

KENT

They say Gloucester's bastard son is.

GENTLEMAN

I hear that Edgar, Gloucester's exiled son, is with the Earl of Kent in Germany.

KENT

You can't trust all the rumors. It's time to reassess the situation. The British troops are coming near.

GENTLEMAN

It will likely be a bloody fight. Goodbye, sir.

He exits.

KENT

My life and my plans completely depend on how today's battle ends.

He exits.

ACT FIVE
SCENE 1

Enter with drum and colors EDMUND, REGAN, *gentlemen, and soldiers*

EDMUND
    (to a gentleman) Know of the duke if his last purpose hold,
    Or whether since he is advised by aught
    To change the course. He's full of alteration
    And self-reproving. Bring his constant pleasure.

                        Exit gentleman

REGAN
5   Our sister's man is certainly miscarried.

EDMUND
    'Tis to be doubted, madam.

REGAN
                    Now, sweet lord,
    You know the goodness I intend upon you.
    Tell me but truly—but then speak the truth—
    Do you not love my sister?

EDMUND
                    In honored love.

REGAN
10   But have you never found my brother's way
    To the forfended place?

EDMUND
    That thought abuses you.

REGAN
    I am doubtful that you have been conjunct
    And bosomed with her as far as we call hers.

EDMUND
15   No, by mine honor, madam.

ACT FIVE

SCENE 1

EDMUND, REGAN, *gentlemen, and soldiers enter with drums and banners.*

EDMUND

(to a gentleman) Go find out from the Duke of Albany if his decision still holds, or if he's changed his mind. He's always going back and forth and second-guessing himself. Come back and tell me what his final decision is.

Gentleman exits.

REGAN

My sister's servant Oswald has certainly run into trouble.

EDMUND

I'm afraid that may be the case, madam.

REGAN

Now, my sweet lord, you know how much I like you. Tell me truthfully, do you love my sister?

EDMUND

Yes, truly and honorably.

REGAN

But have you ever gone in my brother-in-law's bed and had sex with her?

EDMUND

No. You dishonor yourself and our relationship by thinking that.

REGAN

I'm just worried that you've been cozying up to her, and gotten intimate with her.

EDMUND

No, I swear on my honor, I haven't, madam.

REGAN
I never shall endure her. Dear my lord,
Be not familiar with her.

EDMUND
                              Fear me not.—
She and the duke her husband!

Enter with drum and colors **ALBANY** *and* **GONERIL**, *with troops*

GONERIL
(aside) I had rather lose the battle than that sister
20 Should loosen him and me.

ALBANY
Our very loving sister, well bemet.—
Sir, this I hear: the king is come to his daughter,
With others whom the rigor of our state
Forced to cry out. Where I could not be honest
25 I never yet was valiant. For this business,
It touches us as France invades our land,
Not bolds the king, with others whom I fear
Most just and heavy causes make oppose.

EDMUND
Sir, you speak nobly.

REGAN
                              Why is this reasoned?

GONERIL
30 Combine together 'gainst the enemy,
For these domestic and particular broils
Are not the question here.

ALBANY
Let's then determine with the ancient of war
On our proceedings.

EDMUND
35 I shall attend you presently at your tent.

REGAN

I can't stand her. Please, my lord, don't be friendly with her.

EDMUND

Don't worry about me.—Your sister and the duke are here.

ALBANY, GONERIL, and soldiers enter with drums and banners.

GONERIL

(to herself) I'd rather lose this battle than allow that sister of mine to come between me and Edmund.

ALBANY

My dear and loving sister-in-law, I'm happy to see you. *(to EDMUND)* Sir, I've heard that the king has joined up with his daughter as well as others who have complained about our strict policies. I've never fought for a cause I didn't believe in. I'm concerned about the French because they have invaded our soil, not because they support King Lear or those others—who, I'm afraid, may have legitimate grievances against us.

EDMUND

Noble words, sir.

REGAN

Why are we talking about this?

GONERIL

We must join forces against the enemy. Our domestic squabbles are not the issue here.

ALBANY

Then let's meet with our senior command and discuss what to do next.

EDMUND

I'll meet you at your tent.

REGAN
Sister, you'll go with us?

GONERIL
No.

REGAN
'Tis most convenient. Pray you, go with us.

GONERIL
(aside) Oh ho, I know the riddle.—I will go.
Enter EDGAR *disguised*

EDGAR
40   *(to* ALBANY*)* If e'er your grace had speech with man so poor,
Hear me one word.

ALBANY
(to EDMUND, REGAN, *and* GONERIL*)*
         I'll overtake you.—

            Exeunt all but ALBANY *and* EDGAR

               Speak.

EDGAR
(giving ALBANY *a letter)*
Before you fight the battle, ope this letter.
If you have victory, let the trumpet sound
For him that brought it. Wretched though I seem,
45   I can produce a champion that will prove
What is avouchèd there. If you miscarry,
Your business of the world hath so an end,
And machination ceases. Fortune love you.

ALBANY
Stay till I have read the letter.

EDGAR
50   I was forbid it.
When time shall serve, let but the herald cry,
And I'll appear again.

ALBANY
Why, fare thee well. I will o'erlook thy paper.

REGAN

Goneril, are you coming with us?

GONERIL

No.

REGAN

It's the best thing to do. Please come with me.

GONERIL

(to herself) Oh ho, I know her little tricks.—Okay, I'll go.

EDGAR *enters, disguised as a peasant.*

EDGAR

(to ALBANY*)* If you can stoop to speak to a man as poor as I am, then listen to me, please.

ALBANY

(to EDMUND, REGAN, *and* GONERIL *exiting)* I'll catch up with you.—

Everyone exits except ALBANY *and* EDGAR

Go ahead.

EDGAR

(giving ALBANY *a letter)* Before you go into battle, open this letter. If you win, then blow your trumpet as a signal for me. I may look wretched, but I'll bravely stand up to defend my claims. If you die in battle, all your projects and this plan are off. Good luck to you.

ALBANY

Wait until I read the letter.

EDGAR

I was ordered not to. When the time comes, tell the herald to blow the trumpet and I'll return.

ALBANY

Goodbye, then. I'll take a look at your letter.

Exit EDGAR

Enter EDMUND

EDMUND
The enemy's in view. Draw up your powers.
(gives ALBANY *a document)*
55   Here is the guess of their true strength and forces
By diligent discovery, but your haste
Is now urged on you.

ALBANY
We will greet the time.

Exit ALBANY

EDMUND
To both these sisters have I sworn my love,
Each jealous of the other as the stung
60   Are of the adder. Which of them shall I take?
Both? One? Or neither? Neither can be enjoyed
If both remain alive. To take the widow
Exasperates, makes mad her sister Goneril,
And hardly shall I carry out my side,
65   Her husband being alive. Now, then, we'll use
His countenance for the battle, which being done,
Let her who would be rid of him devise
His speedy taking off. As for the mercy
Which he intends to Lear and to Cordelia,
70   The battle done and they within our power,
Shall never see his pardon, for my state
Stands on me to defend, not to debate.

Exit

EDGAR *exits.*

EDMUND *enters.*

EDMUND

The enemy's in sight. Prepare your troops. *(gives* ALBANY *a document)* The reconnaissance operation has returned this estimate of the enemy's manpower and weaponry. But now, please hurry.

ALBANY

We'll be ready when the time comes.

He exits.

EDMUND

I've sworn my love to both of these sisters. They're jealous of each other like poisonous snakes. Which one of them should I pick? Both? One? Neither? I can't enjoy either of them as long as the other one's alive. Goneril would go crazy if I chose Regan, but it would be hard to get in with Goneril while her husband's still alive. I'll use Albany's power and authority for now to win the war, but afterward one of the sisters—whichever one wants to—can get rid of him. Albany wants to spare Lear and Cordelia, but once they are my prisoners after the battle, they won't stay alive long enough to see his pardon. I have to defend my position with actions, not words.

He exits.

ACT 5, SCENE 2

Alarum within
Enter with drum and colors the powers of France over the
stage, and CORDELIA *with her father* LEAR *in her hand*
                                                     And exeunt

Enter EDGAR *disguised and* GLOUCESTER

EDGAR
          Here, father, take the shadow of this tree
          For your good host. Pray that the right may thrive.
          If ever I return to you again,
          I'll bring you comfort.

GLOUCESTER
                              Grace go with you, sir.

                                             Exit EDGAR

Alarum and retreat within
Enter EDGAR

EDGAR
5   Away, old man. Give me thy hand. Away!
          King Lear hath lost, he and his daughter ta'en.
          Give me thy hand. Come on.

GLOUCESTER
          No further, sir. A man may rot even here.

EDGAR
          What, in ill thoughts again? Men must endure
10   Their going hence even as their coming hither.
          Ripeness is all. Come on.

GLOUCESTER
                              And that's true too.

                                             Exeunt

ACT 5, SCENE 2

Sounds of battle offstage. CORDELIA *enters hand in hand with* LEAR, *accompanied by drums, banners, and French troops. They cross the stage and exit.*

EDGAR *enters, disguised, along with* GLOUCESTER.

EDGAR

Here, father, rest awhile in the shade of this tree. Say a little prayer for our side in battle. If I ever come back, I'll bring you good news.

GLOUCESTER

Good luck, sir.

EDGAR exits.

Sounds of battle offstage. They grow fainter.

EDGAR *returns.*

EDGAR

We have to get out of here, old man. Let me help you up. Let's go! King Lear's been defeated. He and his daughter are captured. Give me your hand. Come on.

GLOUCESTER

I can't go any further, sir. This is as good a place as any to die.

EDGAR

Are you depressed again? You can't choose your time of death any more than your time of birth. We live and die when our time comes. Come on.

GLOUCESTER

And that's true too.

They exit.

ACT 5, SCENE 3

Enter in conquest with drum and colors EDMUND*, with* LEAR
and CORDELIA *as prisoners, and* FIRST CAPTAIN *with soldiers*

EDMUND
Some officers take them away. Good guard
Until their greater pleasures first be known
That are to censure them.

CORDELIA
(to LEAR*)*
                              We are not the first
Who with best meaning have incurred the worst.
5   For thee, oppressèd King, I am cast down.
Myself could else outfrown false fortune's frown.
Shall we not see these daughters and these sisters?

LEAR
No, no, no, no! Come, let's away to prison.
We two alone will sing like birds i' th' cage.
10   When thou dost ask me blessing, I'll kneel down
And ask of thee forgiveness. So we'll live,
And pray, and sing, and tell old tales, and laugh
At gilded butterflies, and hear poor rogues
Talk of court news, and we'll talk with them too—
15   Who loses and who wins, who's in, who's out—
And take upon 's the mystery of things
As if we were God's spies. And we'll wear out
In a walled prison packs and sects of great ones
That ebb and flow by the moon.

EDMUND
                              Take them away.

LEAR
20   Upon such sacrifices, my Cordelia,
The gods themselves throw incense. Have I caught thee?
He that parts us shall bring a brand from heaven
And fire us hence like foxes. Wipe thine eyes.

ACT 5, SCENE 3

EDMUND *enters, victorious, with drums and banners.*
LEAR *and* CORDELIA *enter as prisoners, led by the* FIRST
CAPTAIN *and soldiers.*

EDMUND

Officers, take them away. Guard them carefully until
we decide how to punish them.

CORDELIA

(to LEAR*)* At least we're not the first ones in our position. The road to hell is paved with good intentions.
But I'm worried about you, my poor King. If it were
only me, I would just wait out my bad luck. Should we
meet with my sisters?

LEAR

No, no, no, no! Come on, let's go to prison. The two of
us together will sing like birds in a cage. We will be
good to each other. When you ask for my blessing, I'll
get down on my knees and ask you to forgive me.
That's how we'll live—we'll pray, we'll sing, we'll tell
old stories, we'll laugh at pretentious courtiers, we'll
listen to nasty court gossip, we'll find out who's losing
and who's winning, who's in and who's out. We'll
think about the mysteries of the universe as if we were
God's spies. In prison we'll outlast hordes of rulers
that will come and go as their fortunes change.

EDMUND

Take them away.

LEAR

My Cordelia, even the gods admire how much you've
sacrificed for me. Have I hugged you yet? Anyone
who wants to separate us will have to smoke us out of
the cave of our togetherness like foxes. Wipe your eyes.

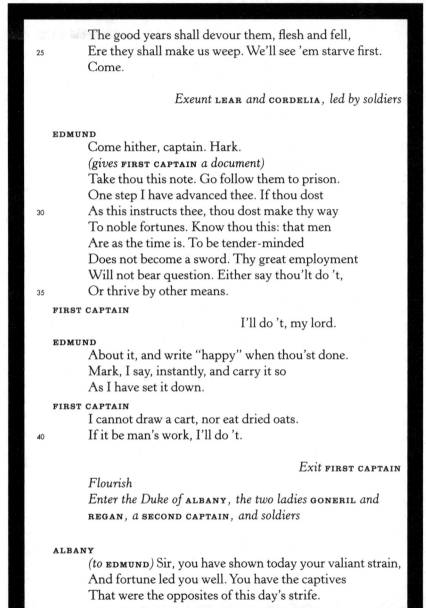

The good years shall devour them, flesh and fell,
25 Ere they shall make us weep. We'll see 'em starve first.
Come.

Exeunt LEAR *and* CORDELIA, *led by soldiers*

EDMUND
Come hither, captain. Hark.
(gives FIRST CAPTAIN *a document)*
Take thou this note. Go follow them to prison.
One step I have advanced thee. If thou dost
30 As this instructs thee, thou dost make thy way
To noble fortunes. Know thou this: that men
Are as the time is. To be tender-minded
Does not become a sword. Thy great employment
Will not bear question. Either say thou'lt do 't,
35 Or thrive by other means.

FIRST CAPTAIN
                                        I'll do 't, my lord.

EDMUND
About it, and write "happy" when thou'st done.
Mark, I say, instantly, and carry it so
As I have set it down.

FIRST CAPTAIN
I cannot draw a cart, nor eat dried oats.
40 If it be man's work, I'll do 't.

Exit FIRST CAPTAIN
Flourish
Enter the Duke of ALBANY, *the two ladies* GONERIL *and*
REGAN, *a* SECOND CAPTAIN, *and soldiers*

ALBANY
(to EDMUND*)* Sir, you have shown today your valiant strain,
And fortune led you well. You have the captives
That were the opposites of this day's strife.

Our jailers will shrivel up with old age before they make us cry again. We'll watch them starve to death first. Come on.

> LEAR *and* CORDELIA *exit, led by soldiers.*

EDMUND

Come here, captain. Listen. *(gives the* FIRST CAPTAIN *a sheet of paper)* Take this note. Follow those two to prison and follow these instructions. I've already promoted you once. If you do as you're told, you'll be richly rewarded. Just remember this: you have to go with the times, and these are the times for being tough. A soldier can't afford to be a ninny. There'll be no quibbling about this assignment. Either you accept it, or go find some other way to support yourself.

FIRST CAPTAIN

I'll do it, sir.

EDMUND

Then off you go. When you've finished, you'll be a happy man. Go immediately, and do exactly as I wrote down.

FIRST CAPTAIN

Jobs are hard to come by. I can't pull a cart or eat dried oats like a horse. If it's work for a man, I'll do it.

> *The* FIRST CAPTAIN *exits.*
> *Trumpets play.* ALBANY *enters with* GONERIL *and* REGAN, *a* SECOND CAPTAIN, *and more soldiers.*

ALBANY

(to EDMUND*)* Sir, you've shown your true courage today, and luck was on your side. You've taken prisoner the leaders of the opposition. I need to take cus-

I do require them of you, so to use them
45   As we shall find their merits and our safety
May equally determine.

EDMUND
                              Sir, I thought it fit
To send the old and miserable king
To some retention and appointed guard—
Whose age has charms in it, whose title more—
50   To pluck the common bosom on his side,
An turn our impressed lances in our eyes
Which do command them. With him I sent the queen,
My reason all the same, and they are ready
Tomorrow or at further space t' appear
55   Where you shall hold your session. At this time
We sweat and bleed. The friend hath lost his friend,
And the best quarrels, in the heat, are cursed
By those that feel their sharpness.
The question of Cordelia and her father
60   Requires a fitter place.

ALBANY
I hold you but a subject of this war,
Not as a brother.

REGAN
                              That's as we list to grace him.
Methinks our pleasure might have been demanded
Ere you had spoke so far. He led our powers,
65   Bore the commission of my place and person—
The which immediacy may well stand up
And call itself your brother.

GONERIL
                              Not so hot.
In his own grace he doth exalt himself
More than in your addition.

REGAN
                              In my rights,
70   By me invested, he compeers the best.

tody of them so I can do what's best out of concern for
their honor and the safety of the kingdom.

EDMUND

Sir, I decided it was appropriate to send the pathetic
old king to a guarded prison cell. His old age and his
title make him so popular among the commoners that
I was worried our enlisted soldiers would turn against
us on his behalf. I sent the French queen with him too,
for the same reason. They're ready to meet with you
tomorrow, or whenever you like, wherever you'd like
to hold your hearing. These are difficult times. Many
have lost friends in battle, and soldiers will curse even
a justified war if it causes them pain. We need a more
appropriate place to discuss Cordelia and her father.

ALBANY

I'm sorry, sir, but in this war I consider you a subor-
dinate, not my equal.

REGAN

That's for to me to decide. You might have asked my
opinion before saying something so rude. Edmund
has led our forces well, and implemented my wishes—
and his close connection with me gives him the right
to be considered your equal.

GONERIL

Not so fast. He has distinguished himself as a great
soldier in his own right, deserving more than any
honor your can bestow on him.

REGAN

I'm the one who gave him his military commission,
and it is as my proxy that he fought bravely.

ALBANY
That were the most if he should
husband you.

REGAN
Jesters do oft prove prophets.

GONERIL
Holla, holla!
That eye that told you so looked but asquint.

REGAN
Lady, I am not well, else I should answer
From a full-flowing stomach.
(to EDMUND*)* General,
75   Take thou my soldiers, prisoners, patrimony.
Dispose of them, of me. The walls is thine.
Witness the world that I create thee here
My lord and master.

GONERIL
Mean you to enjoy him then?

ALBANY
The let-alone lies not in your good will.

EDMUND
80   Nor in thine, lord.

ALBANY
Half-blooded fellow, yes.

REGAN
(to EDMUND*)* Let the drum strike and prove my title thine.

ALBANY
Stay yet. Hear reason.—Edmund, I arrest thee
On capital treason, and in thine attaint
This gilded serpent.*(indicates* GONERIL*)*
85   *(to* REGAN*)* For your claim, fair sister,
I bar it in the interest of my wife.
'Tis she is subcontracted to this lord.
And I, her husband, contradict your banns.
If you will marry, make your loves to me,
90   My lady is bespoke.

ALBANY

He'd really be your proxy if he married you.

REGAN

Don't joke, it might come true.

GONERIL

Whoa, whoa! You're so infatuated with him that you're hallucinating.

REGAN

Hey, lady, if I weren't feeling a little sick, I'd give you a piece of my mind. *(to* EDMUND*)* General, take my soldiers, my prisoners, my whole inheritance, and do as you like with them. I surrender myself to your good judgment. Let the whole world see that I hereby make you my lord and master.

GONERIL

Are you trying to sleep with him?

ALBANY

(to GONERIL*)* It's not up to you to say "Yes" or "No."

EDMUND

Nor is it up to you, my lord.

ALBANY

Yes it is, you half-blood.

REGAN

(to EDMUND*)* Let the drums beat. Prove your right to me by defeating any challenger.

ALBANY

Hang on a second. Listen to me.—Edmund, you're under arrest for capital treason. Along with you, your co-conspirator, this snake of a woman. *(points at* GONERIL. *Then, speaking to* REGAN*)* My dear sister-in-law, I veto your marriage announcement for the benefit of my wife, who is already engaged to Edmund. So if you want to get married, you'll have to woo me. My wife's already spoken for.

GONERIL
An interlude!

ALBANY
Thou art armed, Gloucester. Let the trumpet sound.
If none appear to prove upon thy person
Thy heinous, manifest, and many treasons,
There is my pledge. *(throws down his glove)*
95   I'll make it on thy heart,
Ere I taste bread, thou art in nothing less
Than I have here proclaimed thee.

REGAN
Sick, oh, sick!

GONERIL
(aside) If not, I'll ne'er trust medicine.

EDMUND
(throwing down his glove)
100   There's my exchange. What in the world he is
That names me traitor, villainlike he lies.
Call by thy trumpet. He that dares approach,
On him—on you, who not?—I will maintain
My truth and honor firmly.

ALBANY
105   A herald, ho!

EDMUND
A herald, ho, a herald!

Enter a HERALD

ALBANY
(to EDMUND*)* Trust to thy single virtue, for thy soldiers,
All levied in my name, have in my name
Took their discharge.

REGAN
My sickness grows upon me.

ALBANY
110   She is not well. Convey her to my tent.

GONERIL

What a farce!

ALBANY

You've got a sword, Gloucester. Blow the trumpets. If nobody else comes to challenge you and prove what an abominable traitor you have been, I'll have to challenge you myself. *(he throws down his glove)* I'll prove soon enough that you're just as wicked as I say you are.

> *Throwing down a glove was a way of challenging someone to fight.*

REGAN

Oh, I'm sick, sick!

GONERIL

(to herself) If she's not ill, I'll never trust drugs again.

EDMUND

(throwing down his glove) You're on. Whoever calls me a traitor is a vicious liar. Blow the trumpet. Anyone who dares to step forward and make that accusation— you or anyone else—go ahead. I'll uphold my truth and my honor.

ALBANY

A herald! Call a herald!

> *"herald"=person who reads proclamations aloud.*

EDMUND

A herald, a herald!

A **HERALD** *enters.*

ALBANY

(to EDMUND*)* You're on your own now. The soldiers were all drafted in my name, and now they are discharged in my name.

REGAN

I feel sicker and sicker.

ALBANY

She's not feeling well. Take her to my tent.

Come hither, herald.—Let the trumpet sound,—
And read out this. *(gives the* HERALD *a document)*

SECOND CAPTAIN
Sound, trumpet!

A trumpet sounds

HERALD
(reads)
"If any man of quality or degree within the lists of the
115   army will maintain upon Edmund, supposed Earl of
Gloucester, that he is a manifold traitor, let him appear by
the third sound of the trumpet. He is bold in his defense."

EDMUND
Sound!

First trumpet

HERALD
Again!

Second trumpet

HERALD
120   Again!

Third trumpet
Trumpet answers within
Enter EDGAR, *at the third sound, armed, a trumpet before him*

ALBANY
(to HERALD*)* Ask him his purposes, why he appears
Upon this call o' th' trumpet.

HERALD
What are you?
Your name, your quality, and why you answer
125   This present summons?

REGAN *is helped to exit*

Come here, herald.—Let the trumpet sound!—Read
this out. *(he hands the* HERALD *a document)*

SECOND CAPTAIN
Blow the trumpet!

A trumpet sounds.

HERALD
(reads)
"If any noble man in the army asserts that
Edmund, so-called Earl of Gloucester, is a traitor many times over, let him step forward by the
third trumpet blast."

EDMUND
Sound!

First trumpet sounds.

HERALD
Again!

Second trumpet sounds.

HERALD
Again!

Third trumpet sounds.
Another trumpet answers inside.
EDGAR *enters, wearing armor.*

ALBANY
(to HERALD*)* Ask him why he's stepping forward.

HERALD
Who are you? What's your name and rank, and why
are you stepping forward?

EDGAR
                    O, know, my name is lost.
By treason's tooth bare-gnawn and canker-bit.
Yet am I noble as the adversary
I come to cope withal.

ALBANY
                    Which is that adversary?

EDGAR
    What's he that speaks for Edmund, Earl of Gloucester?

EDMUND
130   Himself. What sayst thou to him?

EDGAR
                    Draw thy sword,
That if my speech offend a noble heart
Thy arm may do thee justice. *(draws his sword)* Here is mine.
Behold: it is the privilege of mine honors,
My oath, and my profession. I protest—
135   Maugre thy strength, youth, place, and eminence,
Despite thy victor sword and fire-new fortune,
Thy valor and thy heart—thou art a traitor,
False to thy gods, thy brother, and thy father,
Conspirant 'gainst this high illustrious prince,
140   And from th' extremest upward of thy head
To the descent and dust below thy foot
A most toad-spotted traitor. Say thou "No,"
This sword, this arm, and my best spirits are bent
To prove upon thy heart, whereto I speak,
145   Thou liest.

EDMUND
              In wisdom I should ask thy name.
But since thy outside looks so fair and warlike,
And that thy tongue some say of breeding breathes,
What safe and nicely I might well delay
By rule of knighthood, I disdain and spurn.
150   Back do I toss these treasons to thy head,
With the hell-hated lie o'erwhelm thy heart—

EDGAR

I've lost my name and title to a traitor. But I'm as noble as my opponent.

ALBANY

And who is that?

EDGAR

Who's the spokesman for Edmund, Earl of Gloucester?

EDMUND

I'm my own spokesman. What do you have to say to me?

EDGAR

Draw your sword. If I offend you by what I say, you can use your sword to take revenge . Here's mine. *(he draws his sword)* Look at it. It's the symbol of my honor, my rank, and my status as a knight. In spite of your youth, rank, strength, and excellence at warfare, in spite of your courage, your recent victory, and your good luck, I declare that you're a traitor. You've betrayed your gods, your brother, and your father. You've plotted against this noble duke. You're a rotten traitor, through and through, from the top of your head to the soles of your feet. If you disagree with me, I'm ready to use this sword and my courage to prove that you're a liar.

EDMUND

Normally I would ask you what your name is first. But since you look so fine and noble, and since you're so well mannered in your speech, I'm prepared to over-look the rules of knighthood, which say I should refuse to fight a man I don't know. I throw your accusations back in your face. Your lies can hardly hurt me,

Which, for they yet glance by and scarcely bruise,
This sword of mine shall give them instant way,
Where they shall rest for ever.—Trumpets, speak!

Alarums
EDMUND and EDGAR fight
EDMUND falls

ALBANY
155   Save him, save him!

GONERIL
This is practice, Gloucester.
By th' law of arms thou wast not bound to answer
An unknown opposite. Thou art not vanquished,
But cozened and beguiled.

ALBANY
                              Shut your mouth, dame,
160   Or with this paper shall I stop it.—Hold, sir,
(gives the letter to EDMUND)
Thou worse than any name, read thine own evil.—
(to GONERIL) Nay, no tearing, lady. I perceive you know it.

GONERIL
Say, if I do? The laws are mine, not thine.
Who can arraign me for 't?

ALBANY
                              Most monstrous, oh!
165   *(to EDMUND)* Know'st thou this paper?

EDMUND
Ask me not what I know.

Exit GONERIL

ALBANY
Go after her. She's desperate. Govern her.

Exit a soldier

but I'll still fight you and embed your lies back in your hellish heart.—Trumpets, blow!

Trumpets play. EDMUND *and* EDGAR *fight.* EDMUND *falls.*

ALBANY

(to EDGAR*)* Save him, save him!

GONERIL

You were tricked into fighting, Gloucester. According to the laws of war, you didn't have to fight a stranger. You haven't lost this fight; you've been tricked and deceived.

ALBANY

Shut your mouth, woman, or I'll shove this paper in it.—Stop, sir. *(gives the letter to* EDMUND*)* You despicable criminal, read your crime. *(to* GONERIL*)* Don't try to tear it up, madam. I take it you know what this letter says.

GONERIL

And what if I do? I make the laws, not you. Who can prosecute me for it?

ALBANY

Oh, monstrous! *(to* EDMUND*)* Do you know what letter this is?

EDMUND

Don't ask me what I know.

GONERIL *exits.*

ALBANY

Follow her. She's desperate. Make sure she doesn't do anything stupid.

A soldier exits.

EDMUND
What you have charged me with, that have I done—
And more, much more. The time will bring it out.
170 'Tis past, and so am I.
(*to* EDGAR)
                                    But what art thou
That hast this fortune on me? If thou'rt noble,
I do forgive thee.

EDGAR
                            Let's exchange charity.
I am no less in blood than thou art, Edmund.
If more, the more thou'st wronged me.
175 My name is Edgar, and thy father's son.

The gods are just, and of our pleasant vices
Make instruments to plague us.
The dark and vicious place where thee he got
Cost him his eyes.

EDMUND
                              Thou'st spoken right. 'Tis true.
180 The wheel is come full circle. I am here.

ALBANY
Methought thy very gait did prophesy
A royal nobleness. I must embrace thee.
Let sorrow split my heart if ever I
Did hate thee or thy father.

EDGAR
185 Worthy prince, I know 't.

ALBANY
Where have you hid yourself?
How have you known the miseries of your father?

EDGAR
By nursing them, my lord. List a brief tale,
And when 'tis told, oh, that my heart would burst!
190 The bloody proclamation to escape,
That followed me so near—O our lives' sweetness,

EDMUND

I've done everything you accuse me of—and more, much more. You'll find out everything in due time. It's all over now, and so am I. *(to EDGAR)* But who are you, you who've managed to defeat me? If you're a nobleman, I forgive you.

EDGAR

Let's forgive each other. I'm no less noble than you are, Edmund. If I'm more noble than you, you've done me wrong. My name is Edgar, and I'm your father's son.

The gods are fair, and they use our little vices to punish us. The woman he committed adultery with, your mother, cost him his eyes.

EDMUND

You're right. That's true. It's all come full circle, and here I am.

ALBANY

I suspected that you were noble when I saw how you walked. Let me embrace you. I swear I never hated you or your father!

EDGAR

I know, prince.

ALBANY

Where have you been hiding? How did you know what happened to your poor father?

EDGAR

I knew because I helped nurse him through his suffering. Listen to my little story, and when it's done, oh, my heart will break! To escape the decree condemning

That we the pain of death would hourly die
Rather than die at once!—taught me to shift
Into a madman's rags, t' assume a semblance
195   That very dogs disdained. And in this habit
Met I my father with his bleeding rings,
Their precious stones new lost, became his guide,
Led him, begged for him, saved him from despair.
Never—O fault!—revealed myself unto him
200   Until some half-hour past, when I was armed.
Not sure, though hoping of this good success,
I asked his blessing, and from first to last
Told him my pilgrimage. But his flawed heart—
Alack, too weak the conflict to support—
205   'Twixt two extremes of passion, joy and grief,
Burst smilingly.

EDMUND
                              This speech of yours hath moved me,
And shall perchance do good. But speak you on.
You look as you had something more to say.

ALBANY
If there be more, more woeful, hold it in.
210   For I am almost ready to dissolve,
Hearing of this.

EDGAR
                              This would have seemed a period
To such as love not sorrow, but another
To amplify too much would make much more
And top extremity.
215   Whilst I was big in clamor came there in a man
Who, having seen me in my worst estate,
Shunned my abhorred society, but then, finding
Who 'twas that so endured, with his strong arms
He fastened on my neck, and bellowed out
220   As he'd burst heaven, threw him on my father,
Told the most piteous tale of Lear and him
That ever ear received—which in recounting

me to death, I disguised myself as a madman beggar and became a creature despised even by dogs.—Oh, how sweet our lives must be if we prefer to die gradually by debasing ourselves rather than dying all at once!—In that disguise I met up with my father with bloody sockets where his beautiful eyes used to be. I became his guide, I led him and begged for him, and kept him from suicide. I never—oh, what a mistake!—revealed myself to him until half an hour ago, when I was in my armor. With hope in my heart I asked him for his blessing, not sure that he'd give it to me. He did. I told him everything that had happened on my journey. But his frail heart, too weak to grapple with such a conflict between joy and sadness, gave out.

EDMUND

Your words have moved me, and maybe it'll do some good. But go on. You look like you have something more to say.

ALBANY

If there's anything more sorrowful left to add, keep it to yourself. I'm almost ready to break down hearing this much.

EDGAR

This may have seemed like the pinnacle of sadness, but if I went on I could outdo it. While I was sobbing loudly, a man came in. He had seen me in my ragged clothes and shunned me, but when he found out who I was, he clasped my neck with his strong arms and cried to high heaven. He threw himself on my father and told the saddest story you've ever heard about Lear and him. As he was telling that story he grieved

His grief grew puissant and the strings of life
Began to crack. Twice then the trumpets sounded,
225   And there I left him tranced.

ALBANY

But who was this?

EDGAR

Kent, sir, the banished Kent, who in disguise
Followed his enemy king and did him service
Improper for a slave.

Enter SECOND KNIGHT *with a bloody knife*

SECOND KNIGHT

Help, help, O, help!

EDGAR

What kind of help?

ALBANY

Speak, man.

EDGAR

230   What means that bloody knife?

SECOND KNIGHT

'Tis hot, it smokes.
It came even from the heart of—oh, she's dead!

ALBANY

Who dead? Speak, man.

SECOND KNIGHT

Your lady, sir, your lady. And her sister
235   By her is poisoned. She confesses it.

EDMUND

I was contracted to them both. All three
Now marry in an instant.

EDGAR

Here comes Kent.

more and more, until his heart started to break. Then I heard the trumpets blow twice, and left him there in a trance.

ALBANY

But who was that man?

EDGAR

It was Kent, sir, the exiled Kent, who, after the king treated him like an enemy of the state, put on a disguise and followed his king, carrying out tasks unworthy of even a slave.

The SECOND KNIGHT *enters with a bloody knife.*

SECOND KNIGHT

Help, help, oh, help!

EDGAR

What kind of help do you need?

ALBANY

Say something, man!

EDGAR

What is that bloody knife?

SECOND KNIGHT

It's still warm from the cut. It was just removed from from the heart of—oh, she's dead!

ALBANY

Who's dead? Speak, man.

SECOND KNIGHT

Your wife, sir, your wife. And her sister's dead too, poisoned by your wife. She confessed.

EDMUND

I was engaged to both of them. All three of us will marry now in death.

EDGAR

Here comes Kent.

ALBANY
Produce their bodies, be they alive or dead.
This judgment of the heavens that makes us tremble
240   Touches us not with pity.

Exit SECOND KNIGHT

Enter KENT

Oh, is this he?
The time will not allow the compliment
Which very manners urges.

KENT
I am come
To bid my king and master aye good night.
Is he not here?

ALBANY
Great thing of us forgot!—
245   Speak, Edmund, where's the king? And where's Cordelia?—

REGAN*'s and* GONERIL*'s corpses are brought out*

Seest thou this object, Kent?

KENT
Alack, why thus?

EDMUND
Yet Edmund was beloved.
The one the other poisoned for my sake,
250   And after slew herself.

ALBANY
Even so.—Cover their faces.

EDMUND
I pant for life. Some good I mean to do
Despite of mine own nature. Quickly send—
Be brief in it—to th' castle, for my writ
Is on the life of Lear and on Cordelia.
255   Nay, send in time!

ALBANY

(to SECOND KNIGHT*)* Bring the bodies here, whether they're alive or dead. We tremble at the gods' wrath, but we don't mourn these deaths.

The SECOND KNIGHT *exits.*
KENT *enters.*

Oh, is that Kent? There's no time for polite greetings.

KENT

I've come to say farewell to my king and master. Isn't he here?

ALBANY

What an enormous thing for us to forget!—Edmund, tell us, where's the king? And where's Cordelia?—

GONERIL*'s and* REGAN*'s bodies are brought out.*

Do you see this, Kent?

KENT

Oh, why is this so?

EDMUND

Still, Edmund was beloved. One of the sisters poisoned the other out of love for me, and then killed herself.

ALBANY

Apparently so.—Cover their faces.

EDMUND

I wish I could live longer. I want to do a little good despite my evil nature. Go quickly—hurry—to the castle, for I've given orders to have Lear and Cordelia killed. Hurry, send someone immediately!

ALBANY
                    Run, run, O, run!

EDGAR
          To who, my lord?—Who hath the office? Send
          Thy token of reprieve.

EDMUND
          Well thought on. Take my sword. The captain—
          Give it the captain.

ALBANY
                              Haste thee for thy life.

                                        Exit a soldier

EDMUND
260   He hath commission from thy wife and me
          To hang Cordelia in the prison and
          To lay the blame upon her own despair,
          That she fordid herself.

ALBANY
          The gods defend her!—hear him hence awhile.

                    Exit soldiers with EDMUND
          Enter LEAR *with* CORDELIA *in his arms, a* THIRD KNIGHT
          following

LEAR
265   Howl, howl, howl, howl! Oh, you are men of stones.
          Had I your tongues and eyes, I'd use them so
          That heaven's vault should crack. She's gone forever.
          I know when one is dead and when one lives.
          She's dead as earth. Lend me a looking-glass.
270   If that her breath will mist or stain the stone,
          Why then, she lives.

KENT
                              Is this the promised end?

EDGAR
          Or image of that horror?

ALBANY

Run, run, oh, run!

EDGAR

Whom should we look for in the castle?—Whose job is it? Send something along to prove you're withdrawing the orders.

EDMUND

Good idea. Take my sword. The captain—give it to the captain.

EDGAR

Run as if your life depended on it.

A soldier exits.

EDMUND

My wife and I ordered him to hang Cordelia in prison and then to make it look as if she committed suicide in despair.

ALBANY

Heaven help her!—Get him out of here for now.

Soldiers exit with EDMUND.
LEAR *enters with* CORDELIA *in his arms, followed by the* THIRD KNIGHT.

LEAR

Howl, howl, howl, howl! Oh, you men are made of stone! If I were you with eyes and a tongue to speak with, I'd crack heaven wide open with my laments! She's gone forever. I know how to tell when someone is alive or dead. She's as dead as the cold ground. Let me borrow a mirror. If her breath steams up the glass, then she's alive.

KENT

Is this doomsday? The end of the world?

EDGAR

Or just a foretaste of it?

ALBANY
                                        Fall and cease.

LEAR
          This feather stirs. She lives. If it be so,
          It is a chance which does redeem all sorrows
275   That ever I have felt.

KENT
                                        O my good master!

LEAR
          Prithee, away.

EDGAR
                              'Tis noble Kent, your friend.

LEAR
          A plague upon you, murderers, traitors all!
          I might have saved her. Now she's gone for ever.—
          Cordelia, Cordelia, stay a little. Ha?
280   What is 't thou say'st?—Her voice was ever soft,
          Gentle and low, an excellent thing in woman.—
          I killed the slave that was a-hanging thee.

THIRD KNIGHT
          'Tis true, my lords, he did.

LEAR
                                        Did I not, fellow?
          I have seen the day with my good biting falchion
285   I would have made them skip. I am old now,
          And these same crosses spoil me. *(to KENT)* Who are you?
          Mine eyes are not o' th' best, I'll tell you straight.

KENT
          If Fortune brag of two she loved and hated,
          One of them we behold.

LEAR
                                        This a dull sight.
290   Are you not Kent?

KENT
          The same. Your servant Kent.
          Where is your servant Caius?

ALBANY

Let the world collapse around us.

LEAR

This feather moved because of her breath. She's alive. If that's true, it makes up for all the sorrows I've ever known.

KENT

Oh, my good master!

LEAR

Please, go away.

EDGAR

It's noble Kent, your friend.

LEAR

Curse you all, you're all murderers and traitors! I could have saved her. Now she's gone forever.— Cordelia, Cordelia, stay a while. Ha? What are you saying?—Her voice always was so soft and gentle. That's a good thing in a woman.—I killed the scum who was hanging you.

THIRD KNIGHT

It's true, my lords, he did.

LEAR

Didn't I? Back in the old days I would've made him dance with my sword. But I'm old now, and suffering has weakened me. *(to* **KENT***)* Who are you? My eyesight's not the best, I'll tell you straight.

KENT

We're looking at the unluckiest man who ever lived.

LEAR

My vision is dull. Aren't you Kent?

KENT

Caius is the name Kent took when he disguised himself and became Lear's servant.

That's me. Your servant Kent. Where's your servant Caius?

LEAR
> He's a good fellow, I can tell you that.
> He'll strike, and quickly too. He's dead and rotten.

KENT
295   No, my good lord. I am the very man—

LEAR
> I'll see that straight.

KENT
> That from your first of difference and decay
> Have followed your sad steps.

LEAR
>   You're welcome hither.

KENT
> Nor no man else. All's cheerless, dark, and deadly.
300   Your eldest daughters have fordone themselves,
> And desperately are dead.

LEAR
>   Ay, so I think.

ALBANY
> He knows not what he says, and vain it is
> That we present us to him.

Enter **THIRD MESSENGER**

EDGAR
>   Very bootless.

THIRD MESSENGER
> Edmund is dead, my lord.

ALBANY
>   That's but a trifle here.—
305   You lords and noble friends, know our intent.
> What comfort to this great decay may come
> Shall be applied. For us, we will resign
> During the life of this old majesty
> To him our absolute power.

LEAR

He's a good fellow, I can tell you that much. Not afraid to fight, he's a feisty one. He's dead and rotting in the dirt now.

KENT

No, my lord, that was me. I'm the one who—

LEAR

I'll get right on that.

KENT

—followed you on your sad wanderings, ever since your bad luck began.

LEAR

Nice to see you.

KENT

It was me, no one else. Everything is gloomy, dark, and dreadful. Your eldest daughters destroyed themselves and died in despair.

LEAR

Yes, I think that's true.

ALBANY

He doesn't know what he's saying. It's useless to try to talk to him.

The **THIRD MESSENGER** *enters.*

EDGAR

Yes, it's pointless.

THIRD MESSENGER

Edmund is dead, my lord.

ALBANY

That doesn't matter much with everything else that's going on.—Gentlemen, I will announce my plans. I'll do everything I can to ease the king's suffering. As for me, I'm surrendering all my power over to him, giving him absolute authority for the rest of his life.

(to EDGAR *and* KENT*)*
                                        You, to your rights
With boot, and such addition as your honors
310   Have more than merited.—All friends shall taste
The wages of their virtue, and all foes
The cup of their deservings. O, see, see!

LEAR

And my poor fool is hanged.—No, no, no life?
Why should a dog, a horse, a rat have life,
315   And thou no breath at all? Oh, thou'lt come no more,
Never, never, never, never, never.—
Pray you, undo this button. Thank you, sir.
Do you see this? Look on her. Look, her lips.
Look there, look there. O, O, O, O.
(dies)

EDGAR

320   He faints!—My lord, my lord!

KENT

Break, heart. I prithee, break!

EDGAR

(to LEAR*)* Look up, my lord.

KENT

Vex not his ghost. O, let him pass. He hates him
That would upon the rack of this tough world
325   Stretch him out longer.

EDGAR

                                        Oh, he is gone indeed.

KENT

The wonder is he hath endured so long.
He but usurped his life.

ALBANY

Bear them from hence. Our present business
Is to general woe.
330   *(to* KENT *and* EDGAR*)* Friends of my soul, you twain
Rule in this realm, and the gored state sustain.

(to EDGAR *and* KENT*)* You will get back your rightful property and titles, along with new honors that you have more than deserved.—My friends and allies will be rewarded for their support, and my enemies will get what they deserve. Look, look!

LEAR

> Lear seems to be talking about Cordelia, using the word "fool" as an endearment.

And my poor fool was hanged.—No, no, no life left? Why should a dog or horse or rat have life, but not you? You'll never come to me again, never, never, never, never, never.—Please help me undo this button. Thank you, sir. Do you see that? Look at her. Look, her lips. Look there, look there. Oh, oh, oh, oh. *(he dies)*

EDGAR

He's fainted.—My lord, my lord!

KENT

My heart will break, break.

EDGAR

(to LEAR*)* Look at me, my lord.

KENT

Don't disturb his soul. Let it go up to heaven. His soul would be angry at anyone who tried to keep him in the torture chamber of this life any longer.

EDGAR

Oh, he's really gone.

KENT

What's amazing is how long he lasted. He was living on borrowed time at the end.

ALBANY

Carry them away. Our business now is mourning and grief. *(to* KENT *and* EDGAR*)* My friends and soulmates, you two will reign over this kingdom and keep the wounded country alive.

KENT

> I have a journey, sir, shortly to go.
> My master calls me. I must not say no.

EDGAR

> The weight of this sad time we must obey.
335 > Speak what we feel, not what we ought to say.
> The oldest hath borne most. We that are young
> Shall never see so much, nor live so long.

Exeunt with a dead march

KENT

I will have to go on a journey to death soon, sir. My master's calling me. I can't say no.

EDGAR

We must remember the gravity of this sad day. We should speak what we feel, not what we ought to say. The oldest one suffered the most. We young ones will never see as much as he has seen, or live as long.

They exit in a funeral march.

SPARKNOTES LITERATURE GUIDES

1984

The Adventures of
 Huckleberry Finn

The Adventures of Tom
 Sawyer

The Aeneid

All Quiet on the Western
 Front

And Then There Were
 None

Angela's Ashes

Animal Farm

Anna Karenina

Anne of Green Gables

Anthem

Antony and Cleopatra

Aristotle's Ethics

As I Lay Dying

As You Like It

Atlas Shrugged

The Autobiography of
 Malcolm X

The Awakening

The Bean Trees

The Bell Jar

Beloved

Beowulf

Billy Budd

Black Boy

Bless Me, Ultima

The Bluest Eye

Brave New World

The Brothers Karamazov

The Call of the Wild

Candide

The Canterbury Tales

Catch-22

The Catcher in the Rye

The Chocolate War

The Chosen

Cold Mountain

Cold Sassy Tree

The Color Purple

The Count of Monte
 Cristo

Crime and Punishment

The Crucible

Cry, the Beloved Country

Cyrano de Bergerac

David Copperfield

Death of a Salesman

The Death of Socrates

The Diary of a Young Girl

A Doll's House

Don Quixote

Dr. Faustus

Dr. Jekyll and Mr. Hyde

Dracula

Dune

Edith Hamilton's
 Mythology

Emma

Ethan Frome

Fahrenheit 451

Fallen Angels

A Farewell to Arms

Farewell to Manzanar

Flowers for Algernon

For Whom the Bell Tolls

The Fountainhead

Frankenstein

The Giver

The Glass Menagerie

Gone With the Wind

The Good Earth

The Grapes of Wrath

Great Expectations

The Great Gatsby

Grendel

Gulliver's Travels

Hamlet

The Handmaid's Tale

Hard Times

Harry Potter and the
 Sorcerer's Stone

Heart of Darkness

Henry IV, Part I

Henry V

Hiroshima

The Hobbit

The House of Seven
 Gables

I Know Why the Caged
 Bird Sings

The Iliad

Inferno

Inherit the Wind

Invisible Man

Jane Eyre

Johnny Tremain

The Joy Luck Club

Julius Caesar

The Jungle

The Killer Angels

King Lear

The Last of the Mohicans

Les Miserables

A Lesson Before Dying

The Little Prince

Little Women

Lord of the Flies

The Lord of the Rings

Macbeth

Madame Bovary

A Man for All Seasons

The Mayor of
 Casterbridge

The Merchant of Venice

A Midsummer Night's
 Dream

Moby Dick

Much Ado About Nothing

My Antonia

Narrative of the Life of
 Frederick Douglass

Native Son

The New Testament

Night

Notes from Underground

The Odyssey

The Oedipus Plays

Of Mice and Men

The Old Man and the Sea

The Old Testament

Oliver Twist

The Once and Future
 King

One Day in the Life of
 Ivan Denisovich

One Flew Over the
 Cuckoo's Nest

One Hundred Years of
 Solitude

Othello

Our Town

The Outsiders

Paradise Lost

A Passage to India

The Pearl

The Picture of Dorian
 Gray

Poe's Short Stories

A Portrait of the Artist as
 a Young Man

Pride and Prejudice

The Prince

A Raisin in the Sun

The Red Badge of
 Courage

The Republic

Richard III

Robinson Crusoe

Romeo and Juliet

The Scarlet Letter

A Separate Peace

Silas Marner

Sir Gawain and the Green
 Knight

Slaughterhouse-Five

Snow Falling on Cedars

Song of Solomon

The Sound and the Fury

Steppenwolf

The Stranger

Streetcar Named Desire

The Sun Also Rises

A Tale of Two Cities

The Taming of the Shrew

The Tempest

Tess of the d'Urbervilles

The Things They Carried

Their Eyes Were
 Watching God

Things Fall Apart

To Kill a Mockingbird

To the Lighthouse

Treasure Island

Twelfth Night

Ulysses

Uncle Tom's Cabin

Walden

War and Peace

Wuthering Heights

A Yellow Raft in Blue
 Water